P9-BAT-911

WITHDRAWN
~~~~~~~~~~~~~~~~~~~~~~~~~ of
~~~~~~~~~~~~~~~~~~~~~~~~ New York Public Library
~~~~~~.

DON'T EVER CHANGE

Also by M. Beth Bloom
Drain You

DON'T

EVER

CHANGE

by M. BETH BLOOM

HARPER TEEN

An Imprint of HarperCollinsPublishers

HarperTeen is an imprint of HarperCollins Publishers.

Don't Ever Change
Copyright © 2015 by M. Beth Bloom
All rights reserved. Printed in the United States of America. No part
of this book may be used or reproduced in any manner whatsoever
without written permission except in the case of brief quotations
embodied in critical articles and reviews. For information address
HarperCollins Children's Books, a division of HarperCollins
Publishers, 195 Broadway, New York, NY 10007.
www.epicreads.com

Library of Congress Cataloging-in-Publication Data
Bloom, M. Beth, date
Don't ever change / M. Beth Bloom. — First edition.
        pages   cm
Summary: Aspiring author Eva takes to heart the words of
her high school English teacher and spends the summer before she
goes away to college trying to figure out just what she knows and
enjoying new experiences that she can draw from in her writing.
ISBN 978-0-06-203688-9 (hardcover)
[1. Self-actualization (Psychology)—Fiction. 2. Camp
counselors—Fiction. 3. Dating (Social customs)—Fiction.
4. Authorship—Fiction.] I. Title. II. Title: Do not ever change.
PZ7.B62294Don 2015   2014034849
[Fic]—dc23   CIP
                                                              AC

Typography by Torborg Davern
15 16 17 18 19 PC/RRDH 10 9 8 7 6 5 4 3 2 1
❖
First Edition

PREFACE TO A CLASSIC

AMERICA, I, AMERICA is a play about freedom and being an American girl, and it's the first thing I ever wrote. I was in the sixth grade. For my middle school's Fourth of July celebration, I picked Erica Bordofsky to play the lead role, which she accepted with a bit too much humility, and that made me question her star power. "You've got to *sell* it," was what I told her. "It's about *America!*"

But ultimately, the final production turned out totally shallow and historically inaccurate and extremely disappointing. At that age, when we're still so young that we can do anything—be nurses or astronauts or princesses or cops—I chose to do this: write. So I began thinking of myself *as* a writer, but a frustrated one, because Erica insisted on mispronouncing her final line as "America, I am Erica," over and over, to a confused assembly of students and teachers.

That's the first thing you learn: being misunderstood.

The second thing is all those old, "classic" books they make you read. They're all about the same themes—the Plight of Man, Man's Epic Nature, Man Versus Society, and whatever else—and there's *always* some depressing metaphor like a river or a war. The overall message I learned about Coming of Age is that if it's a true "classic," then only a boy is allowed to do it, and that's why I hate Holden Caulfield and I hate Huck Finn.

If I'm either going to be left out because I'm a girl, or I'm going to be misunderstood, then I'd much rather be misunderstood; I'd rather have Erica Bordofsky bombing onstage, missing the entire point.

And I'd rather it be because *I* wrote it. Because it's *my* story.

1.

WHAT DO I KNOW

IT'S ONE OF my last classes of my last week of high school. So I don't know why Mr. Roush even has to get into it.

"It's not that your story isn't good," he says. "It *is* good. Better than most."

"Okay," I say.

"But honestly, the truth is there are other subjects you might be better at writing about. Things you know more about. Things you've actually experienced."

"But what I know is just . . . it isn't *dramatic*," I say. "I don't want to write about mean girls in chem class, or babysitting."

"I'm not telling you to," Mr. Roush says.

"I don't want to write about high school."

"Why not?"

"Because it's kind of . . . *trite*," I say.

"The rest of my students don't think so."

"Exactly."

"What are you saying?"

"Nothing, Mr. Roush. I'm saying they don't think it's trite, that's all."

But they should. Most of the stories in class this semester were about fairy-tale proms or teen geniuses or cliques of high school vampires, while mine touched on divorce and cervical cancer and domestic baby adoption. I don't quite consider myself a Teacher's Pet, but I *do* think of myself as a Star Student. I also think when you're a writer everyone's life and everyone's story is what they call Fair Game, so it doesn't make sense to limit yourself to your own boring reality when there's so much good material just a search engine or magazine article away.

Mr. Roush sighs, and hands me the printout of my story. On the inside of the cover page is a single word written in red ink. The word is *WHY*.

"Do you know why I've written this?" Mr. Roush asks.

"Because you want to know why?"

"I wanted to know why you chose to write this specific story."

I shrug. "It was just an idea. I tried to think of something kind of sad and, you know, moving."

"There's nothing wrong with that. But it has to go deeper," he says. "This story doesn't have . . . depth. It doesn't feel real."

"When we were workshopping it, I thought you said you liked it."

"I do like it, Eva. It's well written. But that's all it is." He pauses, choosing his words. "There's a difference between writing that's *fictional*, and writing that's *false*," Mr. Roush continues. "Does that make sense?"

"You think my story is fake," I say.

"Eva, listen."

"You want me to write what I know," I say.

"It's clichéd advice, I admit."

"But nothing around here inspires me."

"Well, what about a boy?" He raises his eyebrows, smiles. "A love story."

"What? No."

"Just a suggestion," Mr. Roush says. "There's a million suggestions. You just have to ask yourself: what do I know?"

I stand there, trying to look like I'm pondering the question. I do all the crucial gestures: slow head nodding, fingernail nibbling, even straightforward head scratching (not on top like "A Thinker," that's too goofy, just gently behind the ear, "A Thoughtful Person"), but what I'm really doing is counting. I decide if Mr. Roush doesn't dismiss me by the time I get to twenty then I'll say something respectful, like "I'll think about it over the summer." But if he hasn't said anything by the time I'm at forty then it'll actually be awkward, so I'll just interrupt with an upbeat "See you at graduation, Mr. Roush," and cruise.

Eleven, what do I know, *twelve*, what do I know, *thirteen*, what do I know.

I make it to fifteen when Mr. Roush sighs and stands with a distant, foggy look in his eyes, like he's just remembered something he hasn't thought about in a really long time. For a moment he holds that pose, gazing past me at the empty room full of little personal desks, each with their own little personal writing tray. I wonder if he's picturing all the fake writers like me who have flooded in and out of his class over the years.

"It's a lot to process," he says, still sort of daydreaming. "There's so much a writer can draw from. Every life is rich. Just because you've read books about adult dramas doesn't mean those are the only subjects worth writing about."

"Don't serious writers write about serious things?"

Mr. Roush's eyes refocus. He smiles at me, warmer than before. "It doesn't work like that. You just write and then you're a writer. And you're a good writer, Eva."

"Thanks. You're a good teacher, Mr. Roush."

"Well, thank you. And *congraduation*, by the way," he says, amused by his pun.

I smile at him and turn to leave, but something catches in my thoughts that makes me pause, and it isn't just the fact that at that exact moment Mr. Roush says, "Oh, and one more thing." It hits me that this whole conversation, what's happening right now, could be a scene, part of a story. Since it's not fictional, it can't be false.

"Can I give you a tip for future writing workshops?" Mr. Roush asks, without waiting for my answer. "You might want to ease up a bit on your peer-editing notes."

"Why, what's wrong with them?"

"They're a little harsh." Mr. Roush reaches for some stapled papers stacked on his desk. "See, here you wrote, 'There's something missing from this story, and that something is everything.'"

"Right. That's just how I felt about it."

"That's not the point. The point is to be constructive in your criticism."

"But Foster has a death in *every one* of his stories," I say. "It's like every story's a dream where it ends with a murder and then the narrator saying, 'And it was all just a dream.' Isn't *that* fake, Mr. Roush?"

"Well, there are gentler ways to express that feeling is all I'm saying."

I start to say more but Mr. Roush leans over, pats my shoulder, picks up his briefcase, and strolls out the door, as if all this time *I* had been keeping *him*, and not the other way around. But once he's gone, I realize I have nowhere to be anyway. This was my last class of the day—one of my last classes in high school, ever. I linger in the doorway, wondering what to do. The cafeteria closed hours ago. I'm not in the mood to try on my cap and gown, or prewrite thank-you notes for incoming graduation checks from relatives, and I definitely have zero desire to go study for my European history final tomorrow.

So instead I stand there, letting time drain away.

Just for the sake of whatever, let's say I *don't* know anything about anything I've written. But if that's true, then what *do* I know that I can write about? I scan around the classroom for inspiration, and this is all I see: seventeen personal desks on which to write personal (but not too harsh) constructive criticisms; an oversize hand-painted Shakespeare quote hanging above the door (THE PLAY IS THE THING); a hardback thesaurus, fat and old, perched on Mr. Roush's desk like a movie prop.

This is all I know: that I'm young and I'm about to finish high school and I write.

But what else, what else.

2.

STANDING IN IT

COURTNEY'S STRETCHED IN a crazy yoga position when I go into her bedroom, but my entrance breaks her concentration. She looks up at me, concerned.

"Your vibes are seriously heavy right now," she says.

"Roush hated my story," I tell her. "He thinks I'm a phony."

"Is he right?"

"Are you asking if he's right that I'm a phony?"

"Yeah."

"How can I even answer that?"

"Well, do you feel like a phony?"

"No," I say. "I don't know. I feel like a regular person."

"There you go then," Courtney says.

Then she closes her eyes and lowers her head to the carpet, her legs crossed under her in a complicated way. She's facing the wall with windows, but she could be facing any direction, she could be facing her stupid mini-fridge, because the blinds aren't open, the windows aren't open, and it's almost nighttime anyway. Once my sister turned twenty-one, she suddenly decided she was "deep," even though she still lives at home and only enrolled in community college so she could major in ceramics (or "pot," as my dad calls it) in hopes of eventually switching to an actual university, where she can study agriculture (or "grass," as my dad likes to say). At least we don't share a room anymore, which makes me think of our old bunk bed, which then makes me wonder about the new bunk bed I'll have this coming fall.

The college roommate questionnaire my school sent me last month asked mostly about your intended major and study habits and one's basic overall level of cleanliness. But the first question was about sex, as in which gender you are, and the last question was about location, as in where you're from. It made me realize that if the pairings had been chosen solely based on people's answers to the first and last questions, then I could've potentially been matched with someone like my sister. She's a girl, like me, and she's from Los Angeles, also like me. But that's where the similarities stop and the differences begin.

"Courtney."

"What?"

"Are you already meditating?" I ask. "Has it started?"

"I'm in the middle of *trying* to do it."

"Can we talk?"

"You always want to talk," Courtney says.

"So?"

"So try to stop sometimes. Try to just stop talking, stop doing anything for a few minutes."

"But I'm a Virgo."

"Well, stop being a Virgo too. At least for a little bit."

Courtney pats the carpet next to her, and I go and sit down. I cross my legs like hers and stare ahead at the closed blinds without moving, holding my back straight, mimicking her posture. I glance at her out of the corner of my left eye but keep my right eye shut because both of her eyes are closed.

If every girl can be described as having the face of a particular animal, then you'd say Courtney has a mouse's face and I have a cat's or kitten's. That's one of our differences. She's also the only Californian I've ever known who acts like a stereotypical "Californian," like she's from the Land of Fruits and Nuts. She calls Beverly Hills "the nine-oh," like the beginning of its zip code, and she calls Malibu "the Boo," or sometimes even "Downtown Boo," which I think is just embarrassing.

"Keep your eyes closed, Eva," she warns.

"Okay, sorry."

"Visualize the number five," Courtney says. "Not just five things, but the number itself, like the icon five. Okay . . . now let five slowly fade. Now create it in your mind two more times. Five. Five. Do the same with the numbers four, three, two, one, and finally zero. Make the zero three times. Picture them big and bold and defined, one at a time, three tall rings, Oh, Oh, Oh. Now hold the last one and picture yourself standing inside the zero."

"Okay, yeah," I say, my eyes closed tight. "I see it."

"Are you standing in it?" she asks.

"I'm standing in it, yeah."

"Now breathe." Courtney breathes. "Whoooooooo."

I do it too: "Whoooooooo."

I listen to Courtney's breath and imitate her, until we're breathing together. Long inhales and long exhales. In one part of my mind I can still see the zero encircling me, hugging my body, but in another I start to think about what I usually think about when my mind wanders: Making It.

Most of the time when people say they want to Make It, what they mean is that they want to become famous and successful. People like to say to me, "Well, what if your life takes a turn? What if you stop writing, then what?" Well, then nothing. I don't want anything else. Since forever, since always, even right now, it's Making It as a Real Writer or else it's me inside a big, bold, defined zero.

"Whoooooooo."

A Writer. A Virgo. A Vegan. Two months ago I went vegan after having been vegetarian for about a year and macrobiotic for two months. I know it's sort of shallow, but labels like Vegan and Virgo and Writer comfort me because they help distinguish me not just from other people, but also from other versions of myself that I could have become, or could one day be. Like how I used to consider Straight Edge another one of my labels because I thought I was *abstaining* from drugs and alcohol, but then I realized I just wasn't being offered any to abstain from.

"Whoooooooo." I breathe.

"Let's go deeper," Courtney says.

"Okay."

"So there's your perfect self, and your injured self. Can you envision them?"

"I'll try."

"Don't picture the injured you getting better, because that only feeds energy to your problems. Instead see the two selves as distinct, separate things. Now gradually overlap them so your perfect self *consumes* your injured self, becoming one. Until you're healed, and always have been."

"Um, okay."

"It's called visual healing," Courtney says. "Are you feeling it?"

"I think so. . . ."

I don't know what I used to imagine college was going to be like before I actually applied, but the one thing I do remember is that for some reason I always pictured my roommate as being a blonde. And then when I finally got the letter telling me my roommate had been selected and I Google Imaged her name, she was. *Is.* But she's also from San Diego, which annoys me because I want her to be from somewhere far away, somewhere I know nothing about, like how Courtney's best friend in community college is from New Hampshire. Now my roommate situation feels like just another part of the Roush Problem. She doesn't expand what I know; she's what I *already* know.

"Do you see it, Eva?" Courtney says.

"I can't tell yet."

What I mainly see is the widening gulf between my expectations and my reality. Like how I totally assumed Mr. Roush would love my short story, and not even just love it like another good short story by a promising senior, but love it better than any of the *other* stories he'd graded the entire semester. But he didn't love it at all. He saw right through it, and right through me. In my encyclopedia of expectations, I thought I knew more than most of my class and, by knowing more, that I'd be able write about more, and impress Mr. Roush with all of it. But now this expectation seems like the numeral 1 I'm trying to visualize: a puny, thin line, going straight down. And reality looks like the tall ringed 0 around me, fencing me in. Oh, Oh, Oh.

"That's it," Courtney says. "You're meditating. You're self-healing! Think of a question—"

WHAT DO I KNOW WHAT DO I KNOW WHAT DO I KNOW.

"Got one?"

"Got it," I say.

"First, as your big sister I have to tell you: there is no answer. Because ultimately, there is no question. You have to see questions and answers as just games that keep us from enlightenment."

"What kind of games?"

"Games of postponement," she says. "Every question is already answered. The only thing to do is let go, to know *beyond* knowing."

"I don't get it," I say. "You're making this up."

"Don't open your eyes yet," she says.

"Too late."

My eyes peek open and I see Courtney, who's already

looking at me, not smiling. We stare at each other, and I wonder if we lock our eyes together long enough without blinking, whether maybe we can communicate our thoughts back and forth, wordlessly. I try and empty my mind. I throw out my old question, What Do I Know, and come up with a new thought to transmit: Tell Me What to Do. I keep staring at Courtney, exerting all my mind power, but nothing happens. I keep beaming at her anyway, until it feels like there isn't anything else in my head, until I'm thinking it so hard I realize my lips are pursed, my forehead's scrunched, and my eyes are just narrow slits. Courtney's mouse-face stays motionless, in a state of total Zen. I don't let it faze me, though; I keep beaming and beaming. I visualize my thought filling the entire space of the room: *Tell Me What to Do.*

I'm five seconds from the beginning of a bad headache when I notice a packet of papers on her otherwise empty desk, which means I probably wasn't meditating very deeply at all.

"What's that?" I ask, pointing.

"What's what?" Courtney says.

"On your desk."

"Just some forms."

"Fine," I say, "don't tell me."

"Chill, Eva. I'm just applying to study abroad next semester."

"Are you serious? I could never do that," I say. "It's not my kind of thing."

"You're seventeen. You don't have a thing."

"Yes, I do. I'm very specific."

"Whatever. What are you going to do all summer while I'm packing for Amsterdam?"

"Amsterdam's not where you go," I say, thinking about it. "Paris is where you go."

"Paris is where *you* go, Ms. Not My Kind of Thing."

"I guess I'll get a job," I say.

"Okay," Courtney says. "Close your eyes again."

"Okay."

"Picture the ideal place you'd want to work this summer, if you could work anywhere. Like, if you could do anything, what would it be?"

"Something in the sunshine," I say. "Maybe, like, doing some *good*. But nothing too dirty, and it still has to be fun, but I also have to learn about myself and other people and hopefully meet a boy—or a few boys."

"Got it," Courtney says. "Easy. Camp counselor. I'll call Steven at that camp I used to work at, Sunny Skies."

"Kids," I say. "Like, little kids?"

"Doesn't Dad say he learned everything in life from raising two girls?"

"That's Dad," I say. "What does Dad know?"

3.

THE USUAL

AT GRADUATION I'M seated between boy Alex and girl Alex. They converse across me through the whole ceremony about some big party at boy Leslie's house tonight, which they assume I'm going to. Tiffany Lee's valedictorian speech is literally called "The University Is the Universe," and near the end she breaks into intense, choking sobs. I try to spot Courtney and my parents in the bleachers, but since I'm not wearing my glasses (thanks to AP English last semester I've become haunted by the Dorothy Parker quote, "Men seldom make passes at women who wear glasses"), it's impossible to distinguish faces that far off. It's even hard to tell boy Alex apart from girl Alex, but mainly because we're all wearing the same thing.

During our principal's speech I wonder what the party will be like tonight and if I should go. I've been to fewer than ten *party* parties in all of high school, but this seems like the one not to miss—mostly because it's the last one. I assume at least a few of my friends will be going, so I decide I'll go too. Plus, it sounds kind of nice to get sentimental. Not in a Tiffany Lee meltdown kind of way but just appreciating right now, what we all went through. It feels like all this obsessing over *just getting to college already* is somehow missing a point. But when I ask boy Alex who's coming to the party, he says, "The usual," and I realize I've probably been missing the point for years.

Then someone in the row in front of me turns around and waves. I lean forward to see who it is, and it's Foster Hoyt, which makes me wish I hadn't leaned forward.

"Hey, Eva," he says.

"Oh hi, Foster."

"Tiffany Lee really went for it, huh?"

"She'd been waiting for that moment her whole life," I say. "Considering that, she did all right."

Foster nods. I notice he's holding some black blurry thing, which at first I think is a camera, but when I squint I see it's a mini tape recorder and the red recording light is on. I laugh because it seems ridiculous to record our graduation ceremony, but then stop laughing when I realize

Foster's taping *our* conversation.

"I'm working on my dialogue," he says.

I can't help but have a Harsh Eva reaction: Foster *should* be working on his dialogue. He should also be working on his plot ideas and his characters and everything else. The problem is that Foster's a terrible writer precisely because he's *actually* a pretty decent writer who refuses to get better by just evolving a little. He always writes about varsity baseball team fights that somehow end in an innocent freshman getting stabbed in the eye, and not only is it like, *who cares*, but he wastes whatever interesting imagery he might've been able to tap into on an unbelievable narrator who ends up blind anyway. Even though Foster's pretty smart—maybe smarter than me— he just doesn't *get it*, and wasn't it someone important who said, "You're either born with taste or you're not"? I like Foster fine, but there's no teaching him good taste.

What's most frustrating of all is that the answer's right in front of him. Like me, like how I'm right in front of him (or in this case, right behind him).

For instance, if everyone in his stories just talked like I talk and acted like I how I act, he'd write the best story of his life. If, just once, his protagonist did something natural, like walked out to the parking lot, got in her car, turned on the radio, rolled down the windows, and didn't even drive anywhere, just put on some lipstick and stared at herself in the rearview mirror, hinting at some kind of emotional epiphany, and then ended it with an ambiguous final line—well, that would be an absolutely legendarily good Foster Hoyt short story.

"Your dialogue is fine," I tell him.

"Come on, dude," Foster says.

"What?"

"I read what you wrote in workshop."

"No," I say, "it's not like that."

"I don't mind," he says. "I want the feedback."

"Foster."

"Seriously, don't worry about it."

I expect Foster to turn back around when there's a lull in the conversation, or start scanning around me for other less harsh people whose dialogue he can record, but he doesn't. He just sits there, looking at me, while our class president rambles on about the game Simon Says and how we should all stop listening to Simon and just be ourselves. I want to tell Foster how I'm not this awful person who insults his stories, I'm just a serious girl who's sort of his rival but only in a healthy, challenging way. Like how if I'm better it makes Foster better, and isn't that a positive influence? Something about the moment, the finality of high school maybe, makes me feel connected to Foster, and I can't let this end with him thinking I'm some jerk.

"You know," I say, "Roush hated my final story. He ripped it apart."

"That's not true," Foster says.

"No, really."

"Well, I liked it," Foster says. "If that matters."

"It does," I say, not lying.

Foster nods in a sweet way and then his eyes catch someone behind me, and he waves. I make a gesture with my hands like I'm dismissing him, like, "Go ahead, I'm fine," and he does, and I am.

4.

HERE'S A DOOR AND IT'S OPEN

COURTNEY GOES TO real college parties sometimes. "Classic" college parties, as she calls them.

An acquaintance or friend of a friend at USC or UCLA will invite her to their dorm room, where the beds have been cleared off and the mini-fridge stocked with wine coolers and soda (which my sister calls "mixers"). The rooms are small, they only hold like twenty people, so eventually everyone spills out into the hall and common area. Apparently there's always a DVD playing, like *The Sopranos: Season One*, but the volume's muted and no one really watches it. And there's also always a stereo on, turned up loud—usually some Velvet Underground album, she says, rolling her eyes—so the video and audio overlap in this particular mashed-up cliché that Courtney swears has been reenacted in similar dorms in similar colleges across the country since basically the beginning of time. It's part of this "sucking black hole" she calls the Generic College Experience, which also includes stuff like *Taxi Driver* posters, shower shoes, standard-issue single beds, Nag Champa incense, one Great Book (like *The Iliad* or *Ulysses* or *Moby-Dick*), clove smoke, and lots of spilled beer.

Still, Courtney loves going and never says no when invited. I assume that's how I'll be one day, especially once I institute my new motto: Walk Through Every Open Door. It's actually something Jesus did, and although I'm not that interested in him, I'm pretty impressed by his dedication to Making It.

The last high school party I remember going to was Derek Hoff's Anti-Prom Prom my junior year, so I'm definitely not the most qualified person to identify the Generic High School Experience, but it seems like it's way less Classic somehow. Courtney says the difference is that in high school everyone still mainly likes what they like. They haven't started worrying about what they *should* like, which happens later. This is why high school parties are sort of a little more genuine: people still get really excited and enthusiastic because it's not cool yet to act numb and blasé about everything.

Tonight is my first door, and it's open, and it's fake to pretend you don't want to walk through it.

Later, at the graduation party, the Usual do come and they're mixed in with the Unusual, yet overall everyone seems pretty happy to be together.

"Remember when you tutored me?" our class treasurer, Hayley Rubin, asks. We're by the iPod dock. She's scrolling through songs impatiently.

"I tutored you for two summers," I say.

"Yeah, remember?"

I laugh. It's mindless chitchat, but I don't mind.

"Remember all your flash cards?" she asks.

"Uh-huh," I say.

"You always held them too low. I could see all the answers."

"Yeah, that was on purpose."

"No."

"I thought if you could read the answers they'd be easier to memorize than if you just guessed and got them wrong and then waited for me to give them to you."

Hayley looks up from the iPod with thankful eyes. "Aww," she says, hand over heart, "you were trying to trick me into thinking I was smarter than you."

"Something like that."

"Awwwww," she says again, and grabs me for a hug. "I love you, Eva," she tells me, and then—spying a few members of our student council approaching, quickly dropping her arms—"but only as a friend."

I expect to see Shelby here, basically running things, since she's single now and avoiding Zack, but she's a no-show, which is also very Shelby, always having cooler plans. Michelle texts that she'll be there soon and so does Steph, but while I'm waiting for them I chat with some random classmates I haven't interacted with since freshman year. I'm the only one who brought their yearbook, which makes me feel like an insane dork, but everyone's cool about it, and I get it signed like a hundred times and hear a hundred stories about which college everybody's going to and what they're doing this summer to save money. Most of them are applying for jobs at the mall (with a heavy emphasis on ice cream/frozen yogurt places, for some reason) or interning with their dad or a family member—except for Foster, who blows my mind when he tells me this'll be his fourth summer in a row as a *camp counselor* at Sunny Skies Day Camp.

The fact that Foster's plans are *identical* to mine makes me think originality is basically dead, because whatever you decide to do someone else has already done it, and is still doing it. So all you can really hope for is to add your own twist somehow.

Around midnight Michelle and Steph finally show but by then the house is packed, mostly with kids who clearly never even went to our school. The social vibe is getting fairly out of control. During my second trip to the bathroom, I see a keg for the first time, ugly and metallic and buried in a bathtub of ice. Some boy hands me a plastic cup of beer, but it smells like moldy white bread so I pour it down the sink.

Everyone seems pretty buzzed, talking too loud, and this guy behind me in line for the bathroom keeps rambling to his friend about how many bitches there are here tonight, and it's seriously making me pissed.

"Look at them all, man," the guy says again to his friend, who's so drunk he's swaying, until he stumbles into me, knocking my bag off my shoulder. Everything spills everywhere. I crouch to gather up my key chain and notebook and change pouch and whatever else and the guy—not his friend—stoops down to help too. That's when I get a closer look at this jerk for the first time, and what I see is a boy with an oddly round head on top of a very skinny, very tall body. He looks like an orange on top of a celery stick, but in an okay way.

I don't want his help, though, so I scoop up all the rest of the stuff myself and throw it in my bag. Doesn't matter if he's trying to be nice and doesn't matter if he's kind of okay-looking; I'm positive he's a jerk because I heard him saying, "Bitch, bitch, bitch," under his breath, pointing to every girl in the room.

"I heard you," I tell him.

"What?"

"I heard you calling those girls bitches," I say.

"And?"

"And nothing, it's just *offensive*."

"Why, are they your friends?"

"Some of them, yeah."

"They don't look like it," he says.

"What the hell does that mean?"

"Nothing," he says. "It's a compliment."

"Do you even go to our school?"

"I go to Westlake," he says. "I *went* to Westlake. A year ago."

"Then why are you here?"

"Tiffany Lee invited me."

"That's not possible."

"We take guitar lessons at the same place. Tiffany shreds," he says, and then smiles and plays air guitar in my face.

"But Tiffany's a bitch," I say. "According to you."

"Tiffany's cool," he says. "You're probably cool."

We're nearly to the front of the line; there's only one girl before me. When she finishes and leaves the bathroom, I go in, but this toothpick guy rushes in behind me and shuts the door so we're crammed in the bathroom together.

"Get out," I say.

"I won't look."

"I don't care," I tell him. "Go get a beer from the bathtub and leave."

"I don't drink beer. I just want to hang out."

"We can hang out later."

"When later?"

I hesitate because I don't know what to say, because I don't know if I even want to hang out with this guy later, or ever. Someone pounds on the door and starts chanting, "Do it! Do it!" which somehow amuses me and makes me wonder if maybe high school parties *are* Classic, and maybe if I want to be Classic or have a Classic Moment, I should let this guy stay while I pee.

"Fine," I say.

"Awesome," he says, and then flips on the faucet and turns around, even putting his fingers in his ears, which makes me think he might not be such a huge jerk after all.

"What's your name?" I ask, but apparently he doesn't hear me because he answers, "I'm in a band."

"What's your name?"

"We're going on tour."

I wipe and flush and then tap his shoulder, and when he turns around he smiles this pretty unbelievable smile. We leave the bathroom and walk through the house together, while I get texted nonstop by Michelle (where r u) and

Steph (whoz that???). Then we go outside on the patio, where everyone's drunkenly put back on their graduation gowns and are all hugging each other, exchanging really heartfelt good-byes, backlit by the glittering faraway LA skyline. In their gowns everyone sort of looks like little teenage judges, but I know I've been judge-y too, for four full years, judging all of them. Foster comes outside to join the group, his tape recorder still in hand, and I wonder if I should also be documenting this, so I reach in my bag and grab a pen and my pocket notebook.

"What are you doing?" the guy asks.

"Writing all this down," I say. "What's your name?"

"Elliot," he says. I write down *ELLIOT*.

"I'm Eva."

We're not facing each other, we're facing forward, out at the horizon and the distant palm trees. Suddenly I feel like I'm about to lose it, have a Tiffany Lee crying fit, because here I am on my graduation night with a total stranger (who didn't even graduate today, who never even went to my *school*), instead of with my friends or with people who at least *could* have been my friends if I hadn't been so judge-y. The palm trees seem so beautiful rustling in the night, which I know is an LA cliché, but what about when it's just true? And what about when they seem extra beautiful because you know you have to leave them for college in Boston in less than three months?

Then Elliot takes my hand, holds it. "Want to go hang out somewhere?"

"Can a person leave their own high school graduation party without saying good-bye?"

"Duh they can," he says.

Then we're at his car and he's opening my door, and once we're driving away Elliot turns the radio to K-Earth 101, the oldies station, and they're playing "Strawberry Letter 23," a song I used to sing along to with my mother in the car when I was younger. It occurs to me this would be a really perfect song for me and Elliot to have as "our song," if something like "our song" ever became necessary.

I write STRAWBERRY LETTER 23 in my notebook as Elliot pulls into the In-N-Out drive-through, the singer singing, "I am free, flying in her arms, over the sea." And while I don't normally respond to any of these themes—not freedom or flying, and not the sea *especially*—the manufactured nostalgia of a classic LA burger "joint" actually washes over me. I order a bun with only lettuce, tomato, and grilled onions, and Elliot gets a chocolate milk shake with fries and that's it. We eat quickly and then I'm dying to kiss Elliot and see where that leads but remember I have my camp interview in the morning and it's late anyway, especially for a school night, even though technically it's not one.

5.

GREAT

STEVEN THE CAMP director shows me around the Sunny Skies grounds, his hands in his cargo pocket shorts, fidgeting with his keys. I'm wearing a dress because I thought it'd be smart to try and look nice and responsible and clean for an interview, but I realize now this position is more about being outdoorsy and into sports and having a good spirit and a positive attitude. For some reason on this particular day there isn't a single kid anywhere, so the camp is oddly peaceful, almost idyllic, which makes me know for sure: *I want this job.*

"We loved having Courtney here," Steven says.

"Oh, thanks."

"Have you ever babysat?" Steven asks.

"Sure. For one of my neighbor's daughters, a bunch of times."

"How'd that go?"

"Okay," I say. "Though maybe not great. But it wasn't my fault. The girl was really . . . *antagonistic*."

"At this camp we as counselors have to have realistic expectations," Steven says.

"Like how?"

"Well, we *want* the kids to like us, that's fantastic, but even when they don't, we're still here to do a job. And that job is to give them an incredible camp experience."

"Even if they don't want one, you mean," I say.

"Every kid wants it to be incredible," Steven tells me. "Kids love camp."

We pass by an archery field, two pools, some volleyball courts, and a muddy lake with canoes docked against a pier. He shows me the nurse's station and the amphitheater and the kitchen, which has a walk-in refrigerator stacked with thousands of school-size paper milk cartons. There's a bead-and-feather closet in the craft lodge and a stable with two old Clydesdales and maybe a half mile of grass so green it looks neon, where the kids play capture the flag and freeze tag.

That's when I come up with an idea for a story: a girl who has the power to actually freeze someone during freeze tag, which makes her the most popular and feared girl in camp. It's kind of like that Stephen King book *Firestarter* mixed with that part in *The Lion, the Witch, and the Wardrobe* where the Queen freezes Mr. Tumnus and the other animals of Narnia. It's kind of sci-fi, but maybe with sci-fi Mr. Roush would agree that you don't have to live it first, or really *know* it.

"What would you say you're best at?" Steven asks.

"Um, in what sense?"

"At Sunny Skies, where do you think you'd shine brightest?"

"Maybe arts and crafts? Or I could be a song leader at assemblies," I suggest. "Or maybe even just a floater who roams around helping wherever needed?"

"I don't think you're giving yourself enough credit," Steven says. "Foster Hoyt told me you're funny and smart and very dependable."

"Thanks, Foster."

"Well, it seems like you'd fit in great here. I'd like to give you a group. They're the nine-year-old girls," Steven says. "They're nine really great girls."

"Nine," I say. "That sounds like a lot."

"You'll have Alyssa for help. She's your very own CIT—counselor-in-training," Steven says. "The CITs are a great group of thirteen-year-olds."

"So I have to watch a thirteen-year-old too."

Steven laughs. "That's funny," he says.

Back in the office, Steven puts together a massive packet of papers for me, running down the basic info. There's so many rules and guidelines and suggestions I can tell I won't be able to read them all. It's not that I think the job is a sleepwalk, but I feel like in each day's schedule I'd prefer to try and spend as little time as possible managing the girls so I can focus on just absorbing the overall experience, gathering writerly research.

Steven hands me a clipboard with a Sunny Skies pen in the clip (perfect for jotting notes on plot ideas and character stuff). Then he hands me two Sunny Skies Counselor shirts, both size XL, a hat, and my camp songbook, which is also so XL that it comes housed in a fat three-ring binder. I'm so loaded up with booklets and info and embroidered baseball caps I can't even shake Steven's hand when I get up to go.

"We had our Counselor Kickoff last weekend," Steven says. "Just a chance to get to know each other a little better before the kids arrive in two weeks."

"Trust falls, right? Role-playing," I say.

Steven laughs.

"I'm sure it's all here in the Trust Fall and Role-Playing packet," I say.

"The girls are going to like you," Steven says, still laughing.

Then Steven tells me I have spunk, whatever that is, and then he gets serious and reminds me it's always okay to ask for help. He doesn't seem to be referring to anything specifically, so he must just mean in general. I ask him to help with the door to make sure he knows I *get it*, but as Steven's walking me to my car I worry that even though I've already been given the job, maybe I haven't impressed him enough, haven't fully won him over with my spirit and enthusiasm.

"We can do one of those role-playing exercises right now if you want," I say.

I throw the camp stuff in my backseat and stand up straight and squint my eyes, and not just because I'm not wearing my glasses, but also because it's my concentrating face.

"I'm ready," I tell Steven.

"Okay," he says. "Okay, pretend I'm a girl who wants to play prisoner ball when everyone else in the group has decided on TV tag."

"Does it matter that I don't know what either of those things are?"

"No," Steven says, and laughs.

"Listen," I say, "think about all the times in your life that you'll be able to play prisoner ball. It's a long, long life. Think about all the times you'll be able to play TV tag. Hundreds of times, I bet. Aren't the differences between them so tiny that in the end it's more about just playing and having fun and being out in the sunshine and bonding with your friends? So why even attach yourself to any *one* game?"

"But I love prisoner ball, it's my favorite game," Steven says.

"Do you know what the word 'open-minded' means? You have to be open-minded. Like, what if you play TV tag and then it becomes your favorite game of all time and you forget all about prisoner ball?"

"But can't the other girls just try prisoner ball for a minute?"

"It's kind of like mob mentality—have you ever heard of that?"

"No."

"It's like how maybe TV tag *isn't* what all the girls want to play. Maybe it's only what *one* girl wants to play, but she convinced another girl and then another and by then you have three girls who all want to play TV tag, which makes the other less-sure girls feel nervous because they want to be liked and they want to belong. Does that make sense?"

"Not really."

"What I'm saying is, good for you for standing out and being super opinionated even if it means you're an outcast for a minute. Good for you! And you know what, you don't have to play TV tag if you don't want to. You can just keep score on my cool clipboard."

"But the girl wants to play, Eva."

"Great," I say. "Problem solved then."

6.

AUSTEN'S DARCY, MILNE'S POOH

I CAN TELL Elliot's not going to ask me out on a *real* date, which is fine, because honestly that's never how the Classic books about romance, love, etc., start off anyway. No stuffy, priggish nineteenth-century novels begin with the sentence, "First he asked her out on a date," because obviously Darcy or Heathcliff have to be super cagey and repressed about everything. Asking someone out shows *vulnerability*, and apparently a thousand years ago it was considered totally unsexy for a guy to be vulnerable.

But we're in the future now, and in my opinion inviting a girl on a real date displays a lot of confidence and strength.

Still, that's just not Elliot's style. He's part of that

long, dumb lineage of guys who have to maintain a cool distance about everything. It's a clichéd convention stretching back into ancient history, which would usually bore me, but in this particular instance I'm choosing to be intrigued by it.

"The Black Lips are playing at the Echo tonight," Elliot tells me when he calls. "It's all ages. Only eight bucks."

"Uh-huh," I say.

"I'll probably get there at like ten, and stay till last call."

"When's last call?"

"Two—don't you know that?"

"Okay, so you'll be there from ten to two," I say. "Four hours."

"Or maybe longer," Elliot says, mentally calculating, "'cause I'm driving myself."

"You're going alone?"

"Yeah. So I'll probably bump into you there," he says, and hangs up.

That's as official an invite as I get.

But later, once I drive there and park and walk inside, Elliot's the first person I see, loitering by the girl at the ticket counter stamping people's wrists. It's obvious he was waiting for me, and I can't fake not being turned on by that.

Inside the lights aren't that low or smoky and it's not even very loud, both of which I associate with live music venues. Usually watching bands play twenty feet in front of my face isn't something I find too thrilling—I guess it just doesn't feel that Classic to me—but being here now I'm realizing there's an aspect to the performance that's a lot like a play. It lives and breathes right there on the stage, and you have to truly be in the moment to understand and appreciate it. One of the quotes Mr. Roush kept up on the board for the first half of senior year was this Emily Dickinson one: "Forever—is composed of Nows."

"Didn't she only leave her bedroom, like, once in her whole life?" Elliot asks. We're outside the club now, standing in the back area with the grungy, smelly smokers.

"That might be true, but what reason did she have to leave?" I say. "The outside world was so *antique* and cruel, and inside was probably mellow and comforting."

"What's comforting about being alone?" Elliot asks. He shoves his hands into his jean pockets and leans against a graffitied wall, pulling a James Dean. And the thing about James Dean is that he wasn't just cute, he was *symbolic*, and I'll never get enough of that.

"You're not alone if you have your books and your pen and your ideas," I say.

Elliot crinkles his forehead at that.

"*Aaaannnd*," I continue, "the awareness that you're

like a poet VIP, and people will be studying and worshipping you forever."

"What's the quote again?"

"'Forever—is composed of Nows.'"

"I've got a better one," Elliot says, then interrupts himself. "Wait, hang on." Then he goes back inside, the heavy door sealing behind him.

I wave away the cigarette smoke, give a small fake cough. It's not cold out, but I hold my arms around my body anyway, shifting from foot to foot. I resist the impulse to mess with my phone because I don't want Elliot to come back and find me that way. I pride myself on having a very long attention span, so I'm not afraid to just stand here alone, touching nothing and looking at nothing, just *thinking*—which makes me a true original. Maybe not compared to Emily Dickinson, but at least to people who're still alive.

When Elliot returns he's holding two sodas, sucking on an ice cube, and smiling.

"You bought me a soda?" I say.

"I know the bartender," Elliot says. "It was free."

"I only want it if you bought it," I joke. "If it took some *effort*."

"Well, I tried pretty hard not to spill," he says, and sticks out his tongue. The cold of the ice has turned his tongue hot pink.

"Do you want to go and actually watch the band?" I say. "You know, see the music play?"

"You can't see music," Elliot says, like it's his deep personal philosophy.

"What was the better one then?" I ask. "You were saying you had a better one. . . ."

"Oh yeah. It's by A. A. Milne—know him?"

"The guy who wrote Pooh," I say.

"C'mon, it wasn't that bad," Elliot says.

"Okay, what's the quote?"

"So Christopher Robin asks what day it is and Piglet says, 'It's today,' and then Pooh says"—here Elliot leans down, his face close to mine—"Pooh says, 'Today. My favorite day.'"

"Is this a real date?" I ask, my eyes right beneath his, my nose just below his nose.

"It's a little date," he says. He chomps on another cube of ice. "A half date."

"Still *half* to ask me," I say, pretty pleased I left my bedroom for once in my whole life.

7.

CHINESE BOMBS

I MEET MICHELLE and Steph at the Thousand Oaks Mall on the Friday before our last weekend as do-nothing ex-seniors. Michelle's been hired as a personal assistant by some rich woman who makes jewelry in Santa Monica, and Steph got a job folding at the Gap. What I like about Michelle is that she's tough and never moody, and what I like about Steph is that she's sensitive and really pays attention. I guess I round out the group by being some mixture of both. I like to think of myself as the glue that holds us together, and I also like to think that if I wasn't around, maybe Michelle and Steph would never really see each other, that's how much I connect us all.

Michelle's trying on a fitted blazer that feels very East Coast, very Boston, so I try one on too. Someone makes a Sisterhood of the Traveling Blazers joke, and it kind of makes me feel old, like I wish it was the summer *before* senior year and not the summer after. I don't want to get a job, or rather, I don't want to *have* a job, but I do, and can't stop complaining about it. What I don't like about Steph is that she lets everyone complain, on and on, because she thinks it's therapeutic to just get everything out, even though sometimes it isn't.

The three of us are definitely cliquish, though, which has been getting a bad rap lately in movies and books and overall culture. There's this backlash against people "wanting to belong," but the truth is I don't want to belong *in general*—I want to belong to *these* two, and I want them to belong to me. Courtney says that being too close to people can become toxic, and that you have to watch out for that, especially with high school friends. She also says I shouldn't forget to "spread my wings," because in a year I might not even know Michelle and Steph—maybe in less than a year. Which makes this blazer, this iced coffee with soy milk, these receipts for candles and hoop earrings, all feel like ticking bombs, and that gives me an idea for a story: a seventeen-year-old girl is visited by two forty-seven-year-old women claiming to be the future versions of her two best friends from high school come back to make sure the girl keeps up their friendships so as to change the course of all three of their lives. This is a good one; Mr. Roush might like it. I scribble it down on something.

"Anyway," I say, "Foster will be at camp with me. So that's something."

"Foster, huh," Michelle says.

"Don't say his name like that."

"I like Foster," Steph says. "We all think he's cute."

"We don't all think that," I say.

"What about that guy Elliot?" Michelle says.

"Has he called?" Steph asks.

"He texted."

"That's better," Michelle says. "It's like, 'Hey, boys, text me, don't call me, okay?'"

"Calling is committing," Steph says.

"And Eva doesn't want to commit."

"You're leaving for Boston in, like, two months anyway."

"And he's leaving for tour. . . ."

"There's also Foster. . . ."

"Guys," I say, interrupting. "I'm not the protagonist in some rom-com, and you aren't my pushy, sentimental sidekicks."

"Hmm," Michelle says, and then Steph says, "Yeah, hmm."

Later we're at the food court, and since I can't find anything vegan at Panda Express I just watch Michelle and Steph go wild on some chicken chow mein. Michelle keeps dangling the noodles in front of me, saying if I want to take a bite she won't tell anybody. This is what everyone thinks: that I'm dying for their chicken chow mein but because there's some noble agenda, some lofty idea to stand behind, I won't let myself indulge. They think at home, alone in my room, I'm slamming turkey cheddar sandwiches, and they also think I just need a friend, or anyone, to convince me to chill on my principles for a minute so I can enjoy life and a big piece of lasagna. But what they don't know is that their egg rolls are time bombs, that they're ticking, because these could be the last egg rolls Michelle and Steph ever share, and isn't that a bigger deal than my dietary choice to slowly save the planet? I tell them all of this, then pound on the food court table and take away their forks so I can hold their hands.

"You have to stop listening to Courtney so much," Michelle says.

"Your sister doesn't know how it is with us," Steph says.

"Yeah, we'll be friends for a supremely long time," Michelle says.

"We're in no danger of not being friends," Steph tells me.

"And didn't someone say something about absence and the fonder heart?"

"And don't our key chains say something about friends and forever?"

"Guys, are we being naive?" I ask.

"Of course we're not being naive," Michelle says, and then Steph says, "Two of us are eighteen, Eva."

I force Michelle and Steph to make firm promises for the summer concerning multiple weekly hangouts and lengthy phone call catch-ups and constant text and email updates. I don't know why but I feel a little desperate, and even though I'm not that interested in the daily business of handmade jewelry from Santa Monica or ribbed V-neck tees and tanks, I feel like I need to hold on to this connection or else I'll be so lonely. So I promise not to slip if they won't slip, and I know that I won't slip because it's *summer camp*, and really, after a long day of being stuck with nine nine-year-olds, all I'll want to do is bond with my friends before we have to say good-bye in August.

"You'll also want time to write, though," Michelle reminds me.

"And talk to Elliot on the phone," Steph says.

"And what about Foster?"

"Or some other counselor you might meet that you want to hang out with."

"Guys!" I say, frustrated. Then I pick up Steph's fork

and shove a big bite of greasy noodles in my mouth, to show that I *can* commit and that I *will* commit, all summer long, until the day I get on the plane for Boston. I think they're impressed, because they immediately feel bad and hug me and tell me I don't have to swallow the chow mein.

So I don't; I rush to a trash can and spit it out before it explodes.

8.

JENNIFER AT BAT

LATER THAT NIGHT Elliot wants to see/not see another band play, but this time it's at this place downtown called The Smell. Elliot knows the girl working the door, so I get my hand stamped—with a unicorn jumping over a rainbow—without having to pay, which I guess in some countries is the same as a person buying a ticket for you. I realize I should be thankful, but mainly I'm just curious what Elliot did to get owed so many favors and complimentary beverages and free admissions into places no one's particularly excited to go or be. It's very Big Man on Campus, only without the campus part because Elliot claims "life" is his campus, which makes me fake gag instantly.

"So you love college?" Elliot asks. "You're in love with going to college?"

"Well, I'm into *knowledge*," I say, trying to discreetly smear the unicorn stamp off my hand. "I know, '*God, what a nerd*.'"

"No, knowledge is cool, but you're not into knowledge—you're into the *illusion* of being at college."

"How's it an illusion when I'm literally there?"

"You know what I mean," he says, rolling his eyes, which reminds me of an episode I saw once of this boring eighties sitcom, where Michael J. Fox is a Republican. In it, the character Jennifer has to pretend like she doesn't know anything about baseball to get a guy on the baseball team to like her, even though she knows everything about baseball—more than him even—and that's why it's supposed to be funny. But I don't find it funny at all; I find it disturbing that girls in the eighties had to dumb themselves down just to get a cute boy.

"What are you looking for?" Elliot asks.

"Nothing," I say, looking around the venue, at zine racks and show flyers and boys in band shirts.

"I mean at Emerson."

"Oh. At Emerson." I ponder it for about one second, then say, "Everything."

Elliot laughs. "All things?"

"Extreme intelligence and immense depth."

"I'm living life after depth," he says.

"I *thought* you looked pale," I tell him, then lick the back of my hand and rub it until the unicorn is a purple smudge.

"The stamp is like a rite," Elliot says, nodding at my inky fingers. "Shows you've experienced something."

"Yeah, well, I told my parents we were going to Barnes and Noble at the Brand, and you don't get your hand stamped for buying *The Portable Thoreau*."

"You lie to your parents?" he asks, turned on.

"Only about where I'm going."

"That's kind of naughty," Elliot says, then Dean-leans against a brick wall, raising his eyebrows suggestively.

"I can be naughty," I say, remembering Jennifer again, the way she sheepishly asks the hunky pitcher if there's a difference between home and fourth base. "I do believe in casual text," I tell Elliot, trying to be simultaneously flirty and clever.

"Casual sext?" he asks, smiling.

"Too naughty."

"I bet you're the type of girl who believes everything they told you in D.A.R.E."

This is what my father means when he says someone has your number.

"Every. Single. Word," I admit.

"You're not into drugs then?"

"They're so sixties," I say. "They're so eighties. People on drugs are depressing."

"You've got a lot of opinions, don't you? 'I think, therefore I am' and all that shit."

"Yeah, I do," I say, starting to get indignant, "and if you don't like it—"

"I like it," Elliot interrupts.

Whatever band was playing finishes, and the doors to The Smell swing open, and we all migrate out into the alley to wait for the next group to set up. No one's being rowdy like you'd think they might be at a DIY rock show; they're conversing politely, hands in their pockets, nodding in agreement that whatever they just saw and heard was pretty good. A few guys come over to us, but Elliot doesn't introduce me, and I don't expect him to. One of them asks when his band's playing next, and Elliot gives a long, detailed response. I zone out to the sound of his voice, and when I zone back in, he's still talking. Elliot's acting like he knows everyone here, like this world is basically another home, and maybe to him it is.

Then the next band kicks into their first song and everyone floods back inside the venue, and it's just me and Elliot alone in the alley.

"Why do you like it?" I ask. "I mean, what about my having so many opinions do you like *in particular*?"

"Can't I just like it *in general*?"

"No," I say.

Then Elliot laughs really loud, like he's got all my numbers, like they couldn't be more obvious, stamped in permanent ink all over my hands.

9.

WHAT'S UP

COURTNEY'S STANDING OVER my shoulder, telling me what to do. "Compose, *compose*," she keeps saying, but I'm not ready yet. I still don't know what the first thing I write to my new college roommate should be.

"Well, what do you know about this girl?" Courtney asks, impatient. "Get the paper."

"Okay," I say, reading. "She's from San Diego, she keeps her room 'moderately' clean, she wants to major in theater, and she likes to wake up early."

"That's it?"

"Yeah, that's it. It's not a *Cosmo* quiz, it's . . . *utilitarian*."

"That's a good word," Courtney says. "Start using that more."

"Courtney, I don't need your help."

"Yes, you do."

"Not really."

"Fine. You write Lindsay's email and then I'll edit it."

"Fine," I say.

I sit for thirty minutes drafting and saving and deleting, poring over this stupid utilitarian message, trying to draw assumptions from the little I have to work with. Lindsay might surf or boogie board or she might have OCD and be addicted to caffeine or she might know every lyric to every song from the musical *Annie*, or have even played Annie or some other orphan, or maybe she actually *is* an orphan. Or maybe she just has an older sister like mine, who's so completely sure of everything that you might as well let her do everything, since she's twenty-one and learning Dutch and you don't even remember a word from the three years of French you took because it's summer and high school's over.

San Diego, what do I know, *theater,* what do I know, *Lindsay,* what do I know?

"Move," Courtney says.

I get up from the desk and pace the room once and Courtney's already clicking the send button.

"There," she says.

"There?" I ask. "You sent it?"

"Eva, it's Go Time, you know?"

"Then go, Courtney. It's time to go."

After Courtney leaves, I search my sent box to read what she wrote. It says, Hey, Lindsay, I'm your new roommate Eva, just wanted to say what's up, so write back when you can.

That's all. That's it.

10.

SAD STORY

WHEN ELLIOT SITS down on the edge of my bed, I pretend not to notice how moody he's being. I know why he's annoyed—he wanted us to go to an indie show at the Troubadour instead of coming here—but I didn't want to do that, and I'm not sorry for saying so. I flip through DVD boxes, trying to find something fun we can watch, and wait for him to speak. He never does. Elliot can go a pretty long time without saying anything, but I can go longer. I'm not even close to cracking when he finally says, "We should have just gone to the Troubadour." I don't reply. Then he says, "I should have brought my guitar," and still I don't say anything.

(First of all) it's Saturday night, our last date before he

leaves, so no, I don't want to go see another band play at a dumb club where I can't hear what Elliot has to say and he can't hear me, (second) while I drink Tropicana orange juice the bartender uses as a "mixer," (third) just so we can be out too late like the last few times and never really get to kiss. (Not to mention fourth) I also have no money and don't feel like standing in a line just to find out Elliot hasn't got any money left either and that maybe this time he doesn't know the door girl and then have it be awkward. And also (fifth!!!) we're in my bedroom, basically alone in the house for the first time, and isn't that sort of sexy and doesn't watching a movie in the dark on my bed sound incredible?

"I said I should've brought my guitar," Elliot says.

"Why?"

"So I could play you something."

"I have an old Casio from when I took piano lessons in third grade."

"Do you have a Gibson SG?"

"Is that a guitar?"

Elliot just looks at me. Maybe he's as amazing a guitar player as he swears he is, and maybe it would blow my mind to hear him play, but the way he's pouting makes me want to throw his Gibson SG off a cliff, or at least dangle it out a window. Although picturing that now—a guitar hurtling off a seaside cliff into the Pacific Ocean, splashing down, floating away tenderly to the horizon—reminds me of a scene in one of Mr. Roush's sample stories, which seems kind of romantic. And this makes me remember when Elliot first took my hand and held it, standing underneath the crossed palm trees in front of the Brentwood In-N-Out Burger.

And here, now, seeing him sitting on my high school bed, in my high school bedroom, among all my soon-to-be-packed-up-or-thrown-out high school things, I can't believe how bad I want to make out with him. So I sit down at the other edge of the bed and wait for Elliot to scoot closer, but then *he* starts flipping through DVDs. I assume if Elliot could take the strings off his guitar and stick his tongue in the hole of his Gibson SG he probably would, and he then wouldn't need my mouth. Because it's not like we're talking anyway.

"Tell me about the tour," I say.

"We're going across the country and back, like, forty cities," Elliot says.

"That sounds awful."

"No way, man."

"So you're leaving Monday."

"Yeah, Monday," he says.

"That's when I start camp too," I say.

"Yeah, what's up with camp?"

"I thought it was important to not get some boring

mall job and instead do something that'll provide me with real experiences. And also I'm helping kids and getting sunshine, which stops depression. I mean, I'm not depressed now, but this way I definitely won't be later because of all the sun, and also the positivity of working hard and helping children."

"Are you kidding?"

"Why would I be kidding?" I say.

"It's just dodgeball and lanyards and wading in the shallow end," Elliot says.

"I guess," I say. "Maybe it's just running around and singing songs."

"Hey, that's what I'll be doing."

"Yeah," I say.

"I get it, though. That was like your warm-up speech," Elliot says. "Like your preshow ritual. You're pumping yourself up, getting psyched for the big gig."

"Yeah, I guess so."

"God," Elliot says, "now I *really* wish I'd brought my guitar."

But before I can say anything about guitars hurtling over cliffs, Elliot says, "I'm hungry."

Downstairs I make two soy cheddar and Tofurky sandwiches on sprouted soy bread while Elliot waits up in my room. My mother's at the kitchen counter watching me while she picks at a Weight Watchers thing, shaking her head. She wants us to come downstairs and eat with her so she can watch me chew and swallow for one of the last fifty times. My dad's scrolling through the Netflix queue with Courtney, but they can't decide and end up aimlessly flipping through TV channels, which is so irritating I try to spread the mustard faster to get this over with. I don't know how Courtney can even watch anything with Mom, because she likes the volume all the way up and the lights on, or with Dad either, since he always gets up in the middle to look through some book or take a shower. I hear Elliot start to come down the stairs, but I rush to meet him in the middle so he doesn't have to witness my family being so ADD and annoying.

Elliot sits Indian-style across from me on the carpet, holding his sandwich with two hands like a little kid. He's already gotten mustard on his pants and fingers, which is the sweetest thing ever, because he's supposed to be some cool guy in a band and not some weirdo covered in mustard. I think about whether it's normal to already miss Elliot, or be sad that he's leaving in two days when I honestly still don't really know him that well. It seems a little crazy, but since I can't help it, that means I'll just have to get to know Elliot better *faster*. Like, immediately.

"Say a bunch of things about yourself that you haven't told me yet," I tell him. "Go."

"Is this about speed?" Elliot asks. "Or more about order of importance?"

"I'm just trying to get to know you super, super well," I say.

"Okay but that takes time, Eva."

"We don't have time, remember?"

"I'll call you from the road," Elliot says. "I'll call you all the time if you want. I'll call you now."

Elliot picks up his phone and calls mine, and it rings and rings but I don't pick it up because this is stupid—Elliot's sitting right in front of me, and I don't want to play any games of postponement. Elliot calls me again, though, and this time he turns his body around so he's facing the wall and he's sighing, saying to himself, "Why won't she pick up, is she mad at me?" And for one minute it's actually cute and makes me smile, so I finally pick up on, like, the seventh ring.

"Hello, who's this?"

"This is Elliot."

"Hi, Elliot, how's Akron, Ohio?"

"It's industrious. How's Los Angeles, California?"

"Glamorous, but I miss you," I say.

"Wait, you do?"

"Yeah. I mean, I'm sure I will when you're gone, and I'm sure I'll tell you when we're on the phone."

"I miss you too."

"When are you coming back?"

"At the end of summer. Like August twenty-eighth or something."

"That's only three days before I leave," I say.

"That's kinda sad," Elliot whispers.

Elliot and I don't say anything after that; I just sort of lean forward and slump my chest on his back, my head on his shoulder. This isn't like a love story really, because no one's in love yet, but it is a sad story because maybe we could've been in love if there'd only been more time. I also don't have enough details yet to tell the story, and for a character to fall for someone this fast won't seem real or realistic and then Mr. Roush will think I'm still a fake.

Then Elliot grabs my arms and pulls them around him, and though it's an awkward way to sit, it's also comfortable. We're just quiet for a while, and I guess I'm getting to know Elliot like I'm getting to know my new roommate, Lindsay, through these small random stats. Elliot is a guitarist and singer in a band; he's nineteen and he graduated from Westlake High last year; he likes extra mustard on his sandwiches; he's leaving for the whole summer; and he's going to miss me. My dad says Patience Is a Virtue, but whenever I ask him what the other virtues are, he just shrugs and says, "Oh, they're all virtues, Eva," so that doesn't help. But I can tell I'll have to be patient with Elliot, because I'm sure sweet boys are virtues too, and I'm almost sure now that Elliot's sweet.

We play Super Mario Kart and I win, and then we watch the news, which is something Elliot does every night at eleven because his mom's a senator's aide and these are more stats for my file. We kiss every once in a while, nothing long and wet, just like open-mouth and soft. We even kiss during the news, during some story about a missing ten-year-old girl. My mind wanders from thinking about Elliot's lips to thinking about how scary it'd be if I lost a girl. Elliot says the news is sexy when he's with me, and then I tell him I *do* wish he'd brought his guitar because no one's ever played to me before and now I'll have to wait all summer for a serenade. Elliot says it's okay, he'll just play me something over the phone.

By the time Elliot and I go downstairs, the whole house is dark and Courtney's and my parents' doors are both shut. I walk Elliot to his car. I don't know quite what to do because this is already another good-bye; there'll be a ton more coming so soon.

"Don't go on tour," Elliot jokes.

"But my band needs me," I say, playing along.

"I'll think of you when I'm wiping up snot and skinned knees," he says.

"And I'll think of you when I'm . . . shredding."

We hug and kiss some more, so much that Elliot eventually opens the door to his backseat, and without stopping, we maneuver our way in. Now I know I full-on like him, that I'm seriously going to miss him, and his fingers are so strong and calloused from playing guitar that when he kneads them up and down my back, it feels like he needs me. Just as we're starting to fog up the car, the McNutt family's dog across the street launches into a frenzy of barking, followed by our porch light flashing on in three short flickers, which is Courtney's signal for warning me when Mom and Dad are up.

Elliot and I separate. We catch our breaths.

"Are you a good writer?" he asks.

"I'm trying to be," I say.

"I bet you are," Elliot says. "You should write about me."

"I should," I say.

Then Elliot drives off and it's sad, but what's the point of crying when I guess I barely even know him, and other than the fact that I'm a writer, he maybe barely even knows me?

11.

GO AHEAD, CHECK

WHEN I WAKE up on the first day of camp my first thought is: *I hate camp.* And my second thought is: *I'll just quit.* I go downstairs and try to convince my mother to call in sick for me, but not just sick for today, sick for the whole summer—sick for life. She won't do it, though. I ask my dad next, but he just says, "Work shall set you free," and then Courtney reminds him that's something the Nazis used to say, and then everyone goes silent. I beg Courtney to call for me, and she says she'll do it but she wants a hundred bucks, like, *right now,* so I give up.

She agrees to help cut my jeans into shorts, though, since it's scorching outside, while I put on Johnson & Johnson's SPF 45 and what feels like ten pounds of Sunny

Skies apparel. I also pack a lunch, because who knows what they're going to try to feed me there. I grab my clipboard and pen on the way out and drive to camp so distracted I can barely pay attention to the road. Jessica Avery. Alexis Powell. Lila Kissling. Jenna Litvak. Zoe Weisberg. Maggie Lamar. Renee Sprout. Rebecca Lovey. Billie Westerman. Right now they're just names on a roster, but those are my girls, with Alyssa Barber as my CIT. What do they look like, what do they sound like, what do they want? My brain goes blank.

When I get to camp, it's like a crazy carnival shit show, with kids running everywhere. I assume I'm going to get some alone time with my group at some point, but the first day is all games and getting-to-know-yous, and suddenly we're mixed up and separated.

"Where am I supposed to go?" I ask a girl counselor, and all she does is point and walk away.

"What are we supposed to be doing?" I ask a boy counselor.

"What do you mean?" he says. "You're doing it."

I grab another counselor by the arm. "Can I just follow you?"

"You're lost," he says, turning his Dodgers hat around backward so he can squint at me better.

"So lost."

"What's your name?"

"Eva." I watch him flip through pages on his clip-board. "Kramer."

"Foster's friend," he says without looking up.

"Yes!" I say. "Exactly."

"I'm Booth."

"Help me, Booth. I'm not afraid to ask for help."

"It's the first day," he says, showing me how on the monthly schedule, today's block simply reads *FIRST DAY*. "No big deal, always a little hecky."

"*Hecky*," I repeat. Everyone gets it but me, and I'm not into conspiracy theories, but it feels like they want to keep it that way. It's annoying.

"Upup," he says, pointing behind me, "there's an easy one."

Upup?

I turn around and see a huddle of five campers strug-gling over a knotted jumble of jump ropes. Each one yanks in an opposite direction, groaning, to pry theirs loose from the pile.

"See ya," Booth says before strolling away, leaving me to spend the next ten minutes helping kids loop and unloop tangled ropes. At least it's ten minutes gone.

I want to just be with my girls, but they're all spread out in different clusters, and I keep getting stuck with various rotating groups of *interlopers* who I'm hesitant to bond with, because what if there's only so much bondage this summer and what if it's wasted on them? So instead of participating in the team-building exercises, I pass most of the day playing the game I often play in classes I don't really care about, and that game is Minimum Effort.

The only goal's to test the limit of how much you can get away with *not* doing and, if possible, find a good hiding place. From ten to eleven thirty I dodge dodgeball, sit out soccer, and avoid the deep end, the shallow end, and the poolside changing room altogether. I help push the canoe out, but I don't get in. As a concession I organize the lanyard string in neat rows on the table and sit at the head, scissors in hand, Eva Scissorhands, helping boys and girls cut pieces.

At noon there's a camp sing-along, but I only mouth the words because I never finished reading the camp packet, so I don't know the lyrics. I make sure I'm peeing during the ropes course, peeing during lice check, even during most of lunch. If I can't pee I at least pretend to, sitting on the toilet, reading graffiti. I don't go anywhere near the horses, and I don't pet the bunnies. I linger at the lost and found station, even though it's the first day and nothing's been lost yet. I sign a list volunteering to stay at camp with future sick kids on future field trip days.

I let the littler ones from the younger groups climb on me, pull my arms, braid my hair, and assault me with questions:

"Do you have a boyfriend?"

"Are you going to college? To be a doctor, a teacher, an actress?"

"Do you know any famous people?"

"Are you a camp counselor all year long?"

"Will you be a camp counselor forever?"

I tell them I have zero boyfriends, that I'm going to write novels and a bunch of other things, that I know one girl on a Nickelodeon show because we had the same geometry tutor, and that I'm not really a camp counselor. That I must be magical like Mary Poppins because I was never even here today.

"Go ahead," I tell them, "check. There's no evidence of me anywhere."

No one knows who Mary Poppins is.

I barely get ten minutes alone with my girls.

I never see Foster once. I even try looking through my glasses for a change, sneaking peeks when a Foster-shaped polo shirt or pair of cargo shorts jogs by.

At three as I'm heading home, I call Michelle and then Steph, but neither of them is off work yet. I call Elliot, but he's on his way to Tempe and doesn't pick up. I squeeze the steering wheel a little tighter as I dial Courtney's number, and when she finally answers, I vent to her how I screwed up majorly, that I can basically never go back. She reminds me about Roush.

"What about the open door and the walking through it?" she asks. "What about an open *mind* at least?"

I try to visualize what the worst camp counselor looks like, but all I can picture is me. Then I try to visualize what the best camp counselor must look like and nothing materializes—I don't even have a reference point.

I drive the rest of the way home in a daze, rolling through who knows how many stop signs while trying to picture this ideal dream counselor, who doesn't even exist. Courtney's waiting for me when I walk in. All she does is hand me a photo of myself—eleven years old, smiling, my arms linked with some girls I used to be best friends with at Camp Hollywoodland—and I'm, like, completely comatose.

I go upstairs and collapse in my room, wondering how to bounce back. I may have never been Teacher's Pet, but I'm still a Star Student. I don't have to necessarily ace this summer, but I absolutely have to pass it. Tomorrow it'll just be me and my group. Jessica, Alexis, Lila, Jenna, Zoe, Maggie, Renee, Rebecca, Billie, Alyssa—I repeat the names a dozen times, like I'm cramming for a Civil War exam.

Later I check my email. Lindsay's written.

Hey gurl, sweet 2 meet. Wanna chat? Roomies, yay.

I forward it to Michelle and Steph for deeper analysis and then keep studying my names.

12.

TWO VERY IMPORTANT
CONVERSATIONS IN BETWEEN
TWO VERY DISAPPOINTING TEXTS

AFTER I'VE MEMORIZED all the names and feel confident I know them, something else starts to stress me out, and that something is: What Next? Just knowing their names isn't anything. I'm sure Foster knows the names of all the campers in the entire camp—and I bet they know his name too, first and last.

I'm lying on my bed, rolling from side to side, sighing, restless. I text Elliot something vague like where do we go from here? and he texts me back Albuquerque. I'm still staring at my phone, my eyes itchy from not blinking, when Michelle calls.

"What's wrong?" Michelle says, right away.

"I'm angsty," I tell her.

"You're *angsty*?"

"Antsy. I said *antsy*."

"No," Michelle says. "You said angsty. That's amazing, Eva. What a hilarious Freudian slip."

"It'd only be a Freudian slip if I actually *was* angsty. Which I'm not."

"Uh-huh."

"Anyway—I'm antsy."

"Remember when Steph and I used to call you Shakes?"

"Yeah, but that was for Shakespeare."

"And for other reasons," Michelle says.

"My eyes are itchy," I say. "Camp is making me itchy. I can't stop rubbing my eyes."

"It's been one day."

"Tell me about *your* day," I say.

"Well, there are about fifteen different closures for a necklace," Michelle says. "I also learned that only a few of them are technically called 'clasps.'"

"It's the summer before leaving for college and you're learning about *closures*?"

"I knew you'd like that," Michelle says.

"I'm writing it down."

"Have you talked to Elliot?"

"Talked or . . . *communicated*?"

"What about Foster?" Michelle asks.

"What *about* Foster?"

"You're not in the mood to talk," Michelle says. "Obviously."

"Noooo, we *have* to talk," I whine.

But Michelle doesn't say anything else, and I can't think of anything to say either. The nerves around my eyes twitch, like they always do when I'm stressed, so I press against the lids until I can feel my heartbeat in my eyelashes and see a thousand stars.

"My eyes," I say, and that's it. Then I hear a beep and it's Steph on the other line. "Steph's calling."

"Tell Steph about your eyes."

"They really hurt," I say.

"You could start wearing your glasses again."

"Eh."

The other line beeps a second beep.

"What did Shakespeare say?" Michelle says. "Eye, there's the rub."

"I'm writing that down too."

"Take it, it's yours."

I click over to Steph.

"I was just telling Michelle that my eyes hurt," I tell Steph.

"You're just stressed," Steph says. "How was the first day of camp?"

"There have been times in history when the word 'camp' has been used to describe a very, very bad place."

"Does a place called the Gap sound any better?"

"I'm warning you," I say, "I've been whining."

"Eva, I'm sure you'll start to like the girls."

"But will *they* start to *love* me?"

"Try harder," Steph says.

"I know, I know."

"I called to tell you that Lindsay seems nice."

"Does she seem illiterate?" I ask. "She seems sort of illiterate to me."

"You're being a snob."

"And you're living off campus, in a studio apartment, less than a mile from the beach."

"You hate the beach," Steph reminds me.

"I hate the *ocean*," I remind her.

"And you're going to *Boston*," Steph says. "That's awesome."

"Maybe we should trade colleges. Like, have you ever thought about swapping futures with someone? Maybe you'd have more fun in my future than I would. Maybe you'd make the best of it and we'd both learn more if it wasn't our *own* lives we had to learn from."

"You're just stressed," Steph says again.

"I need a writing assignment," I say, rubbing my eyes more. "I suck at being a counselor, and I can't write unless someone tells me what to write about."

"Okay, here's something: write like you're me," Steph says. "Write something I'd write, or write me as your main character."

"I'm too jealous of you," I say. "Why are we always so jealous of each other?"

"Because we're girls."

"Don't admit that."

"I love you, Eva," Steph says. "And you're *not* jealous of me. I'm going to a state school for hippies and you're going to a private school for geniuses. Tomorrow I fall back into the Gap, but you get a second chance at being Camp Champ."

"Did you just say Camp Tramp? Because that's not nice."

"Champ, not *tramp*. But how *is* Foster?" Steph asks.

"My eye's twitching, that's how Foster is."

"Don't you feel better now, though?"

"So-so," I say. "Hey, why'd you and Michelle used to call me Shakes? Because I'm a writer, right? Because I'm an awesome writer and you think of me as, like, the Shakespeare of the group?"

"That—and other reasons," Steph says, laughing, and then we say good-bye.

Later I text Elliot something cute like **the best friends are breast friends** and he texts me back **curl powder and whirled peas**, which I assume means he tried to type *girl power* and *world peace* some wacky way but his autocorrect changed them.

I write it all down.

13.

WE'RE GOING TO HAVE A MOTTO

EACH MORNING WE have what's called Morning Ceremonies, where all 179 campers and counselors and staff gather in the outdoor amphitheater to sit on stiff seats and listen to various announcements. Today there's a badly sung sing-along about friendship and letting your light shine, and then Steven introduces the new lifeguard, Marta, and calls an eight-year-old up to the front because it's his birthday. We tunelessly sing the "Happy Birthday" song and all shout "Hi, Marta!" like a day-care center full of reformed, upbeat addicts.

Foster's sitting with his group of nine nine-year-old boys (who Steven swears are a *"really* great group") just off to our left, and they keep swiveling their heads around to sideways-scope my girls—maybe because we're huddled around Alyssa poring over our schedule for the day, not really paying attention and talking too loud. Underneath *MORNING CEREMONIES* it says *FREE PLAY*. My girls can't shut up about it because they're too excited, even me, I'm *dying* to play free, but then we look up and I guess we've missed some dismissal, because everybody's up and leaving, even Foster.

I lead my group out to an empty patch of grass not far from the archery field and climb onto a nice big rock, gesturing for the girls to gather close. Alyssa lies down on her stomach, her head on her elbows, and then all the other girls want to lie the same way, so for a few minutes there's a steady chatter of who's going to lie where and who gets to be closest to Alyssa. I try to give Alyssa a coded look, psychically instructing her to *lead by example*, but it doesn't work because Alyssa's totally oblivious, and why wouldn't she be, she's thirteen and not at all intimidated. None of my girls are intimidated by me, actually, which is the *exact opposite* of how I thought it'd be when I took this job.

When everyone's finally quiet, I get a chance to do what I really wanted to do yesterday: take a good long look at each of them, at their faces and their whole presented selves. Then, without making a big deal of it, I start taking notes.

Jessica is small; she's the redhead dressed all in pink. Lila and Renee are best friends, I assume, because they're wearing matching best friend necklaces and bracelets and rings, and they've braided their hair the same way in a high fishtail with matching scrunchies. Jenna is mean; she has a mean face with a hoodie pulled tightly around it. Zoe must be into sports, because she's dressed like a mini-Olympian: Nike everything and a backward visor. Maggie's generic, instantly forgettable; I can't think of anything to write about her. Rebecca wants to be called Becks and tries to give everyone a similarly nickish-name, which is sort of overbearing. Billie's bright, a smarty, so I like her right away—she's an early favorite. Alexis is very, very chubby. And Alyssa's obviously the coolie; she's got bangs and high-top purple Converses and her ears pierced four times. I write down *Don't be competitive with your CIT* because she's thirteen and who cares, but it's already being hard because Alyssa's brought her makeup and also because she *is* my competition. The girls can't grow to love me if they're too busy obsessing over her.

I read my notes, pleased with my character descriptions. I fold the page and put it in my pocket. I look around at the girls, who're just blankly staring up at me, and then it hits me where to begin.

"Everyone tell me your favorite thing about camp." I say. "Lila, you first."

"Swimming," Lila says.

"Yeah, swimming," Renee says after Lila.

I point to Jessica next. She says, "Meeting friends," and Alyssa dramatically rolls her eyes, makes a *pbbth* sound.

Zoe shouts, "Tetherball!" and Rebecca/Becks says, "Field trips," and Maggie says, "Swimming," and then someone reminds her that two girls have already said swimming, and then *I* have to remind *them* that it's okay to have the same answer as long as we're all thinking for ourselves.

Jenna's favorite thing about camp is going home from camp.

Then Billie raises her hand. "I like making lanyards and I like outdoor cooking and the skits are fun and so are the sing-alongs."

"Anything but the horses," Alexis says.

I look over at Alyssa.

"What, you want me to answer too?" she asks, sort of indignant. "Uh, lunchtime."

"Okay, well, we're going to do *all* those things," I say. "But right now is free play and next is"—I glance at the schedule—"capture the flag, with the boys." I look at the schedule again, because that doesn't seem right.

"Ooh, the boys," Alyssa says, and some girls squirm while other girls giggle.

"Alyssa," I say, whispering, "are we always going to have an hour with Foster's group?"

"They're our Brother Group," Alyssa explains. "So, yeah, every day we have an hour with them. Some days two, if swim overlaps."

"Shit," I say, and the girls go quiet. "Shoot," I say.

"Corey's hot," Alyssa says.

"Who's Corey?"

"He's Foster's CIT."

"Oh my God," I say, burying my head in my hands. I stay like that for a second, sighing, and when I look up, the girls haven't moved. They're waiting for some instruction from me: an order to stay, permission to go, anything. "It's free play," I say. "Go, go."

The girls scatter. Alyssa pulls out her phone—which she's explicitly not supposed to use during camp hours— and starts texting. I'm too overwhelmed by the heat and our schedule to bother scolding her. I consider taking out my phone too but don't, even though I know now would be the perfect time to call Elliot, because he's probably just woken up and hasn't started his long drive to the next city. I think, *Let Alyssa text, let her get in trouble, let her get fired*, and then I realize Alyssa can't get fired, she's just a kid. I'm the one in charge.

"Alyssa," I say, when we're alone. "What are they supposed to *do*?"

"It's free play," she says between texts. "They're doing it."

"What do *we* do? You and I."

Alyssa sits up. "I don't know. Some counselors make up group mottos or, like, little songs for their group to sing. Some groups have a color and then they wear a bandanna that color or something else." Alyssa sends a text. "We can talk about the girls if you want," she says. "I like Becks, she's so funny. She was in a stain remover commercial once, she told me."

"That's cool," I say, looking out at the grassy field, silently counting the number of unsupervised nine-year-olds. I count three together, two together, three together, and then chubby Alexis Powell all by herself pulling up grass in clumps, tossing it in the air.

"No one wants to play with Alexis," I say. Alyssa throws a short glance in Alexis's direction.

"That's their problem," she says. "Girls read too many magazines. They have body image issues," she says, and flips her hair.

"We are going to fix the Alexis problem."

"*Pbbth*."

"But first, what did you say about mottos?"

"I don't know," Alyssa says, ignoring me, so I grab her phone and hold it above my head so she has to deal with me. "You *know*," she says, rolling her eyes, "a motto, like our own saying, like we shout it, y'know?"

"Sure, like 'Go Team,'" I say.

"Yeah, but not stupid."

I hand Alyssa her phone back and call the girls in, and even though I'm telling them to hurry, they're slow, sluggish or distracted by other sights and sounds: butterflies, a dandelion, animal-shaped clouds rolling by. I call them again and this time I clap, above my head like a coach, and I stamp-stomp too. But the girls don't react; I have no control over them. Obviously we need a motto that will bring us together somehow. I pull out my notebook and flip through the pages for something I already know, something I've already thought of, lived through, and this will work toward solving the Roush Problem too. Motto what you know. What. Do. I. Know.

By the time the girls finally make it back to the rock, they already look bored. I imagine what it'd feel like to hate these girls, and if I eventually did hate them, if that'd make me a terrible person.

"We're going to have a motto," I say.

"What's a motto?" Jessica asks.

"It's like our own phrase that we say, like a way to say hello or good-bye or good luck or good one or go team, or whatever."

Hands shoot up; everyone has an idea. Someone says, "Boys are toys!" and someone else shouts out, "Wild things!" and then Jenna says, "When you mouth the words 'F you,' it looks like you're saying 'vacuum,' so how about Vacuum for our motto, because no one will ever know that it really means F you."

I look at Alyssa, and she's trying not to explode laughing. The rest of the girls are scandalized.

"*Orrrr*," I say, "when you mouth the words 'I love you,' it looks like you're saying 'olive juice,' so how about Olive Juice? That's nicer, I think."

No one likes Olive Juice.

"But we want it to be secret, right, like how nobody gets what it means but us. Right?"

They all agree, right.

"How about instead of Girl Power we say Curl Powder? We can yell 'Curl Powder!' whenever one of us scores at a game or dives off the high dive. And then how about Whirled Peas instead of World Peace, and we can say that when we mean hi or bye or when we all have to meet up back here after free play?"

The girls are silent; they think about this.

"Whirled Peas is cool," Alyssa says, weighing it. "And Curl Powder is *definitely* cool."

So that's what it's going to be.

14.

NIGHTMARING

MARCHING THE KIDS from one recreational destination to another isn't so bad, but it is kind of exhausting, and not just because it's ninety degrees and everything's pretty far apart. It also feels weird for me to encourage anyone to do anything that isn't brainy or bookish, let alone a bunch of *kids* who just want to *play*. Being at Sunny Skies is forcing me to remember my own childhood, which is the exact *opposite* of what I'm trying to do, which is focus on my future. When I was seven, my favorite game was called Teacher/Student, and it involved me crafting long, difficult multiple-choice tests for Ariella Klein, and then only giving her ten minutes to complete them. After the time was up I'd collect her pages, grade them, and stick a glittery star sticker at the top before dismissing her for recess. "The best thing about your job," my father would say, tossing me a shiny red apple, "is you get your weekends and summers off." Then he'd wink.

I never got the joke.

I get it now, though. But I'm not teaching anyone. I'm less of a leader than I am just a tour guide for fun, a kid–cattle rancher—which no one in a billion years would've imagined me as.

I didn't really get a chance to talk with Foster during our hour together, or at the pool when our groups swapped places, but when I stop by the nurse's station to ask for an Advil or three, he's there and seems excited to see me. He's waiting for a camper's insulin shot and makes a joke about me doping for the next big capture-the-flag game. It's funny, Foster's funny, and also sort of calm and caring. I can tell by the way he pours a cup of orange juice for his sad-eyed camper and also by the way he laughs when he realizes I'm digging for excuses not to rejoin my group.

"How are you so good at this?" I say.

"How are *you* so good at *writing*?"

"Practice."

"I don't believe you," he says.

"Foster, how should a counselor be? I'm serious."

"You're being it."

"Yeah, Curl Powder," I say, without spirit, raising a limp fist in the air. "I just feel like it should come easier, because I'm sort of cool, so shouldn't a nine-year-old think I'm cool too?"

"Everyone thinks you're *cool*, Eva," Foster says, amused.

"I should write about this," I say. "This is like a real struggle. I'm struggling *for real*."

"Remember when we read *Heart of Darkness* in Mr. Perry's class?"

"No," I say.

"Yes, you do," Foster says. "Remember that line where Conrad's like, 'I should be loyal to the nightmare of my choice'?"

"You're calling camp the *nightmare of my choice?*"

"I guess I am," Foster says, cracking up.

I don't know if I've ever seen Foster really laugh, like how you laugh around friends—all cackling sounds and contorted faces. When I think back about it, I can't remember many times Foster let loose and had fun around me. He's always so self-conscious and, like, *composed*. But maybe that was just Foster trying to impress me, which sounds like it'd be kind of annoying but is actually so sweet. And this is even sweeter: laughing together, away from school, in a totally different *context*, where I can be New Context Eva, seen in a totally new light.

"Anyway," I say, "I hate that book. I hate all books about ships, and I hate Mr. Perry."

"You can't hate that book, it's a classic," he says.

"You know what I say to classics? Vacuum! I say Vacuum! to classics."

"Am I supposed to understand that?"

"Just tell me what you're writing now," I say, "because I know you go home and write every day."

"It's a short story about a boy who dies on accident."

"Wait, a boy who dies on *what*?"

"A boy who dies on accident."

I stop to consider the statement. This is a moment. I'm having a moment, and this is why: Foster says *on accident*, which you can't say because it's not correct. The correct phrase is *by accident*, and normally a mistake like that would kill me, drive me insane, but when Foster says *on accident*, I like it. It makes the boy dying seem even more sad, even more accidental, as if there's this other *kind* of accident and it's even more horrible and unfair.

But I still can't stand that there's a boy dying. Why is anyone dying?! It's the endless Foster Problem. I guess I like Foster, though, he's a sympathetic character, and I have to cure him of this ridiculous, endless Foster Problem.

"Listen," I say, "some people don't know how to begin things and some people don't know how to end them."

"Where would you begin things?"

"In the middle," I say. "Close to the end."

"And where would you end things?"

"Not with a death."

"Why not?" Foster asks, but then his diabetic camper stumbles toward us, holding a cotton ball over the tiny needle hole in his side. The kid is less green but no more coordinated, because he drops his plastic cup of OJ, juice spilling down the front of his Sunny Skies T-shirt. Foster takes him into the nurse's bathroom, where I can hear him splashing water on the boy, telling him not to worry about getting wet, that now he'll be nice and cooled off in the sun. *This* is how a counselor should be. I do like Foster! Foster's a saint! Why were we rivals instead of friends? Why, *on accident*, were we ever such frivals?

"Why not?" Foster says again when he returns with the boy, holding hands, as they follow me out of the nurse's station into the hot day. "People *do* die," Foster whispers. "Death *is* an end."

"Because, Foster!" Then I turn to him and say something I've always wanted to say to him, ever since our sophomore year creative writing class with Mrs. Dubrowski, ever since Foster's first short story about the mailman who gets stabbed in the eye with his own letter opener: "Because aren't things sad enough already?"

"Your stories are sad," Foster says.

"My stories are . . . *hard*."

"And is your life so hard?"

I'm about to answer when Alyssa walks up with the rest of my group. Their hair's all wet, some of them still wearing bathing suits under their jean shorts. Alexis is holding my clipboard, and Billie's gripping a clump of rainbow lanyard string, on their way to the Craft Shack. I scan their faces for frowns, dulled senses, disinterest, and notice they've all got freckles, every one of them, and a sense of duty floods through me, and I suddenly feel super protective. How many more summers are these girls going to have freckles, and how can *I* make these freckle-filled summers as *fun* as humanly possible?

Alyssa tells me the girls want me to pick out our group's colors so they can make beaded necklaces in those colors and wear them to the End-of-Day Ceremonies. I suggest pink and turquoise, which they all love, and then, God, I realize I'm actually feeling loyal to the nightmare of my choice. Then Alyssa counts off, "One, two, *three*!" and that's when they each hold up peace signs and all together yell, "Whirled Peas!"

A few seconds later they wander off, and I feel so sensitive I want to hug Foster because even though I did this, it feels like he did it too.

15.

THERE YOU ARE

AT HOME COURTNEY'S on the couch arguing with Dad about the same stuff as always, while Mom leans against the counter eating soy chips out of the bag, watching the two of them longingly, like somehow even this aimless afternoon bickering is a precious family moment. When I tell them about the Conrad quote, Dad answers back, "Sure, but that guy will say anything to get on a syllabus," and Mom chimes in too, something about how the redeeming things in life aren't happiness and pleasure but the deeper satisfactions that come from struggle. Then she brings up F. Scott Fitzgerald, who wrote about Gatsby and guilt and tycoons and other Classic stuff. Mom actually had a cat when she was little named the Grrr-eat Catsby, and Dad always tells us about his idea for a cookbook called *Recipes for Disaster*. Whenever I think about that, I think about how people always say babies are so cute, but parents can be just as cute sometimes.

Courtney doesn't think so; when I go upstairs my sister follows me, shutting the door behind us.

"I've got two thousand saved," she says, "but Dad's making me put it toward that stupid scratch on his car instead of letting me use it for Amsterdam."

"Mom and Dad were being so cute," I say. "Did you hear when Dad made that syllabus joke? I could *potentially* miss them a lot."

"Potentially," Courtney says. "But Dad's taking my money."

"Yeah, but you hit that guy's speedboat."

"Like a hundred years ago."

"Dad'll forget," I say. "He's literally forgotten every single thing that's ever happened. And Mom doesn't care. She's hit, like, thirteen mailboxes just this year, and she hates Dad's car."

"That's actually helpful," Courtney says, encouraged.

"Hey, I'm on a serious roll today," I tell her.

Then Courtney leaves for a second. When she comes back she's holding the Lonely Planet guide to Amsterdam and sits next to me on the bed. As she flips through the pages, showing me stuff, pointing to everything, her whole face lights up—her whole body even. It's the first time I've been able to tell how Amsterdam really means the world to her—the whole lonely planet to her—and the appeal isn't just that Amsterdam's exotic and in Europe but because it's its *own thing*. It's got its own flavor, which seems obvious—because doesn't everywhere?—but that's what Courtney's attracted to: the substance of what the place truly is.

I don't feel the same way about Boston. I don't care about the city specifically, I just care that it's three thousand miles away. I confess this to Courtney, the shallow truth that I only like Boston because it's far from LA and seems safer than New York and essentially that's it, *that's the only reason I'm going to school there*, and she shuts the book, hands it to me.

"Take this," she says.

"I'm not going to Amsterdam," I say.

"I know, but think of Amsterdam as Boston," Courtney says.

"How do I do that?"

"Just try to think deeply about being somewhere other than where you are."

I skim through the Lonely Planet guide. Nothing looks that interesting. There's a page about Anne Frank's house, but it doesn't seem interesting either, which makes me feel like a bad person.

"Lots of history, I guess," I say.

"Lots of history in Boston too."

"Do you think you'll change when you're in Amsterdam?" I ask.

"Sure, but not that much. I mean, not like *my essence*."

"In Boston I want to change everything," I say. "I'm going to buy a beige trench coat like Mom's Burberry one and carry a newspaper under my arm, and every time I want a book, instead of buying it on Amazon, I'm going to *check it out* from the *library*. And maybe I'll be wearing glasses, too, either round tortoiseshell ones or the kind with clear frames, very *professorial*."

"Ooh," Courtney says, laughing, "how will I *ever* recognize you?"

"Real change can come from the outside first," I say. "It's possible."

"I hope that's not what you're teaching your campers," Courtney says. "I hope you're empowering them, because they're girls and girls need guidance."

I take out my notebook. *Empower them*, I write.

Courtney wants me to look through the guide again, at the photos of old windmills and public parks lined with blooming tulips and beer gardens and canals and a ton of things named after Van Gogh, after Rembrandt, after Anne Frank. Amsterdam is nothing like Boston, but it still gives me an idea for a story: Anne Frank *lives*. Like, she *makes it*, and goes on to lead a secret resistance against the Nazis by hiding other girls and empowering them to fight back. It's historical fiction, or maybe creative nonfiction, which I've never tried, but maybe trying something new beats out writing something you know. Mr. Roush might think so, because he's always so serious about not limiting oneself, and also only a *really* bad person wouldn't be interested in an alternate history of Anne Frank's life.

Then my eyes stop on this super-peaceful picture of the Dutch countryside, and it's not hard for me to imagine my sister there, riding a bike or just picnicking with new Dutch friends. I always thought *I'd* be the only one leaving and so I'd be the one getting wiser, and I always liked that idea, but now I realize that Courtney's better at being the Weird Philosopher and I'm better at being the Absorber, the person who takes it all in. And so maybe I'm not meant to *experience* but to chronicle *other people's experiences*, and now I feel like I totally know how to empower the girls and also how to empower myself so I can totally obliterate the Roush Problem, 100 percent: I'll go to Barnes & Noble and buy ten blank journals and then sneak into Dad's office and steal a fifty-pack of Bic pens; I'll tie pink and turquoise yarn to everything, and then I'll be ready.

I hand Courtney back the book, and even though I

know she won't like me saying this, I say it anyway: "I don't need some Lonely Planet guide. What a stupid name."

"Don't you think the planet *is* lonely, though?"

"I mean, space is lonely. Like, the Arctic tundra's lonely."

"What about Sunny Skies?" Courtney asks.

"I guess," I say. "That can be lonely too."

"Get out your notebook," my sister says. "Write this down: 'Wherever You Go, There You Are.'"

I write it down, look at it.

"It's true, Eva. There isn't a city you could ever travel to where *you* wouldn't be. So you can't rely on a place to change you. You have to do that yourself."

"I know Boston's not going to change *me*," I tell Courtney. "*I'm* going to change *for* Boston."

"By getting a trench coat and a library card?"

"Yeah."

"What about 'Don't Ever Change' or 'Don't Go Changing'?" Courtney says, grabbing my senior yearbook, waving it around. "A bazillion yearbooks can't be wrong."

"Nobody," I say, "*nobody* wrote 'Don't Ever Change' in *my* yearbook."

Courtney flips through the signature pages. "This one says 'Stay Cool,'" she tells me. "That's basically the same thing."

But it isn't the same thing—not even a little, not at all—and I know it. What I don't know is what we're talking about anymore: staying or going, changing or being changed, by someplace, or someone.

16.

SECOND COURSE

"DON'T YOU EVER wish Los Angeles had a Little Italy?" I ask Michelle. It's nine and we're at the Grove, waiting for Steph to finish counting her register and lock up the Gap so we can all share bland Italian food at La Piazza. I'm happy to be out on a summer night and eating late, which feels so European. Even though I usually complain when meals take forever, I understand that there's a sophistication to not rushing through the dining experience.

"The phrase 'Little Italy' really has a vibe to it, doesn't it?" I ask. "Like all the pleasures of somewhere exotic made super easy and brought right to your neighborhood. Little Italy really *conjures* something."

"I thought you didn't even like Italian that much," Michelle says distractedly, fishing through her bag. She pulls out her phone for what seems like the eighteenth time and checks for texts.

"First of all—whose text are you waiting for?" I try to glance at her cell, but she shields the screen with her palm. "I'm already here and Steph's coming any minute."

"Skip to second of all."

"And *second* of all," I say, "it's a cheese thing. I'd love Italian if they didn't put so much cheese on everything."

"Cheeseless lasagna, you're saying."

"Why not?"

"Because it's lasagna. It's like a centuries-old tradition."

"True, but we've evolved into humans who basically can't digest dairy anymore."

"*De*volved you mean," Michelle says. Just then her phone beeps, and as her eyes scan the screen, she smiles privately. I'm about to pry for details when Steph finally arrives, wearing khaki shorts and a sleeveless denim button-up, total Gap-on-Gap—a Gap Attack. It's less that I don't recognize her in her work outfit, and more that I don't recognize her as Steph, my best friend who never has a job or any reason to change out of her own Steph Uniform: velvet leggings and a baggy, boxy top.

"You look like a camp counselor," I say. "And I would know."

"Miranda calls it 'the Basic Bitch,'" Steph explains.

"Who's Miranda?"

"Miranda," Steph says, and then Michelle says, "She told us about Miranda."

"Why does Miranda think it's so casual to call women bitches?" I ask.

Michelle drapes an arm around me in that bemused, Eva-just-can't-help-herself way. "Always looking out for the females," she says, shaking her head.

"It's just not a helpful word," I say. "That's not what it means in the dictionary."

"Miranda's my work-friend," Steph says.

"I don't think you told me about her."

"It's not really news," Michelle says, guiding me through the front door of the restaurant. Once inside she shuffles through her tote again and inspects her phone, scrolling through messages.

Steph's looking around too—not in an ambient way, but purposefully, like someone should be there already. Someone *good*.

"Guys, what's happening?" I ask, but abruptly we're being led to our table, out on a fake piazza under white Christmas lights. "Wait," I say, counting chairs and place settings and best friends, the numbers not matching up: it's a table for five.

"Miranda's joining us," Steph says, and then Michelle says, "And so is Bart."

"Bart—like from high school, *Bart*?"

"Yeah," Michelle says.

"Who invited *him*?"

"It'll be fun," Steph says, opening her menu, hiding from my gaze. "Yum," she says—a word I've never heard her use, ever—"yum, yum, yum."

Miranda keeps insisting we should've gone to Bestia if we wanted pasta. She's Italian—or Italian-American, I think it's important to point out—and apparently that gives her the authority to differentiate good red sauces from bad. She lifts her fork, frowning in disapproval at the watery marinara dripping through the tines of her fork next to our mozzarella sticks. La Piazza was actually Steph's idea, but I don't mention that, especially not after Miranda corrects her pronunciation of *secondo*.

"It means 'main entrée,'" Miranda explains, while my two best friends, plus Bart, all nod, quite impressed. But they shouldn't be; *secondo* sounds and even *looks* like "second." Second—aka second course, aka main entrée—makes perfect sense.

Since Miranda's the only one old enough to drink, she's the only one drinking. She's on her second carafe of red wine, though we still haven't ordered our *secondos*.

"I think I want the linguini," Bart says to no one in particular. Bart's always been pretty *nice*, I guess, but who cares? The problem is he's not *interesting*, which is way more important. Even though everyone changes after high school, it hasn't been that long yet, so there hasn't been enough time for him to change so much that it's actually noticeable. "I used to order it in Rome a lot," he continues, "piled high on top of pizza crusts."

"When were you in Rome?" Steph asks, covering her mouth to ask, which means she's impressed.

"A few times, actually," Bart says, and now maybe I'm impressed. Or jealous. Or both.

"Well, have you been to Florence?" I ask, twirling my angel hair. "Do you know anything about Italian art or history or anything?"

Michelle tries to kick me under the table, but I know her too well and pivot my legs to the side, her shoe thudding against my chair.

"The Vatican is actually really sick," Bart says, rambling. He's so uninteresting he can't even tell that no one cares. He can't even tell that he's not supposed to be here, that it's supposed to just be me and Michelle and Steph, telling our usual jokes, being our usual selves—which means being content. "Content," which if you look it up in the dictionary, means "happy" and "totally satisfied."

"Cheers to the Pope, *salute, cin cin*!" Miranda says, raising her glass. We return her toast with our ice waters and nod. My cup's so full it spills when we all clink glasses, because I'm not drinking any of it because I read you're not supposed to consume liquid while you chew. It weakens the saliva.

"Miranda, you're such a *lightweight*," Steph says, like it's some cute fact she's learned firsthand. Then Steph leans across the table and, in an overly animated way, mouths the word "wasted." Everyone breaks out laughing. At what? At the acknowledgment that if you drink two carafes of wine it makes you drunk? It's so stupid the world doesn't just feel small, it also feels spun around, flipped upside down.

"Bart spent Thanksgiving in Rome," Michelle tells the table.

"No way, what did you eat?" Miranda asks, pink-cheeked and buzzing. It takes her a full three seconds to open her eyes after a blink.

"I had risotto and my brother had something alfredo— or eggplant? One or the other, can't quite remember. No one there even *knew* it was Thanksgiving. I mean, you'd think, 'Oh, of course they don't know, they're not American, so they don't celebrate it.' But then you could also think, 'Oh, I don't know, it's not impossible that maybe Italians know about Thanksgiving. And maybe not just know *about* it, but maybe even know what day it is and that there's special Thanksgiving foods and things like that.' We wondered if the waiter might say something when he brought our plates out—because he spoke perfect English, even asked if we were from New York—but he didn't mention it."

For Bart this many sentences in a row is practically a soliloquy, straight from Shakes himself.

"That's so annoying," I say, killing the table's glow. "That he assumed just because you were American you were from New York City. Ugh, I hate that New York worship, it's such propaganda."

No one bothers trying to kick me under the table this time.

Steph changes the subject: "I bet the linguini in Rome is better than the linguini in Florence. Because it's an older city. They've had more time to perfect it."

"How do you know it's older?" Miranda asks, slightly slurring.

"Because," Steph says, spearing a tortellini, "like the Roman Empire."

"Don't be an idiot, pasta's from China," I say, and this time I don't see it coming: Michelle jabs an elbow and catches me right in the wrist, knocking over Miranda's wine glass, which is already empty.

"Anyway," Bart continues, oblivious to everything, "it was a pretty cool Thanksgiving. We saw the *Pietà* and a bunch of dope sculptures, and the Pope waved from his window, which was awesome."

"Sounds supercool, Bart," I say, glaring at him spreading more butter on more bread. "Better than being in generic-ass New York gobbling some big, nasty turkey at least."

Just then Michelle pinches my arm, stands up, and says sternly, "Bathroom," which in this context means me and her and Steph *now*.

I follow the two of them across the fake rustic piazza and under the fake vine-covered trellises leading to the bathrooms. Michelle shoves the door open and we all file in, even though it's a single—one toilet, one sink, one candle, and one framed painting of a Venice canal with a little gondola bopping along the choppy water.

"Don't look at the art," Michelle says.

"Hey, you guys don't get to be the mad ones here," I say. "You both lied by omission."

"It was a last-minute thing," Steph says. "We didn't know for sure they were coming."

"Lying! You did too know, you planned it."

"We just thought it would be fun," Michelle says.

"It was *already* going to be fun, because it was going to be the three of us and we always have fun, no matter what."

"*More* fun, then," Steph says, and then Michelle says, "A different *kind* of fun."

"No one say 'fun' again or I'm going to flip out," I tell them.

No one does but I flip out anyway, letting loose one sad and lonely scream because I feel left out and lonely, and those are the last two things I should feel when I'm with my two best friends.

"We *like* Bart," Michelle says, and she means all of us—even me.

"I'm okay with that," I say, sighing. "I just don't know why he has to be here."

"Because it's cool sometimes to have other people around, not just us."

"No, we're the coolest," I say.

"Miranda's cool too," Steph says. "She's a writer."

"She doesn't seem like one," I say. "At all."

"Eva, we can't all be Eva," Michelle says.

The toilet in the other bathroom flushes loudly through the thin walls; a man coughs. If everything inside us isn't being dropped down a hole, then it's being hacked up, and I don't want to go back to the table. Not unless we're all laughing, all forgiven, all in agreement about who's on the inside and who's on the outside looking in.

"Well, what does she write?" I ask.

"Really, really beautiful songs," Steph says. "Like poetry."

"Oh," I say. I'd forgotten about songwriting, about even the idea of poetry.

"Even though you were rude," Steph says, collecting

herself, "we're not mad." She looks to Michelle for verbal agreement.

"Even though we have every *right* to be," Michelle says.

"I was just giving them a *pizza* my mind," I say, trying to reconnect.

"Ha-ha," Steph says, not smiling.

"You're the one who put cheese on it," Michelle says to me, accusingly.

She's the first one out the door.

17.

LONELY GETS LONELIER

I'M LYING IN bed at midnight, mentally prepping for my girls tomorrow, visualizing how to introduce the journals and the pens, but it's so absurdly hot in my room I keep getting distracted. I flip open my phone: I've got one message from Shelby, wanting to hang out this weekend and *not* talk about boys (re: Zack), but there are no postgame amendments from Michelle or Steph, obviously. Lindsay emailed again, and it's kind of cryptic (*Comin 2 San D NETime soon? cuz lez hang*), and Foster wrote saying he's trying to figure out a way for the boy *not* to die.

Every summer my mother declares it the hottest summer she's ever felt in Los Angeles, and even though she's factually wrong, I'm still not looking forward to the year when it finally gets cooler and turns autumn right on schedule with the rest of the lonely planet. I hope LA gets hotter and hotter year after year, until one year summer lasts all the way until the next summer, and beyond that even.

One reason I don't mind the heat is because I can't sweat. Not even in the areas where it should be easy: armpits, crooks of elbows, backs of knees. I wish I could, because it feels like there's something inside me that needs to be sweated out. I close my eyes and imagine taking a bath—*aye, there's the tub*—and then I imagine Sunny Skies Day Camp being scorched by sunshine. I try to *will* the sweat out. Maybe if I played prisoner ball. Maybe if I played prisoner ball in sweats. Maybe if I had sex. Maybe if I had the hottest sex.

That's when Elliot calls. I pick up on the first ring, which he wasn't expecting. I can tell he was expecting to talk to an answering machine, because what he says sounds like a speech, but because it's a nice speech I don't interrupt. He's somewhere in Texas, north of Austin, on his way to Oklahoma City, then Little Rock.

"Then Nashville, then Louisville, then Baltimore, then Philly."

"Wow," I say.

"I'm counting off days."

"That's what I'd do."

"Our LA gig is in some parking lot on Melrose outside some record store," Elliot says. "Have you heard of it?"

"I'm not sure."

"I'm having an okay time"—that's the word he uses—"are things being okay at camp?"

"Yeah," I say. "I'd say they've been mainly okay."

"Sorry I haven't called," he says.

And then Elliot exhales in that specific way a smoker exhales, between words, so I ask if he's smoking. He is! I never knew that he smoked—I *hate* that he smokes—so I launch into a tirade about tongue cancer, which to me seems even grosser than lung cancer, and about those tiny electronic boxes they put in cancer patients' throats to help them talk.

"I only smoke when I'm stressed or when I'm having fun," he says.

That makes no sense to me.

Then Elliot brings up how we only have, like, six or seven weeks left before I leave. But I can't tell: is he just counting off days on a calendar, or does he mean we only have six or seven weeks—the rest of this hot, lonely summer—to *do something*, to know each other, or fall in love, or form some bond that'll last into fall when I'm running through the Boston rain with a newspaper covering my head? I don't know and I don't ask, because I'm still mad about the smoking and I won't change that, not for him.

"Well," I say, wrapping up, "don't have too much fun."

"*Don't have too much fun?*" Elliot asks, disappointed.

"How about, 'Don't do anything I wouldn't do'?"

"Okay," he says. "So don't do anything then."

18.

SOBTOWN, MASS.

THE MORNING STARTS great, full of promise. We all sing "Boom Chicka Boom" at Morning Ceremonies—even me, even *Alyssa*—while Foster and I exchange funny looks. During the "Happy Birthday" song for Meghan Bremner, who's turning nine, my girls shout out alternate lyrics ("*you look like a monkey, and you smell like one too*") and erupt into laughter. When I'm handed our schedule, I'm disappointed to see we don't have any overlap with Foster's boys until free play, which isn't until two. But we have Swim as our first activity, and that usually puts the group in a good mood.

But today Alexis Powell doesn't want to get in the pool. She refuses to even wear a bathing suit. I tell her that's fine, she doesn't have to. I let her wear a baggy T-shirt over boys' trunks and let her sit out the underwater test. She wants to just dangle her feet in the water, so I let her. And later, when she wants to lie on a towel and flick her fingers in a puddle, I let her do that too.

But it keeps going like that through the whole day.

"I don't want to ride the horses," she says.

"I don't want to run in the relay race."

"I don't want to be in the skit."

"I don't want to hike Mount Bony."

"That's okay, that's fine," I tell her, because most of it sounds boring to me too, and not that big of a deal. "You can be my second assistant, like a *junior* junior counselor," I say, and for a moment I worry it'll make the other girls jealous, but it doesn't. They don't care, and honestly, they're not paying attention anyway.

The truth is Alexis *isn't* fat, but she's getting there, and I'm not helping. I don't make her do anything all day except hold the clipboard, which she clutches against her hip and occasionally drops in the dirt. I can tell this is how she gets by: pretending to faint at strategic moments like right before archery, or staging a migraine when it's her turn to return the kickballs to the gym. I know it's kind of wrong to enable her—she's here to play, she's here to interact, to exercise, to move her little fat butt—but I also know Alexis Powell *hates* camp, so maybe it was sort of wrong to send her here in the first place. Why should Alexis Powell have to go anywhere or do anything she doesn't want to do? Why should any of us, really?

At two, when it's time for free play, I notice Foster gathering his group around the big rock. I lead my girls to a patch of grass in the shade farther away, so we can have a little privacy. I unzip my backpack and dump out the journals and pens in a messy pile on the ground. I smile, eager, but no one smiles back; I gesture to the books for the girls to each take one. No one moves.

"Take one," I say. "You guys, seriously, they're for you."

"You were carrying those all day on your back?" Alyssa says. "Pbbth."

"They aren't that heavy," I say.

"They aren't heavy," Alyssa says, "but they *are* ugly. I mean, I know you're not supposed to judge a book by its cover, but I mean, really, that's what covers are for."

"You can put stickers on yours," I say, and finally Alyssa picks one up, and then all the other girls do, one after the other—slowly, and not at all enthusiastically. "And a pen," I say, and then they pick those up too.

"If we really want Curl Powder," I start, "and Girl Power too, then our voices have to be heard. Remember Anne Frank? That's what I'm talking about, how if she never wrote that diary, then no one would ever know she was up in that attic, and then generations of societies wouldn't have her amazing story. Now, we all have amazing stories, I'm sure of that, so all we have to do is write what we know and then something unbelievably amazing will come out. There's this saying that the pen is mightier than the sword, and what people mean when they say that is that the written word is superpowerful. I think you're all very specific and interesting, and that means your stories are important to tell."

The girls rustle a little. They flip through the pages of their empty books with equally empty faces. I can't tell if this is working, if I'm empowering them.

"Everyone can personalize their books, like I said, with stickers and whatever else."

"Can we use it as a diary?" Lila asks, and then Renee asks, "Yeah, can we put our secrets in it?"

"That's fine, I guess."

"I'm not good at writing," Zoe says, and then Maggie agrees. Billie's already drawing something in her book, a bunch of smiling puppy faces. Then Jessica gets up and starts looking in the grass for her pen cap, which she's somehow already lost. Jenna's carving a *J* in the spine of her book with a safety pin, and there's no time to wonder where she got the safety pin or whether I should take it away, because Rebecca's throwing more questions at me and Alexis is . . . crying.

"Uhhh-ohhh," Alyssa says, and that launches a minor chaos of everyone talking at once and fighting with sword-pens and writing on each other's arms and using the books to crush ants and other bugs.

"Whirled Peas!" I shout. "Whirled Peas," I say more quietly, hushing them. "Nobody else in camp has a book like ours to write down all their secrets and stories and awesome ideas. Only us, and I think that's cool. Alyssa?"

"It's cool," Alyssa agrees, but sort of annoyed. "*God.*"

"I know it's free play and we can do anything we want for an hour, but what do you guys think about spending that time writing together?"

"Okay," everyone says, "okay, yeah, fine."

"On the very first page, write this down: 'My name is,' and put whatever your name is, and next 'I'm traveling toward,' and then write whatever thing or place or feeling you're traveling toward. Can be anything."

Billie's hand shoots up.

"Just write," I say. "Be creative!"

"Do I have to do it too?" Alyssa whispers in my ear, and I shoot her back a dirty look.

"Let's take ten minutes and then we'll all share," I tell them.

I stare at my own blank book. *My name is EVA KRAMER* and *I'm traveling toward BOSTON.* It's a good answer, but it doesn't look good written down. I move the letters in the word around to read *SOBTON* and then *NOTSOB*, and that sort of works: *I'm traveling toward not sobbing when I leave for Boston.* This feels real and deeply what I know, and even though that means it's *actually working,* something makes me cross the words out. While it's true that the Eva I know *is* traveling toward Boston, there's also a more romantic version of Eva out there, maybe one that doesn't exist yet, who's traveling toward Paris, and she's obviously the more interesting Eva, so of course she's the Eva I want to write about. Mr. Roush is right: I have a serious problem, I'm a fake writer, but there's no time to worry about that now.

"Okay," I say, "what did everyone write?"

"It's only been eight minutes," Rebecca says.

"I'll go first," Billie says. "My name is Billie Westerman and I'm traveling toward finishing all of the books on my summer reading list, including *The Hobbit* and every book in the American Girl series."

Then Jessica goes: "My name is Jessica Avery, and I'm traveling toward peace."

And then Maggie: "My name's Maggie Lamar, and I'm traveling toward peace*fulness.*"

And then all the other girls look down at what they've written, and then no one will go. I pinch Alyssa.

"My name is blah, blah," Alyssa begins, "and I'm

traveling toward Corey," and she waves at Corey across the field.

"Maybe it seems like I didn't give you enough time," I say to the group, "but listen, these are just fun little writing exercises. You can really write whatever you want whenever you want."

"Even when we're supposed to be playing tetherball?" Alexis wants to know.

"Totally," I tell her. "If you're writing, then you don't have to do anything else."

"I don't think Steven will—" Alyssa starts to whisper in my ear, but I stop her, because Steven told me every camper wants a fun camp experience, and I'm sure he doesn't claim to know what every single camper thinks is fun.

"So let's call this Free Write from now on! Go ahead and Free Write, girls. Have fun," I say.

Suddenly I need a minute away from all this. I spy Foster across the field glancing in my direction, so I get up and tell Alyssa she's in charge.

"Wait," she says. "What'd you write in your book? I want to hear."

"I wrote, 'My name is Eva Kramer, and I'm traveling toward Paris.'"

"Paris?" Alyssa says. "Pbbth, Paris is so cliché."

"You don't even know what a cliché is."

"I know the Eiffel Tower's just an overrated tourist place, because I've been there."

"You can't say the Eiffel Tower's overrated," I say.

Alyssa shrugs.

"I'm going to Boston anyway," I say.

"Boston's cool," Alyssa says, and shrugs again.

19.

THE WHOLE THING

FOSTER'S LEANING AGAINST a tree, holding a Sunny Skies baseball cap half-filled with folded slips of paper while his boys play a fluid, lawless game of charades. I peek inside the hat and glance at a few of the clues. Each one is totally ridiculous: *DINOSAUR ROCK STAR, GRENADE WHIPLASH.* I laugh out loud. None of these kids are *ever* going to guess right, but everyone seems happy anyway. Foster's boys are impressively self-sufficient too; they don't even need Foster to help out, so he doesn't, and I don't either.

One thing I've noticed about Foster is that he has really great posture, and I wonder if it's part of the reason his group likes him so much. He stands tall when he's giving them instructions, but when he talks to them one-on-one, he doesn't bend down like the rest of the counselors do—Foster actually kneels on the ground, right at his camper's height, so they're on the same level. I love that, which makes me wonder if there might be something like that he loves about me.

When Foster asks how it's going, I tell him about my empowerment idea and what I've done with the journals. Foster smiles; he says it's a Very Eva Idea. Then he nudges me and I nudge him and we nudge each other back and forth until it's like we're playing our own charades game and the clue is *FLIRTING*.

"Look at this kid," I say, laughing. "His clue is 'Banana Underwear.'"

"That's actually kind of easy," Foster says.

"Oh yeah," I say, nudging again, "act out 'banana' then, Mr. Sean Penn."

"I can act out 'underwear,'" Foster says, and pulls his jeans down just a little, revealing an inch of navy-blue elastic.

"That's vulgar," I tell him.

"You want to see vulgar?"

"I do not."

"Eat lunch with nine boys and a horny eighth grader."

"Maybe I will," I say.

"Tomorrow?" Foster asks, but I don't answer, just

nudge. "Look at all those promising female writers," he says, looking out across the field at my clump of doodling girls. "Intimidating, if they can write like you."

"Foster," I say, "if they can write like me, I want you to drown me in that sludge Steven calls a lake. Just lay my dead body in a canoe and let it drift away."

"Are nine-year-old girls the competition now?" Foster asks. "Because that means I'm out of a job. I was planning on putting 'Eva's Competitor' on my résumé and using you as a reference."

"We're friends now," I say.

"*Now?*" Foster says.

"Yeah, *now.*"

Foster smiles his smile that I guess I've seen a ton of times before, but this time it makes me feel extra crazy good. I know Michelle and Steph think Foster's cute, but they also think we're destined to fall into some predictable summer romance, which is exactly the type of peer pressure that I can't *help* resisting, like with the chow mein and so many other things. But I'm not trying to taste Foster Hoyt just to prove a point and then spit him out, because *we're friends now*, and besides, there's Elliot in the picture, even though he's a smoker.

"Charades," I say. "Ugh."

"Not an Eva Thing?"

"I've never liked it. I hate that you can only

communicate with body language, because you can't learn that. It's like, I've done all this work to be better at talking and writing, and here's this game that forces you to unlearn all that and express yourself through mime gestures and monkey faces and just *being a good sport*."

"You're a good sport," Foster says.

"No one has *ever* called me that," I say. Then I point to the boy whose turn it is, who's still nowhere *close* to impersonating Banana Underwear. "For instance, this might be a lame point to make, it may seem straightforward, but when you're playing charades, you have to remember that no one knows what the clue is, so getting frustrated at your team doesn't help anything. But look at this kid—"

"Oliver."

"Look at Oliver. He's getting pissed the other boys can't tell he's acting out Banana Underwear, but instead of trying a new tactic, some other way of getting Banana Underwear across, he's just getting madder and, like, more *emphatic*. I hate being misunderstood like that over and over."

"Okay," Foster says, "that's fair, but it goes both ways. The guessers have to shout out a lot of guesses, because if they just sit there waiting to guess until they're a hundred percent sure, then they're not really playing."

"Foster, that's like a life lesson, I think."

Then, at the exact same time, I reach for my notebook and Foster reaches for his recorder. We laugh.

"You can have it," I say. "You said it."

"We can share it," Foster says, and then whispers into his tape recorder. I write down *CHARADES*, and that's it, and Foster nudges me. "Do you ever go to readings?" he asks.

"Sure," I say, trying to sound like a Good Sport.

"There's this reading at Book Soup on Sunday that I really want to go to."

This is Foster asking me on a date, and *I know it*. This is so distinctly an Open Door that there's no question I'm going to walk through it, but just as I'm about to say the perfect response, a boy comes crashing into Foster's legs. He wants a new clue because the last one was too hard, so Foster asks me to fish around in the hat and find something more guessable. But each clue I unfold and peek at is more impossible than the one before—not to mention that some of them are outright illegible. Then I unfold *HARRY POTTER AND THE SORCERER'S STONE*.

"Here you go," I say, handing the slip of paper to the kid.

"What do you think, Trevor?" Foster asks, kneeling down, studying his face.

Trevor reads it and then he smiles, the spark of an idea animating his eyes, and it's pretty magical. I feel good about his chances. I squeeze Foster's arm.

Trevor goes back in front of the group, and everyone stops talking. He unfolds and folds the clue a few times, biting his lip, staring down at the dirt, thinking. I'm rooting for Trevor, but I'm also rooting for Foster and me, because it feels like if Trevor can get this one, then Foster and I will get our first date.

Finally Trevor slips the clue in his pocket and begins, raising his arms in the air, making a big circle three or four times.

"What's he doing?" I whisper to Foster.

"That means the *whole thing*," Foster whispers back. "He's going to act out the whole clue instead of just the individual words."

At first I'm annoyed, because the words are so plain, anyone could act them out. "Sorcerer" could be broken down into a few simple gestures (waving a wand, stroking a beard), and for "Stone" you can just pretend to lift something heavy. "Harry" is even easier—just point to your hair. But the Whole Thing? I can't even imagine that. The Whole Thing is like everything, and how do you act out Everything? How do you communicate *Everything*? You can't.

Trevor starts off crouching on the ground, like he's scared and hiding, then there's some bird impressions and a bit where he's pretending to be lost. Later he waves his hand frantically, trying to indicate something that's moving really fast, but no one can tell it's a train. Then he changes strategies, going for more of a wizard thing, miming the costume—a hat and scarf and glasses. Finally he does the wand, but the way he's casting spells looks more like he's hitting somebody with a stick, so no one guesses it, which then derails into an extremely confusing impersonation of a Quidditch game, and after that there's a bunch of gestures I can't interpret at all. The rest of his team aren't even guessing at this point, they're just shouting, "What is that?" and "Do that part again!" and I'm feeling depressed and responsible because I picked it. But Trevor doesn't give up; he keeps trying stuff, experimenting, throwing himself into it, until gradually it's like this emotional one-man performance, and suddenly I find myself really visualizing this frightened and heroic boy-wizard. He's in the midst of mime-fighting some villain like Voldemort or Severus Snape when, magically, a kid yells out, "Harry Potter and the Sorcerer's Stone!" and Trevor throws his fists in the air and cheers and the whole thing's over.

Foster runs to his group and high-fives everyone, and hugs Trevor, and he even hugs me, but he forgets about the reading and Book Soup and Sunday, because that whole thing's over too.

20.

INCENTIVE

WALKING BACK TO my girls, I can't stop thinking about the charades game, how inspiring it was. But more than just inspiring *me*, it inspires me *to inspire*. Even though incentive, as a concept, doesn't really do much for me personally, it usually works on other people, so I assume it'll probably work on the girls. I'm starting to get used to what it feels like to be a leader, and I'm also getting used to giving speeches and just basically trying to share my voice with other females and other potential future writers. I gather the girls near the animal area by the bunny pen and give them a long speech, which they have no choice but to listen to.

"When I was a kid, even younger than you guys, my

mom had a jar that she filled with quarters. It was a big jar, with like a thousand quarters—which used to seem like a thousand dollars, but is really only like two hundred and fifty bucks, which is still a lot. I was seven, and my parents decided that was a good age for me to start receiving an allowance. They said they'd give me a quarter for each chore I did. That was the plan, that there was no set weekly amount; I could earn however much I wanted if I just *did the work*. So I asked my mom what jobs there were, but each week she'd only be able to think of, like, three or four jobs because I was so short and sort of clumsy and also because my older sister'd already done most of the important chores. So every Friday I only earned like four quarters, which I thought was unfair, since I was *willing* to do more work. My dad told me to start inventing new chores, like ironing his ties or separating the mail—Job Creation, he called it—but that felt like a hassle, because there was a chance my mom wouldn't even consider those *real chores*, and then I wouldn't get more quarters.

"I tried to make my mom an offer that I'd do any work she wanted, all week long, for a flat fee of two dollars, or eight quarters. To me that seemed more than fair; she could take advantage of the situation if she wanted and have me washing her hair or something and for only two dollars! I don't know if any of you get an allowance, but I just don't think that's a lot to ask, even with the economy or whatever. But my mom said no. She told me she wasn't bargaining and that I had to *earn* those quarters, quarter by quarter. She called it 'incentive.' Have you heard of incentive? It means, like, motivation or encouragement or *inspiration*.

"So—I was thinking about the journals, which I know some of you want to use as diaries or for doodling or writing notes to each other, and I had this cool idea: we're going to take everyone's favorite things that they write this summer—if it's a story or a poem or a letter or even just like a rant or an essay about something you love or hate—and we'll make a collection. I'll make a zine—have you heard of a zine? It's like a magazine but smaller and photocopied and indie, like *independent*. I'll bind the collection like a little book, and then you'll have a memory of this summer you can keep forever. It'll be all our cool thoughts and feelings, and it'll be just for us, though you can show it to your parents if you want. Then they'll see how you're these smart writers and how you didn't just have fun this summer, you also *used your brain*.

"This is your incentive to care about what you write and care about each other's writing too. It's incentive to love your journal and to love writing and to love our group!"

When I finish, no one says anything. A few girls look

down at their journals, in a daze. But I can see wheels turning in Billie's head, just like I saw those Harry Potter ideas light up Trevor's face.

I tell them tonight's assignment is to think of something you're really good at and then describe precisely how to do it in as few sentences as possible. I tell them this kind of writing is called Second Person, which makes me feel how Mr. Roush must feel when he's teaching a classroom of semi-attentive young minds about Second Person: *excited.*

After camp, out by the bus, Alyssa comes over and tells me there's nothing that she's *so good* at, that she knows *so well,* that she could describe how to do it in just a few steps.

"No way, you're good at a bunch of things," I say.

"Not really," Alyssa says.

"What about that cool friendship bracelet?" I ask, pointing to her wrist.

"I didn't make that."

"Okay," I say, looking all over Alyssa. I look at her shoes and her shirt and then up around her face, but all I notice is her sleek black eyeliner, perfectly straight, with the tiniest flick at the edge of each eye. It's like a cat-eye tutorial in a magazine, pristine as some Kate Moss photo. "What about your eyeliner?" I suggest. "You rule at putting on eyeliner. Way better than me."

"It's just practicing in the mirror. I just do it every day."

"Well, there you go," I say, patting her shoulder. "Now you've got something: Putting on Eyeliner."

And that's another problem solved.

Later, when Courtney and I are setting the table for dinner, I tell her about the assignment and Alyssa's cat-eye talent. Courtney's so impressed she puts down the silverware to give me a hug.

"You're not just stimulating them," Courtney says, "you're also helping with their self-confidence. It's awesome!"

"It feels good," I say. "Self-confidence is major."

"What are *you* going to write about for the assignment?"

"I don't know yet, maybe the best way to play charades."

"But you hate charades," Courtney says.

"I *used* to hate charades," I correct her. I set all the plates and the cups down and it reminds me: "I told the girls about Mom's quarters and our allowance."

"You told them what you did?"

"The story's about *incentive*, Court."

"The *story* is about *indigestion*," Courtney says, raising her eyebrows at me.

But I don't tell my sister that the girls heard an abridged

version, like how sometimes editors shorten Charles Dickens because he's so rambling and annoying and repetitive. With *Great Expectations* it's about the highlights, not about the long dinners with Uncle Pumblechook. So that's what I gave my girls—the highlights—not the long parts about how I started swallowing the quarters, one by one, week after week, until my mother not only gave me the raise I demanded but also started paying me in crisp one-dollar bills.

We were talking about incentive anyway, and besides, I have Great Expectations for these girls, so if a story can be a bridge—from one person to another—then *this* story can be *abridged*, no problem.

21.

GCHATTING WITH LINDSAY

Lindsay: r u there

me: i'm here, hey

Lindsay: can't talk 2 long, have rehearsal in an hour, but wanna at least say hi

me: rehearsal for what

Lindsay: pirates of penzance, i'm n it

me: you're an actress

Lindsay: yah

me: yr a theater major

Lindsay: yah, whut r u

me: wlp

Lindsay: ?????

me: writing, literature, and publishing

Lindsay: oh weird

me: i guess emerson does have a rlly good theater dept

Lindsay: yah but i wanna go 2 london

me: when

Lindsay: i wanna transfer after 2 yrs

me: to london??

Lindsay: u evr heard of the west end

me: i think my parents used to watch that show

Lindsay: no, it's n london, where they do all the plays

me: london

Lindsay: u evr been

me: not really

Lindsay: it's tha best

me: but aren't you excited for boston and for emerson

Lindsay: yah of course but i'm also thinkin bout after that

me: so yr a pirate

Lindsay: no i'm the daughter

me: sounds like a good part

Lindsay: tha leed!

me: i wish i could see it

Lindsay: ever been 2 SD?

me: sea world, yeah

Lindsay: wanna come back?

me: hmm got this job now

Lindsay: sat n sun?

me: maybe

Lindsay: i can get u free tix 2 my play

me: i'll see

Lindsay: can't b leeve we r gonna b roomies

evr shared a room?

me: i have a sister

Lindsay: me 2, she's 11

me: i'm a counselor and my girls are all 9

Lindsay: the worst

me: u think?

Lindsay: they r so mean 2 each other, meaner than hi

skool 4 sure

me: hmm

Lindsay: whut r yr girls like

me: i don't really know

Lindsay: haha

me: got any tips

Lindsay: NO haha

me: i'm teaching them to write

Lindsay: dont they alrdy know how 2 write

me: no, like, to write a story or a poem

Lindsay: oh kool

evr write plays?

me: not really

Lindsay: u shd, i can be in it

me: maybe

Lindsay: 4 emerson, u know

AH! gotta run

me: have fun at yr thing

Lindsay: rad 2 talk! last summer, make it count!!

me: i'm counting

22.

IDEA FOR A PLAY

IT'S A BUMPY rest of the week, mainly because there's so many horseback-riding sessions. On Wednesday it was just me and Alyssa sitting out with Alexis, but by Thursday and especially Friday, *all* the girls are sitting out—it's not just Alexis who doesn't want to do anything. But my incentive *is* working, the girls *are* writing, even if it's partially for the wrong reasons. I'm writing too, though (*My name is EVA, and I'm traveling toward SAN DIEGO*), and when I feel ready to read my stuff to the girls, they'll probably feel like they're ready too. That's called Leading by Example, and it's what Foster does; I know because I watch him, whenever he's around.

I thought I'd find more literary inspirations at camp

and in my experiences here, but so far I haven't really experienced that much. Overall it's been pretty normal, just going from activity to activity, half doing whatever we're supposed to be doing and half working on our journals. Sometimes an hour or so passes with all of us just quietly buried in our books, huddled under a big oak tree or sitting along the edge of the lake, before I realize it's time to gather everyone up and march on to the next station.

I'm proud, though, because we're becoming kind of a unified little front. Foster says our group's totally distinguished itself by never screaming or arguing or getting sent to Steven's office to settle some fight over swim towels or lunch sacks or who called who a stupid bitch. I'm not sure if I should be worried, if that sort of conflict is somehow more healthy than what I've created, which is this odd, isolated, mellow utopia. Mr. Roush once said that in literature there's no such thing as a utopia, because writing about utopia inherently means writing about *dystopia*, because even a perfect world—*especially* a perfect world—is suspect.

I had thought that making it to the first weekend of my first-ever job would feel incredibly satisfying, like I'd been through so much and really come out on top. But when Friday night comes, I don't know, it's not like that. I don't feel like a survivor, and I definitely don't have a million great stories or funny anecdotes. I text Michelle and Steph to see if they want to go to the movies and then wait for them to text back.

It seems like there's a lot of static in the air, because I keep getting shocked when I touch the banister or doorknobs or the DirecTV remote. For a minute there's even a brownout, then a full-on blackout, which makes Courtney scream because she's in the shower. There's a scramble for the candles, but once they're lit I find my phone and still no one's texted. Mom starts saying how the good thing about landlines was that you never lost your phone, while Dad makes jokes about something ancient called a beeper. I'd always rather have a cell phone, because it means that no matter how long power is out Elliot can still call, and Michelle or Steph can still text. Even though none of them do.

Sitting in the dark, watching my sister flipping the switch of her blow dryer on and off, I get an idea for a new play. There're two couples, two families, who live next door to each other. This is the 1980s or nineties, it's a period piece, so that means they have landlines and regular plugged-in phones. After a blackout, their phone lines get crossed. The first couple starts receiving calls meant for the second couple and vice versa. One night the first couple gets a call from a worried friend of their neighbors' teenage daughter. She's missing. She's run away. The two of them were on a summer trip together in Amsterdam or London, and last night she vanished. Just gone. But the first couple doesn't tell their neighbors; they don't say a word about it. To them it's a mystery, like a problem, one they want to solve, so they hide the truth, pose as their neighbors, try to piece together clues, only to get the call at the end of the second act that their daughter is never coming back. Not *their* daughter, their neighbors' daughter. And now they can't keep the secret anymore, because they've got to go over there and do the right thing. The play could be called *Neighbors*, or *Lines*, or *Crossed Lines* maybe.

Knock, knock.

Hello.

You remember that blackout last month?

Yes.

Our lines got crossed.

Yes.

We've got something to tell you.

Then the play ends, before anyone has to say the word "dead."

Maybe I'll give this one to Foster. Or maybe we can share it.

23.

REP

MICHELLE AGREES TO hang at the mall until four, but Steph is busy until seven. I don't want to wait there for three hours, and besides, the point is to all hang out *together*, but when I explain this, they say it's okay because they saw each other last night, so it's fine if there's no overlap today. Then Michelle tells me about this Santa Barbara Jewelry Fair she's working next week—although she doesn't exactly invite me—while Steph describes how Miranda caught a shoplifter at the Gap, but I can't pay attention to either of them, because I want to know where and *why* they were hanging out without me last night. I interrupt our three-way call and, in a weird desperation, start reading back all the texts I sent last night, demanding to know why they didn't respond. They both claim they didn't even receive them. But even if that *is* true, even if the lines were somehow crossed and my texts got sent to two *different* friends, that still doesn't explain why I wasn't invited, why they didn't reach out to me.

"We were just at Kerry's house, watching Kate Mara movies and Rooney Mara movies," Michelle says. "Kerry calls it a *Mara*thon, and since you hate Kerry and don't really have any feelings about the Mara sisters, no one thought to call."

"I don't remember hating Kerry," I tell Steph.

Then, without saying the name Bart, but implying as much, Steph reminds me I hate everyone.

She's wrong, though—I don't hate everyone. It's just that in high school you say mean things about your classmates because you're dying of boredom and dying to graduate and because you're just joking anyway.

"It's not a big deal. You wouldn't have had that much fun anyway," Michelle says, and that hurts too, because why do my best friends assume I wouldn't have fun watching movies with them?

This must be my rep: someone who's Not a Good Sport, someone who's this Very Specific Person, and *not* in a good way. I guess a Classic Eva move doesn't mean a funny, cool, chill move, but a close-minded, judge-y move, which maybe was true before, but I honestly feel like I've begun to change all that.

"Am I that much of a bummer?" I ask.

"Bummer's not the word *I'd* use," Steph says, and Michelle just says, "Eh."

"It's just that you're so rigid," Steph says.

"Yeah, you have a lot of *rules*," Michelle adds.

"Okay, but I'd still like to be extended the *opportunity*, even if sometimes I say no. Is that bratty?"

"I wouldn't call it *bratty*," Steph says, and then Michelle says, "I would."

"Are you mad at me or something?"

"Let's not get into that again," Steph says.

"It's not about being mad," Michelle tells me.

We run out of things to say for a minute, so I check my email and there's a message in my in-box from Shelby, asking if I want to hang out today. I relay this to Michelle and Steph, plainly fishing, hoping they'll say something mean or dismissive about Shelby, but realize that's more something I would do, which is what Courtney calls Classic Projection. Neither of them has a reaction to my news about Shelby, so eventually we trade stilted good-byes and I text Shelby that we should meet for lunch later.

Downstairs my mom's got the fridge open, calling out items to my dad, who's writing a shopping list. They can tell right away that something's wrong.

"You know, water seeks its own level," my mother says.

"What does that even mean?" I ask.

"It means people match up with other people who are on their level."

"Okay, but what do you mean by 'level'?"

"It's advice, Eva," my father says. "Take it or don't take it."

"But how can I take it if I don't understand it?"

"You love Michelle and Steph, but you're also on your way to college, where you'll meet a ton of new people, many of whom will have the same *agenda* as you," my mother says.

"Other writers, you mean."

"Writers, thinkers," my father says. "Other smart young men and women."

"I'm not going to *Harvard*," I say.

"Yes, but you'll be *near* Harvard," my mother says, hopefully.

"Sure, geographically, but not like, *mentally*."

"You could make Harvard friends," my father says. "It's not impossible."

"This is *not* advice," I say.

"Oh, smile," my mother says. "It's Saturday!"

I force a smile and then leave to meet Shelby for lunch at Roxy's Famous Deli. Shelby always picks the place, and she always gets there early so she can pick the booth. She's already eating from a basket of cheesy fries when I slide in beside her.

"Did you get contacts?" she asks. "They look so good."

"Contacts are gross."

Shelby offers me a fry, then remembers the cheese and takes the offer away.

"I'll wear my glasses when I can get glasses that *suit* me," I say. "I have to, like, grow into the look."

"Glasses make everyone look smarter, and I know you, you want to look smarter than everyone."

"I *want* to look sexy."

"Guys will have sex with you even if you don't look sexy," Shelby says. "Fact." She licks cheese and grease off her fingers. "Lasik?"

"Gross."

Shelby shrugs and moves on. "Well, are you crazy excited, like, overflowing with anticipation for Boston?" she asks.

"I guess so," I say.

"Oh, stop moping, Eva," she tells me.

That's the word she uses—"moping"—and when she says it, she rolls her eyes and waves me off like that's also part of my rep, that I'm some Eternal Moper. Shelby says she moped for five straight days after she and Zack broke up, but she's done with moping now.

Shelby's a good friend—not a *close* friend, but a good one—and she does this thing my dad calls Telling It Like

It Is, which really just means she doesn't hold back on honest details, even if a person might not want to hear them. What I like about Shelby is that she's always had such a different agenda from everyone else. She never wanted to go to college or move away, she just wanted to do people's hair for a living and run her own salon in this very posh part of Pasadena. Shelby's very ambitious, which I think is on my level, but her ambitions aren't to be this Important Person or to Make It, which my parents would probably say is some totally different level from mine. Shelby's also the only real adult in our graduating class, because she's always had a job and birth control pills and a silver nose ring, and because she was always dating Zack, who's like six years older.

The breakup happened two months ago, at the food court in the Thousand Oaks Mall. They were eating Sbarro's and talking about the future when Zack invited Shelby to move into his bachelor apartment after she graduated in May. He said he cared about her, and how amazing it would be to live together, and if she did want to move in, maybe they should buy some new furniture together. Gradually, though, the conversation turned into a discussion of *space issues*—not issues regarding their own personal space but issues of where to physically put all this new furniture, like into *what space*. Zack suggested packing some stuff in a storage unit if necessary, or keeping extra furniture at his mom's place, where he still sort of had a room. But Shelby didn't like that idea; she thought the only way it'd work was if they got something bigger, like a one-bedroom or even a two-bedroom, even though that was kind of a huge commitment, since she was only eighteen and her summer job wasn't going to pay much. Still, she told him she didn't want to move into a place where she didn't have space for her photography and her haircutting, so maybe the best thing to do was to just wait and figure it out later in the year. Zack proposed something else: renting a two-bedroom apartment in the Valley they could move into in June. Money wasn't a concern to him; he loved her and would pay whatever she couldn't cover. And as long as they'd be living together, why not get married too? He smiled, asked her what she thought of the idea.

That's when Shelby pushed away her slice of pizza. She couldn't take another bite. She left the food court, left the mall, and left him there with no ride home.

"Really, you're lucky with that guy Elliot," Shelby says. "At least he's not bugging you about marriage, about being some teen bride."

"Shelby, I like barely know him. He's only called me once since he left."

"Ugh, you're being like Zack," she tells me—which means being something I shouldn't be.

Coincidentally, on the drive home from Roxy's, Elliot calls, from somewhere in the middle of the country. He tells me their drummer, Marcus, threw a bottle at Chelsea, the bassist. He tells me things have been getting crazier on the road because the whole band's been drunk so much, except for him, and now the whole band's angrier, and everything's changing. Elliot thinks maybe Marcus had sex with Chelsea. I never knew Elliot had a girl bassist, because he never told me, and now I'm wondering if *Elliot* has had sex with Chelsea.

He wants to know if camp's ruling. I say it isn't. He wants to know if I've started packing. I say I haven't and don't really feel like talking about it. But I do tell him Courtney's packing, that she packs for Amsterdam a little bit each day.

"Where's Amsterdam?" Elliot asks.

"What do you mean?" I say.

"*Where's* Amsterdam?"

"Holland?"

"Holla!" Elliot laughs. Then he says, "You were rushin' but now you're peein'."

"What?"

"You were *Russian* but now *European*," Elliot says, laughing harder.

It's like the worst joke ever, so I hold my forehead in my hands, trying to remember if Elliot's told me other bad jokes or if this is the first one. Is *his* rep as some Joker? Because I can't stand that. Elliot asks what I'm wearing in this fake-sleazy way—another joke, because he knows it's two p.m. and that I'm driving—and I tell him I'm completely naked and that makes him laugh again.

I'm trying to picture what Marcus looks like, and what he looks like with a bottle in his hand, about to throw it. Then I try to picture Chelsea, and every image is like a Mara sister or some Hollywood celeb. And then I hear a match strike on the other end, and a deep inhalation, exhalation. Elliot's smoking—he's *smoking again*—so I just hang up.

Back home, I lie there for a while before realizing I guess now I *am* moping, even though Shelby told me not to. She also told me not to be like Zack, but Zack's older, drives a yellow motorcycle, and has his own dog, which I always thought was cool, Classic even. I always kind of liked Zack in general; he's not some Joker who smokes. In fact, he's not funny at all, which seems like it could be boring but probably in the long run means he'll be *stable* and *respectable*.

Normally only Shelbys can get Zacks, which is important to remember, but normally Evas can't get Elliots, so maybe the rules are changing.

Not that I necessarily *want* a Zack, obviously. It's just that a part of me can't help but be curious what it'd feel like to *have* one, and by extension, what it'd feel like to be a Shelby: Ready for the World. A girl who's intriguing to actual *men* because she can shop and go the movies *alone*, and already has errands and responsibilities, and knows how to live and doesn't have to leave a note for her parents when she goes out. A Pre-Woman, an Almost Adult. But the trick is that Shelbys are born, not made, which means I never had a shot.

But if for the sake of argument I *did* have a shot at Shelbydom, at becoming this evolved, elegant female presence, my only hope would be to add someone like Zack to my résumé.

And I *do* know someone like Zack—Zack.

This is all just a train of thought; I'm not trying to greener-grass the situation. But it might be interesting to at least experience being a tourist over there, to get my passport stamped, take a quick, harmless sightseeing trip. It might be interesting to at least call him.

Call it *Eva*lving.

I should call him.

24.

THE FIFTY-FIRST STATE

COURTNEY DOESN'T HAVE any other plans, but she swears that's not why she wants to spend her Saturday night with me. She says it's because she'll be gone soon and I'll be gone soon and we're *sisters* and isn't that enough? I'm on the tail end of moping—I can actually *feel* the mope fading—because I don't miss Michelle and Steph, because I decided *not* to miss them, which is the mature thing to do: pack it up and move it on. "Just remember these four words," my father said one time, probably misquoting somebody. "Forward, forward, forward, *forward!*" And also, Courtney was right: they're high school friends, and I'm not in high school anymore.

"Okay, but that's not really what I said," Courtney tells me. "I just said you might not be *friends forever*, and that there's nothing wrong with that, but I didn't tell you to let one annoying thing they do end your friendship just because you're moving away and who cares. Stop being so dramatic, Eva. You don't always have to be this dramatic."

"Am I supposed to miss them or *not* miss them?" I ask. "Is this supposed to bother me or *not* bother me?"

"I don't know," Courtney says. "*Not* bother you, I guess."

"Not bother me because I'm moving away, or not bother me because I'm above it and it doesn't really matter?"

"The second one."

"Fine," I say. "I'm above it then."

"How's Elliot?"

"Ehhh," I say.

"How's that Foster guy?"

"He was seconds away from asking me on a date to this reading, but some kid interrupted him," I say.

"*Some kid*," Courtney says. "And how are your campers?"

"Brilliant," I tell her. "I mean, basically brilliant."

"Like you," she says.

"Ha-ha."

"It's only been one week. Give them time for brilliance."

"Yeah but we only have five weeks. A month now."

"You should go to that reading," Courtney says. "Just show up."

"That seems sort of loser-ish, doesn't it?"

"You don't care," Courtney says. "You've never cared what anyone thought."

"I care about other people's feelings."

"That's not the same thing, Eva. This is what I mean about dramatic."

After flipping around for a while, Courtney and I settle on an old movie on AMC about this sort of nerdy, plainly dressed woman who gets discovered by a fashion photographer when he's doing a photo shoot in the bookstore she works in. Audrey Hepburn is the star, and it's called *Funny Face*, because that's what Fred Astaire says she has, this sort of unconventional, funny face. Obviously she has a movie-star face, one of the most glamorous faces ever, but that's not the point. The point is once she's discovered and invited to do a photo shoot for a super-prestigious fashion magazine, she's able to leave New York City for Paris, a city she's always wanted to visit because her favorite French writer/philosopher gives lectures at a bar there and she'd give anything in the world to meet him.

No one in the movie can understand why in a million years she'd skip out on all the tourist attractions of Paris for some dirty hipster bar in some seedy part of the city where some Beat lunatic is giving lectures. No one gets that they chose her specifically because she's smart and unique and unlike the other fashion models because of her funny face, and that wanting to go to this seedy bar is all wrapped up in why they picked her in the first place. But this is also a movie where everyone acts like her underground bookstore in Manhattan *isn't* the coolest spot ever, that it's really grungy and dull and not at all what little girls who dream of moving to a glamorous city would think of as glamorous. And that's what makes Courtney so mad.

"God!" she groans. "This *movie*! This is why there's all those idiot backpackers and tourists wanting to go abroad, because they're brainwashed by Hollywood that Europe's so much more exciting than America. Nobody cares about the history or the art, not really."

"Audrey Hepburn cares," I say.

"And she's totally mocked for it!"

"I thought everyone wanted to go to New York," I say. "Everyone I know thinks New York is a huge deal."

"Except for you," Courtney says.

"*Including* me. New York just also seems really scary and gross. It's like a Split the Difference kind of thing,"

I say. "If I'm from LA and I don't want to go to New York, then that's pretty limiting. What's left for a famous writer—Boston, Chicago, maybe like San Francisco? I know there's the rest of the country, but I have a list of reasons, like a *long* list, of why each city isn't going to work."

"If only there was another state, some fifty-first state, just for you," Courtney says, and then snaps her fingers like, *shucks.*

"You can mock," I say, "but it's true! You know when we go to Whole Foods with Mom and we stand around the produce section, wishing there was just like *one more* vegetable, just a different kind of vegetable, for us to try? Or just one more channel on TV, even though we have a trillion channels and they're all fine, but just *one more* that we haven't already seen or skipped past?"

"This is existentialism," Courtney says. "Now you don't have to take it in college."

"I just want there to be another choice for me to choose from," I say. "I want there to be something *new.*"

"*Everything's* new! You haven't done *anything* yet!"

"I know," I say.

Eventually we finish the movie. It's pretty good, actually, and some parts do feel real, like how even if you're given this interesting opportunity, you'll still do it Your Way, sort of stubbornly and without keeping your mind open. I don't know if the mind is the same as the brain, but it seems like you can have this giant *brain* and be a really smart person but still have a straightforward, totally closed-off *mind*. If you took out the silly music numbers and the stupid church wedding at the end, *Funny Face* could be this really serious short story about Making It but not really Getting It, about trying something new but still not truly being open to the newness.

NEWNESS, I write down. *FUNNY FACE. MIND/ BRAIN. FOSTER. BOOK SOUP. GOING, GOING, GOING.*

25.

SO WHAT

WHEN I GET to Book Soup, there're no chairs left, so I stand at the back of the room, half paying attention to the reading and half staring at Foster's hair. Since I arrived a little late, it's hard to understand the context of what's being read, so instead I try to think of what to say to Foster afterward. Then the writer finishes, closing her book, and the crowd starts clapping really loudly and the people sitting down stand up. Even though I came late and haven't read the book or heard of the writer, I can still feel the awesome energy in the room, and to me it feels like Making It.

That energy carries over into the Q & A portion of the reading, where anyone who wants to can ask the writer if her characters are based on real people or if it was more difficult to write this book than her first or second one. Foster raises his hand, but by then the Q & A is winding down and the writer moves over to start signing books by the front door. The store's so crowded I can't just *casually* bump into Foster, so I have to ditch the low-key approach and walk right over to him. He's alone.

"Foster," I say, tapping him on the shoulder.

"Eva," Foster says, "you came to the reading!"

"It was great."

"Did you like it?"

"It was really great."

"I didn't know you were coming," Foster says. "We could've come together."

"I don't have your number," I tell him.

"Give me your phone," he says, and types his number in my contacts. Then he hands me his phone and tells me I should add my number to his contacts too.

This is the thing about Foster: he's so amazingly direct that he can say stuff like "We could've come together" and then, *no big deal*, get me to program my number into his phone. Being with Foster is too easy, but in a good way; like, it's effortless, but not effort *free*. For instance, I'm still conscious of working hard to get Foster to like me—like *really* like me—and that means doing something as shameless as pretending I read the book.

"I like her imagery," I say, staring past Foster at the writer shaking hands with fans. "It's simple but kind of *vivid*, and I also like the way she writes her characters; they're really *three-dimensional*, don't you think?"

"Actually, I haven't read it," Foster says. "I've never even heard of her. I just thought it would be a cool thing to do."

"Oh my God," I say.

"What?"

"Nothing," I say. "Hey, are you doing anything now?"

"Uh, I'm going to buy a copy of the book and get it signed, I think."

"I'll come with you," I say.

Luckily, there's not much of a line anymore, but the line area is narrow, so Foster and I have to stand really close. Foster actually smells like camp, like sun and sunscreen and chlorine. He's such a perfect counselor that Sunny Skies literally *permeates* his skin. I even notice a knotted leather bracelet around his wrist that's so ugly it could only have been made by one of his campers.

When we're next in line, about to meet the writer, I whisper to Foster that he should ask her the question he was going to ask earlier during the Q & A. I nudge him and he laughs and then we're up, standing in front of the writer, whose eyebrows are raised, her pen ready to sign. She doesn't look that much older than Courtney, or all that brilliant. She is wearing glasses, though, frame-less ones sort of floating in front of her face, and I think they're really helping with the overall Writer Image, and I'm definitely taking note of that. I'm reminded of what Alyssa said ("I know you can't judge a book by its cover, but isn't that what a cover's for?"), and this writer's cover says: Sort of Bookish, Regular Person Who Wrote a Book. And the book's cover says: Sort of Sad, Sort of Sweet, Regular Book.

"Hello," Foster says.

"Hello there," the writer says. She holds her hand out to take Foster's copy of the book.

"We really liked the reading," Foster tells her.

"You're sweet," she says.

"We just graduated from high school and we're writ-ers. We're both going to major in creative writing in college."

"That's wonderful," the writer says. "If I had to give myself advice ten years ago, I would tell myself to write every day. Doesn't matter what."

"What if you're not inspired?" I say.

"That's sometimes when the best writing comes out—when you feel challenged, when you don't want to write because it's too hard," she says. "If you only wrote when you felt inspired, you wouldn't find something new inside of it, you wouldn't *uncover* anything."

"What about writing what you know?" I ask.

"That works for some people, not really for me."

"So this is entirely made up?" I say, holding out the book.

"Well, it's fiction," the writer says. "But there's truth in fiction, right?"

"I think so," I say.

"Me too," Foster says.

"What are your names?" she asks.

"Foster and Eva," Foster says.

"You're cute," the writer says. "Who should I make the book out to?"

"To Eva," Foster says.

"Foster," I say, "that's too nice, don't do that."

"Well, I know you haven't read it yet," he says, smiling, and I nudge him.

Outside Book Soup, Foster's holding his keys, so I reach for mine too. I wish one of us didn't have our keys so we could drive home together. Foster asks where I parked, and I'm sad when I tell him, "That's my car right there," less than twenty feet away. He says he's parked much farther down, out of sight, so I offer to be a *gentleman* and walk with him along Sunset to his meter.

"Are you having a good summer?" Foster asks as we cross the street.

"I am," I say.

"And you like camp?"

"I like my campers. Pretty much."

"What about the other counselors?" Foster asks.

I've barely ever thought about any of the other counselors besides Foster; I only know the names of two or three of them. I shrug, say, "Jen seems cool."

"Do you mean Jennifer, Jenny, or Genesis?" Foster asks.

"Jenny?"

"Trick question. No Jenny."

"Foster, it took me forever just to learn my campers' names!"

"Well, now it's time to move on to the counselors."

"I want to," I say.

Foster shoots me a skeptical look.

"I *do* want to!"

"Making friends is *cool*, Eva."

"Did you read that on a bookmark?"

"I'm serious. You might meet someone you like. You might meet *one person* in the entire camp that you like."

"I already like you."

"You didn't used to."

"But then," I say, tapping on my forehead, pointing to my brain, "I gave you a chance."

"Think of it as extra credit."

"Well, I love extra credit."

When we get to his car, Foster takes a long time to put his key in the door's lock. Then he and I both go to talk at the same time, and then both say, "No, you go first, no, you."

I start: "You know Kerry Ward?"

"From PE freshman year. She was in Roush's class too."

"Right," I say. "To you, did it seem like I *hated* her or anything?"

Foster just laughs.

"What, why are you laughing?"

"I remember you wrote on her short story about that traveling circus, 'I'm excited to see what you write next, especially if what you write next is a lot more interesting than this.'"

"How do *you* know that?!"

"Kerry told everyone," Foster says, laughing again.

"Okay, listen, I'm not a bad person."

"I know, you're awesome, Eva," Foster says, still laughing.

"I wasn't trying to, like, cut her down, or anything."

"So you're a little snobby," Foster says, smiling. "So what?"

If I'd known all through high school that one day there'd be a boy—a boy who sat only two or three desks away from me for *four* years—who would react to my snobbiness with a casual, un-judge-y "So what?" then everything might've gone a lot, lot differently.

But I know *now*. So maybe things can go differently *now*.

Maybe I can grab Foster and kiss him on the lips just for a second, real fast, and then go running across Sunset, dodging cars and laughing, with a Regular Book in my hand and a Regular Feeling too.

Happiness, that's what.

26.

WE SHOULD'VE STAYED ON THE HILL

SUNDAY NIGHT, AFTER dinner, there's an earthquake. Nothing too big, but it means the next day at camp we have to do earthquake drills all day. The drills are pretty pointless—or if not pointless, then at least unnecessary—because basically every camp activity takes place in a giant open outdoor space. So unless the ground split in two and swallowed us whole, there's not much an earthquake could do to harm us. But still, at nine, and then at eleven, and again at two, the special alarm sounds and all the groups gather on the main field. Some come dripping wet, straight from the pool, and some come still chewing, carrying the rest of their lunch or snack. But my girls are the only ones who come carrying pink-and-turquoise-decorated books, already silent when Steven strolls by for roll call.

"Everyone's here," I tell Steven's assistant, a short, mustached man with a bandanna around his head.

He turns to my girls and shouts out the camp cheer. None of them respond with the camp callback.

I smile and shrug, shielding my eyes from the sun. "At least they're quiet and calm," I say. "It's a good way to react."

In a real emergency situation, I actually think my group would do the best. Look at them: Alexis Powell softly spinning my clipboard against the grass; Jessica Avery swatting at a fly; Lila and Alyssa and Renee comparing designs of friendship bracelets. They're unpanicked and undisturbed. When the last drill is over and Steven blows his whistle, I motion to my girls to stand and they do, one at a time, wobbly, wiping grass and dirt off the bottoms of their shorts.

"Okay," I say, rubbing my hands together when I have their attention. "Let's go."

I turn and they start following me, but halfway up a hill I realize, not for the first time, that I have no idea where I'm leading them. But Alyssa seems confident, holding Rebecca's hand, who's holding Billie's hand, everyone all holding hands in a chain, hiking up the hill behind me.

"Alyssa," I say, "how long have you been coming to Sunny Skies?"

"Since I was seven," Alyssa says.

"You really know how camp works."

"What do you mean *works*?"

"I mean, you could take over. Like if I wasn't here."

"Where are you going?" Zoe asks.

"You can't go anywhere," Jenna says.

"Can I go too?" Alexis says, jumping up and down.

"I'm not leaving. I just feel like promoting Alyssa," I say.

"To what?" Alyssa says.

"Co-counselor."

"Then can I be CIT?" Rebecca asks.

"No, all the campers have to stay campers," I explain.

"Co-counselor's cool," Alyssa says. "Even if it's not a real thing."

I look back. From our vantage point on the hill I can see most of camp, laid out below. This is probably what my mom means when she tells me to take a Bird's-Eye View of things, to look at a situation from some faraway point and not from the *inside*. From where I'm standing, the camp looks pretty peaceful, all the different groups in different areas doing different things: playing H-O-R-S-E on the basketball courts, diving off the diving boards at the pool, sitting outside the Craft Shack at the long wood tables gluing glittery junk to pinecones. From up here it all seems to be running smoothly, an ant farm laid on its side, everyone in their zone, doing their thing. And all the ants are people, and any of these people could potentially be a friend. I decide right then: I'm going to be the Un-Eva; I'm going to learn some names, give some chances.

I sit down on the grass, and the girls plop down around me. Alexis hands me the clipboard; it says we were supposed to be at Outdoor Cooking with the boys ten minutes ago.

"Outdoor Cooking." I sigh.

"Sucks," Alyssa says.

"What do you want to do instead?"

Alyssa looks at me like she can't believe I'm asking.

"Seriously, what do you guys all want to do?"

"I like sitting here," Jessica says.

"What if there's another earthquake?" Maggie asks.

"Then we'll slide down the hill and break our legs," Jenna says.

"We're not going to break our legs," I say, in a voice that sounds like my mom's.

"Earthquakes are cool," Alyssa says.

"My cat got lost during an earthquake two years ago," Lila says, and then Renee says, "We put posters all over the neighborhood."

"Did you find him?" Alexis asks.

"No," Renee says, and Lila says, "His name was Mr. Baggy Jeans, but my brother called him BJ."

"You should write about it," Alyssa says.

"Yeah," Billie says, "write a story about Mr. Baggy Jeans."

"That's such a good idea," I say. "Let's all write about something we've lost. Everyone here has lost something, right?"

Most of the girls nod, but some of the girls are already writing. I feel happy and extra proud because we're like the awesome underdogs, and not underdogs like we're the slowest or the dumbest or the ones no one is rooting for. It's more like we're the outsiders, and I love that about my group. I love that we're spending the last hour of camp up on a hill, writing together, doing our own thing, because who says we're not united and who says we're not forming a bond and who doesn't love an underdog?

I look at the clipboard again. *2:30–3:30, Outdoor Cooking w/ Foster's group.* I tap Alyssa on the arm, and she leans in closer.

"I haven't seen Foster all day," I whisper.

"So?" she whispers back.

I lean in closer. "So, you *know* I like Foster."

Alyssa's eyes go wide and she pulls away, hand over her mouth, blown away.

"I want to go see him, but I also want to stay here," I

whisper. "The girls are being so sweet, writing *on their own*, it's amazing. What should we do?"

"You're asking *me*?" Alyssa whispers.

"I'm asking my *co-counselor*," I whisper.

"Hmm. Let's go to Outdoor Cooking then."

"Why?"

"Because then I can see Corey too," Alyssa says.

"Alyssa," I whisper.

"The girls won't care, they'll go wherever you want and do whatever."

"Really?"

"Yeah, really. Duh. You're older, and you're the one in charge."

"Well, now I feel bad," I whisper.

"I never feel bad," Alyssa whispers.

"You should have my job then."

"I'm just a kid," Alyssa says, like I'm dumb.

I rouse everyone and we march down the hill, but when we get to Outdoor Cooking, it's just the boys and Corey; I don't see Foster anywhere. Before I can ask where he is, Steven walks up, looking really serious. He tells everyone that he's taking over Foster's group for the rest of the period and that he'll walk both groups to End-of-Day Ceremonies. I can't tell what's going on and feel afraid to ask, but then Steven gives me a really serious look, so I can tell things are *definitely* not great and maybe Foster's even in trouble. I gather my girls in a circle and tell them there's nothing to worry about, but I have to leave them with Steven for a while.

"Just for a few minutes," I say.

They all shout, "Noooo!" super sad and distressed. Even Alyssa looks a little upset, which means the girls *do* need me and they *do* want me around, even if I don't really know what I'm doing. I wonder if maybe we should've stayed on the hill and then I worry that I'm always learning the wrong lessons in important lesson-learning situations and this is something I have to work on. But now I have to go.

We all huddle together and put our arms around the girls on either side of us, and then I say, "Whirled Peas," Alyssa says, "Curl Powder," and we give a big squeeze.

"Foster's in the counselor break room," Steven tells me.

"There's a counselor break room?" I say, and normally Steven would laugh at something like that, but this time he doesn't. He looks concerned.

"You can go talk to him for a bit and then meet us back at the amphitheater for End-of-Day."

"Is everything okay?" I ask.

"Everything's going to be fine," Steven says without a smile. Then he looks past me, at my girls, his face filling with a new concern as he notices they aren't outdoor cooking at all, but scribbling in journals.

27.

FORESHADOWED

FOSTER STANDS WHEN he sees me. At first I can't tell what to do—give him a hug, or wait to see if *he* hugs *me*—but Foster's so explicitly sad that I just go to him and wrap my arms around him. Instead of hugging back, Foster just shakes his head and rambles. It seems like he finally took my advice, though, because he starts somewhere in the middle.

"Not because of the earthquake," Foster says. "Because of something else, some heart arrhythmia condition, have you heard of that?"

"No."

"But they thought it was the earthquake, because something fell on him and hit him from up on this shelf above his bed."

"Did he . . . *die*?" I say.

"He's dead."

I feel lost so I just start guessing: "Foster, was it your brother? Was it your dad? Was—"

"What?" Foster interrupts, confused.

"Who are you talking about?"

"Didn't Steven tell you?"

I shake my head.

"Brandon Gettis."

I don't know who Brandon Gettis is.

"He's a camper. He's seven," Foster says. "He's in Eli's group."

I don't know who Eli is.

"His brother's *Trevor* Gettis. From my group."

I remember Trevor. I love Trevor. I ask if Trevor's okay.

"He's not coming back to camp."

"That's so sad," I say. "What's Eli going to tell his group?"

"Steven's going to tell them."

"What are *you* going to do?"

"I'll tell the guys tomorrow," Foster says. He looks like he's about to cry. "When I was a CIT, Trevor was in my group too. The Gettises, they're a really nice family."

"Trevor's amazing," I say.

"It was just some sudden heart attack."

"Can kids get heart attacks?" I ask, even though I'm

realizing I guess they can.

Foster nods and covers his eyes.

Even though it's terrible, even though it's *the worst thing ever*, I try to imagine if Lila's brother died, the one who called Mr. Baggy Jeans "BJ." I imagine if he died and I had to tell my girls. I probably wouldn't be able to. I'd probably make Alyssa do it, because she never feels bad about anything. Then my eyes start to get wet, and I choke up. Foster's so good, he's such a *good counselor*, that I know how much this hurts him. I rack my brain for something completely incredible and soulful to say, because I want to make Foster feel better and I also want to be the Best Possible Eva.

"You know, these kids are sort of *precious*." I touch his hand.

Foster looks at me and smiles. He nods.

"It's the saddest story," I say, and I don't need to tell Foster he can have this one, because it's the story Foster's been writing since we were freshmen.

It's the story he's always written, and now that it's become real, it feels like anything's possible. Anything can happen.

Anything can end any way.

28.

FRENCHING FOSTER

THERE ARE CERTAIN very adult, very serious movies about grief and mourning and loss that my parents don't like me watching, probably for pretty sensible reasons. But I watch them anyway, and what I notice happens a lot is that the man and woman become so agonized by the suicide or the baby drowning that their pain, their crushing *heartache*, mysteriously transforms into what I can only call . . . *horniness*.

Standing so close to Foster, being so moved, my emotions feel like they're mysteriously transforming too.

Foster's lips part, and that's my entrance: it's where my tongue goes. We're so literary, Foster and I; our stories have stories inside of them. Like how this is the story of a boy dying unexpectedly, but when you dig deeper, it's also about two people finding one another after years of being right in front of each other's faces. I've read novels where it's like that, and I get what they're saying: *He was always there, he'd been there the whole time, I just didn't realize it!* And sometimes that feels phony, but sometimes it feels like it's absolutely true. And this time, for me, it's absolutely true. And if that's a cliché, *so what*, I'm living it.

It's strangely normal, Frenching Foster. He closes his eyes, and it gets even better: we're licking each other's lips, stroking the sides of each other's face. When I was thirteen, I was obsessed with being an amazing kisser, but later on you realize it's a waste of time, because boys want to kiss you whether you're any good at it or not. Now I just try to match their speed, respond to their motions, and they mainly seem satisfied.

But Foster's so *tender.* He's so vulnerable, and he cares so much. He's so sad about Brandon Gettis that the sadness is making his lips, his tongue, his hands more serious, more intent. He's like some Back from the War kisser, or some Train Station Farewell kisser, which is completely different from Elliot, or from anyone else I've kissed.

Elliot, ugh.

Now, unfortunately, I'm thinking about Elliot and can't stop.

I've always felt ambiguous about the idea of the Bad Boy. Like, I know *morally* we shouldn't find that attractive, but I guess *realistically* we can't always help it. Now I'm realizing maybe it's just the phrase itself that's the problem. Bad Boy sounds kind of cute—there's something dumbly adorable about it. But Bad Person sounds awful. Saying "I'm in love with a Bad Boy" might make your friend giggle or blush, but saying "I'm in love with a Bad Person" is just disturbing. I'm not labeling Elliot as some Officially Bad Person, but I *am* saying he's a Bad Boy, and if the two could be recognized as being part of the same category, we'd all save ourselves a lot of time and trouble.

But right now I'm kissing a Good Guy *and* a Good Person, kissing him all over his face, and not so softly or slowly either. When Mr. Roush thinks a student has style or passion but not much skill, he'll write on their paper: *Artfully messy!* That's what Frenching Foster has turned into—more of a creative chaos than some smooth move.

Just as I'm thinking, *I hope nobody walks in,* immediately someone does.

It's a counselor I've seen around before who has some old-timey name I can never remember. He doesn't even say anything, he just cracks the door, sees us, and abruptly leaves, which is how I know he was weirded out.

"He didn't see anything," I say. "I mean, he saw us,

but he didn't see what we were doing really.

"He's not going to go tell Steven," I continue, talking too fast, already feeling short of breath. "What kind of person would do that?

"It's not like we were having *sex*," I say. I shake my head, gesture confusingly with my hands. "We weren't naked or spooning on the couch or, like, *pressing up* against each other.

"Also, there's nothing illegal about two counselors kissing when they're away from their campers, alone in the *counselor* break room. Only a total jerk would complain to Steven, and there's no way *that* guy would do that—he always seems really nice. I mean, that's how he seems when we're singing 'If I Had a Hammer' at Morning Ceremonies.

"We're *not* going to get fired," I blurt out, but Foster looks like he's thinking about Brandon now, which makes me feel crazy and awful.

"*And also*," I say, "a boy died today, so there are other things to be upset about.

"I can fix all this," I say, finally moving toward the door to leave, "but first, real quick, what's that guy's name?"

29.

NOT THE ONLY ONE

I SPRINT ACROSS camp, past the abandoned swimming pool and the empty archery range, past the bungalow by Steven's office and the outdoor amphitheater, until I get to the parking lot where the last of the big yellow buses is reversing out to leave down the long, curving exit road. I keel over, panting from the run, wiping sweat from my forehead, and spy a few tiny campers' faces peering out through the dirty rear window of the bus, their tiny hands flailing at what they think is my bye-bye wave.

Over on the edge of the parking lot by my car, there're a few other cars still there, and some counselors standing around talking. Even though I can't quite make out their faces, one of them looks like Booth, the old-timey-named nice guy I'm looking for.

"Booth!" I shout. "Booth!"

Booth turns around and looks at me like I'm insane.

"Booth! Can I talk to you for a sec?"

"Sure!" Booth shouts back, standing there, waiting.

"No, can I talk to you over *here*?" I shout again, pointing to the ground next to me. Booth hesitates but then reluctantly jogs over.

"What's up, Eva?"

"What's up with you?"

"Everything's . . . cool."

"It is?"

"Yeah," Booth says with an amused smile, "it is."

"Okay, cool, because I just wanted to make sure you knew that Foster is *really* responsible, and I'm less responsible but still, you know, *competent*."

"You're not the only ones who make out in the break room," Booth says, his smile turning sort of sleazy, like he's looking at me differently, like he's seen me on TV or something.

"Okay."

"You're just the first one to get Foster into it."

"Well, Foster's not *that* into it," I say. "I pretty much forced him."

"Oh ho ho," Booth says, and then there's that look

again, that cable TV look.

"Just don't tell anyone."

"Trust me," Booth says—and I don't, I *do not*—"I wouldn't want a frenzy."

"What do you mean, a frenzy?"

"With the other girls. They're *all about* Foster."

I glance over Booth's shoulder. Everyone's scowling at us. Male, female, all of them.

"Foster?" I say slowly, confused.

"Every summer," Booth tells me. "It's like a contest."

"And is he *all about* any of the other girls?"

"Who cares?" Booth says, grinning.

"Well, please don't tell anyone, okay, Booth? Promise? Pinkie swear, promise?"

"You sound like one of your campers."

"To me that's a compliment," I say, and fold my arms.

"Chill," Booth says. "I'm not going to tell."

"Thanks."

"C'mon," he says, motioning to the cars.

"Totally," I say, but don't move.

In high school, which I admit was basically five minutes ago, a gaggle of girls who might or might not like me wasn't too intimidating. I had my own friends and we had our own *thing* and part of that thing was making fun of everyone, and that felt really solid, really stable. The trick was to exist somewhere between the Bully and the

Bullied, and that somewhere was Above It All. There's TGIF and then there's TGFI: Too Good For It. But every day was TGFI, *four years* of TGFI, which is part of the Roush Problem and the Overlooking/Underestimating Foster Problem, and probably most of the other problems too.

But this isn't high school, and I *am* intimidated.

"Nobody'll find out about you and Foster," Booth says. "C'mon, we're a *grreat grroup*," he says, doing this lame goofy voice, which shows I'm not the only one who's noticed Steven's a dork.

"Seriously, Eva," Booth says, actually serious. "You don't talk to anyone. You don't even really talk to *Foster*." He raises his eyebrows suggestively.

"Ignorance is a blister," my father always jokes, then taps me on the forehead and goes, "Pop!" It's dumb, but he's right; I need to know a lot more before I act so *superior*. And I really wouldn't mind making another friend at camp—and not just Alyssa, who'd probably *pbbth* if she heard me call her a friend. So this is definitely a GTFI moment: Good Time For Improvement.

"I'll hang out by the cars," I say stiffly. "Let's go hang out."

"Convincing," Booth says, unconvinced, and grabs my hand.

When we walk over, he introduces everyone (Jules, TJ,

Kit, Nick, Melly, Amanda, Seth) and then there's a heavy silence like I interrupted some moment, even though no one was talking when we got there. I don't know what to do, so I just say, "Did you guys hear about Brandon Gettis?"

"Yeah," Melly says, and that's it.

No one else says anything. To seem more natural, I start fishing my keys out of my bag but then wonder if that seems rude.

"You don't eat the cookies and milk when I pass them out after swim," Jules says, facing me. "You're like the only one."

"I'm vegan. So . . . that's why."

"Do you eat eggs?" Melly asks.

"Eggnorance is bliss," I say.

"What about eggplant parmesan?"

"No, because it's got—"

"Not even a little chicken?" Seth asks.

"Why do you think they call it *fowl*?" I say.

"That's really funny," Jules says, and it sounds like she means it, but she's not laughing.

"You should come to Nick's," Amanda says.

"When, now?"

"For the party," TJ says. "Counselors only."

"You don't have to say 'counselors only,'" Nick says. "I think she knows the kids aren't invited."

They all look at me.

"I know that," I assure them, with a nod and a smile.

"It's this Friday," Nick tells me.

"Should I bring anyone?"

"It's counselors only," TJ says again, and everyone laughs.

"Fun," I say. "Fun, fun, fun," I keep saying, until it seems real.

30.

JUST REGULAR PRESSING

I LEAVE A desperate message on Michelle's voice mail insisting she hang out with me later, and then I call Steph and beg her to help convince Michelle. Usually I'm more discreet about manipulations like these, but today I'm too worked up. Courtney overhears and shakes her head. She's perched on a bar stool in the kitchen, casually flipping through *LA Yoga* magazine.

"Are you shaking your head at yoga or at me?" I ask.

"Guess," she says, not looking up.

"Things are getting *unusual*," I say.

"That sounds mild."

"My best friends don't even like me anymore. It's real, it's happening."

"You don't seem very devastated."

"That's because I'm *overwhelmed*."

"With camp?" Courtney says.

"With camp, exactly."

"Why, what happened at camp?"

My sister has an endless reserve of wisdom but not an endless reserve of patience. I learned this for the first time five years ago, when I started coming to Courtney for advice about all my high-stakes eighth-grade crises. Courtney always told me precisely what to do, as well as how and when to do it; Dad called her Court-throat and would leave the room whenever she launched into Life Coach mode. The difference was that Courtney hadn't taught herself to *let go* back then; she hadn't discovered how to self-therapize. She was actually more like I am now—while I was even *more* immature and helpless, if that's possible.

"Here's what happened at camp," I say, sighing, prepping myself.

Our dynamic used to be that I would just unload on Courtney—everything times everything, the conflicts and the contexts and the personalities involved—and then she'd process the situation for a moment, think it over, and lay out a hard-line verdict: *Don't ever call her again*, or, *Turn in the paper anyway*. It was a Give a Man a Fish type of thing; Courtney carefully instructed me how a thirteen-year-old girl should behave, but I never absorbed the lesson because I was too fixated on just getting the answer. And that's all that I want from her right now: the Right Answer.

"Foster and I kissed," I say. "For a *while*."

"Uh-huh, and?"

"And then we got caught. By another counselor."

"So are you in trouble?"

I shrug.

"How was the kissing?" she asks.

"Amazing," I say. "He had his hands against my back and pushed up and down my spine like a massage."

"Reiki," Courtney says.

"I think it was just regular pressing."

"When he had his hands on your back, did it feel like this life-force energy was flowing between you?"

"Maybe," I say.

"And did you feel, like, a glowing radiance when he stopped?"

"Okay, I guess you're right, I guess it was Reiki," I say.

This gives me an idea for a new story. Two sisters grow up with this secret power: they can heal people with their touch. They can't cure diseases exactly, it's not like that, it's more like they can provide this calm or relief, the feeling of the Right Answer a person's been searching for. But as the sisters grow older, they become lazier with their power, and eventually, since they don't work on refining it, they lose it completely. But even after the power's gone, they keep on touching people, pressing on strangers' arms and shoulders and spines with their palms, pretending they can heal. I can't tell if the story should ultimately have them being uncovered as frauds or if it's more just about the sisters trying to rekindle their lost power, but maybe a cool, sort of heavy way to end it would be during one of their sessions: *Do you feel that? No. Well, do you feel this? No, I don't feel a thing.*

There's a pen and paper on the counter, but I don't write it down.

"I like Foster," Courtney tells me.

"I like Foster too."

"I like Elliot too, though, and I also like Michelle and Steph. I like Shelby. But I like you the most," she says, making a sweet face. "*Especially* when you wear your glasses, which lately is basically never."

"So you like everyone?" I ask.

"I do," my sister says. "That's the whole point. Liking people is easy, Eva."

"Easy for you," I say.

31.

JOBS

MICHELLE AND STEPH don't show up till eight, which gives me the whole afternoon to redecorate my room into an elaborate flashback museum, with everything the three of us used to love arranged in an imposing pile on the carpet. Their eyes widen when they walk in.

"This is . . . a lot of stuff," Michelle says, clearly weirded out.

"What's this all doing here?" Steph asks, confused.

Looking at it through their eyes, I see it totally differently now, like I've set up a yard sale full of our memories. And nobody's buying any of it. Michelle toes a stack of *Teen Vogue* magazines with the tip of her shoe. Steph grimaces when she notices the hideous sweater we all puffy-painted sophomore year.

"Never mind," I say nervously, and force a laugh. "Forget all that, just sit down."

"Michelle lost her job," Steph blurts out.

"Steph!" Michelle says.

"You lost your job?" I ask. "Like you were *laid off*?"

"It's not a factory, Eva," Michelle says. "They weren't making, like, cutbacks or something."

"She got fired," Steph whispers.

"From the jewelry thing," I say.

"Don't say *jewelry thing*," Michelle says. "I was a personal assistant."

"I'm in trouble at work too," I say.

"Oh, *please*, Eva, tell us about *that*," Steph says sarcastically, and then Michelle says, "Yeah, Eva, please?" in a genuinely mocking way.

I guess I understand the hostility, but not this ganging-upness, because that's never how it's been between us, even when it's been bad. Before this sour summer I can barely recall a specific time when the two of them came to a decision without me; sometimes I'd walk out of the bathroom at school, having only been gone a couple minutes, and find them sitting in silence like two strangers, picking dirt out of their fingernails, scrolling through text messages. How long have I been in the bathroom *this* time? What changed?

"My job," I say, searching for the right words, "is kind of harder than I thought it'd be. It's, like"—just then I notice the family DustBuster over in the corner of my room, above which my mother's stuck a neon Post-it scrawled with the words, *REMEMBER ME!?!??*— "*sucking up* a lot more of my time than I thought it would."

Michelle and Steph exchange eye rolls.

"Typical," Michelle says, annoyed. "Eva the Hypocrite."

"That's offensive," I tell her. "I may be a hypocrite, but I'm not typical."

"Whatever," Steph says. "Ever notice how you're the one who's most clingy and anxious about things changing—"

"And you lean on us super hard when you feel like it—" Michelle cuts in.

"And make us do all these pinkie swears that we're not going to lose touch—"

"But you couldn't be nice through one dumb dinner with two totally nice people, and then it was just one dumb party—and you don't even *like* Kerry, you actually really don't—"

"Not to mention," Steph says, getting even more worked up, "you wouldn't have come anyway! You *know* you wouldn't have, Eva. And even if randomly you did, you would've been so *crappy* to everyone, like you were to Bart and Miranda. Like you were to us because we *like* Bart and Miranda."

"We tried not to be mad."

"Because being mad at you never works, because you always win, because you're so smart—which is really not as good a look on you as you'd like to think."

"But we *were* mad," Michelle says.

"But no one can be mad at *Eva*, because she punishes you for it," Steph says, glaring.

"Because one day later it's like, *poof*"—Michelle mimics an imaginary smoke bomb exploding in her hands—"'if you're gonna have a problem with me, forget you guys.'"

"No, no, no," I say, reeling from the outpouring, "that's not what happened. I was just trying to . . . get ahead of the problem."

"What problem?" Steph asks.

"The problem of missing you both too much, and freaking out about it. Of basically dying inside because I know soon we won't be together anymore."

They both go quiet, caught off guard by this.

In general I've never been a big apologizer, and I wonder if that's also part of the problem. But the real truth is I don't *mind* apologizing; it's super easy if you really mean it, which I really do. "I'm really sorry, guys. Seriously. *Seriously.*"

"We *do* love you," Steph says, looking sadder for it,

and then Michelle says, almost tearfully, "We accept you, even when you *are* judgmental . . . and close-minded . . . and a little mean."

"Don't accept me! Force me to change!"

"Can't," Michelle says.

"Don't know how," Steph admits.

"Six months from now I'll be like a completely different person, you'll be, like, 'Who's *this* Eva?'"

"That's not what we're asking for," Steph says.

Michelle just shrugs.

How can I be this person who likes the way she is, has self-confidence—or at least some *semblance* of what *appears* to be self-confidence—if I still have to spend so much time trying to change? Why am I always having to search deeper for self-improvement and self-love or self-worth or whatever Courtney would call it? I don't know and I don't know, so all I can do is keep saying I'm sorry and I'm sorry. Sorry, sorry, sawry, sari, sari—a bright and colorful sheath to wrap yourself in—sorry!

"Thanks," Michelle says, seeming appeased, while Steph finishes, "For being the bigger person."

"Are you guys calling me fat?" I say, trying to lighten things.

"Your eyes seem better," Steph says, ignoring the joke. "No more twitching."

"Still not wearing your glasses?" Michelle asks. "You're, like, blind."

"*Undiagnosed*," I say, but no one laughs at that either. "Hey, laugh," I tell them, which only makes it weirder.

I want to explain to them that having stayed friends through four full years of high school is an epic accomplishment, it's *monumental*, and so staying friends just four more weeks should be a breeze. I want to convince them that it's not childish or regressive to try and hold on to our high school best friends, even as we inevitably separate and go away to college, but how can I, honestly? All I know is that I'm *working on* becoming a Better Eva, a Bigger Eva, so I want my favorite people to recognize my struggle for, like, inner enrichment and be proud, or uplifted, and like me even more. But clearly that's not happening.

"This is silly!" I say. "I love you guys, you're my best friends, we can tell each other anything—a million different things. Should I start? I can start!"

Michelle smiles, but it's not that big and not that bright.

"Okay, do you want to start?" I ask.

"I've never been fired before," she says. "She found out I was lying about being able to commit to the position for a full year."

"Your six weeks is better than any dumb girl's year," I say. "That jewelry lady is the stupidest woman alive."

"She totally is," Steph says, and then we're all nodding, *Sooo stupid.*

"What am I going to do now?" Michelle asks.

"Ah!" I shout. "I've got it!"

Michelle and Steph wait.

"The Gap!" I scream, punching a pillow we tie-dyed two summers ago.

Steph shakes her head, twists her hair. "I'm seasonal," she says.

"So?"

"So they can't take on *another* seasonal employee now that the season's started."

"Steph already asked," Michelle tells me. "They're not hiring."

"Maybe Shelby knows a salon that needs a receptionist," I offer.

"Shelby?" Michelle says, with a very superior huff.

"What about Sunny Skies?" Steph asks me.

"You think *summer* camp isn't *seasonal*?"

"Can you at least ask?" Michelle says, and then Steph says, "*I* at least *asked*."

"I can't," I say.

"You won't," Michelle says, annoyed.

"It's just that I'm in trouble. I Frenched Foster."

"Is he your boyfriend now?" Steph asks, not in a nice way.

This is one of those impossible friendship crossroads, where every direction is wrong. But I'm also beginning to sense something deeper behind why they're upset with me, and it's not just because I dug out everything we've ever done and created together, everything we poured our love into, and piled it on the carpet to be exposed for what it is: outdated and juvenile. It's because instead of writing about my experiences with Michelle and Steph—all the funny, true, goofy, *epic, monumental* things we went through together—I chose to invent a bunch of sad stories about imaginary strangers. At the time I didn't want to draw from my own life because it felt so un-unique and forgettable, and I think gradually my best friends picked up on that—even though I didn't. So now when they look at me, they don't see an old friend who's trying hard to improve and grow; they see someone who started to leave them years ago, has pretty much already left, and maybe didn't fully care about being there in the first place.

"You put the *art* in martyr," Courtney once told me, "like it's your job."

32.

RINGTONES

MY CELL PHONE rings at four a.m., and it's the last of the several people I expect it to be: Elliot. I have a chest-tightening *Oh yeah, Elliot!* moment that's more shock than surprise, which I can't disguise in my voice as sleepiness. But Elliot didn't call to pay attention to *me*, so I just listen to him ramble about hating his band, hating music, and hating his stupid tour, and hope he doesn't say anything about *love*.

But why would he? This is what I always do: put too much *pressure* on everything. If Elliot was here I'd probably kiss him, and if he'd stayed all summer I probably would have dated him, but since he's *not* and he *didn't*, the reality is much milder. Elliot only calls me because he thinks I'm funny or smart or both. He calls me because we're friends; it's not about love.

I ask Elliot about groupies, like if he has any. He laughs, like that's a joke. I ask him about gigs, and he giggles. I even ask him if he's drunk, because I don't remember the last time someone had this much fun talking to me. But he's not drunk and he's not smoking and he's not taking any pictures, he says, because there haven't been any "Kodak-ota" moments—because they haven't made it to North or South Dakota yet. Ha!

"What was tonight's show all about?" I ask.

"It was in this long, hallway-type room with a small stage at one end and a DJ-slash–sound booth at the other. There was so much slapback I had to stop playing five or six times, and once I even had to unplug. But the rest of the band just kept going, like I didn't matter, even though I'm the singer *and* the lead guitarist."

"I *get* that," I say, in a way I hope comes across as soulful.

"The crowd had their arms folded most of the show and were way too dressed up and mainly awful."

The thing about Elliot I'd sort of forgotten is that he's *cool* and easy to be friends with. He doesn't really expect anything from me except that I'll answer my phone at four in the morning on a work night, and since that's something I have no problem doing, our friendship isn't a burden at all. Also, Elliot's older, so I assume he sees something innocent and puppyish in me, like how excited I was to get to know him when we met and how excited I was to kiss and pre-miss him. That must've seemed naive and sort of sweet, and isn't it okay to want to be seen that way in someone's eyes?

Another surprise: Elliot asks about my writing. I tell him something I've never told anyone, which is that I don't really like to write. What I mean by that is the *act of writing*, which makes me feel stupid and slow. Like when my mother opens the fridge and just stands there, with no idea what she wants.

"Writing's like that a lot of the time," I say, "except when everyone loves your writing, I assume."

Elliot, probably thinking about his own music, agrees.

Then he gets kind of serious, apologizing for not communicating more.

"The road sucks, but at least we're at the farthest point east, which means we'll be looping back west now. Back to Hell-A," he says, "to see you before you go."

First I liked Elliot and felt sad when he was gone. Now I like Elliot gone; I might even like him *more* because he's gone, which feels wrong.

But I'm tired of being wrong.

I'm tired anyway, so we say good night.

33.

"THE TOASTER" BY EVA KRAMER

MY MOTHER WAKES me seven minutes before my alarm, which is a complete injustice. I have no problem telling her so.

"Mom, this is one of the worst things you've ever done."

"Then I'm doing pretty good," she says. "I should run for office."

My mother's holding an old toaster. It looks pretty banged up.

"Have we stopped making toast in the kitchen?" I ask.

"I found it in the garage," she says, extending her arms so the toaster's right in my face. "For your dorm!" my mother exclaims, and then shakes the toaster like I'm supposed to leap out of bed and immediately bubble-wrap it for Boston.

"I don't want that," I tell her. "It's crusty and gross."

"You'll need a toaster."

"Why?"

"You'll have to eat."

I sit up so I can really look at her, to see which way she's acting: lonely or crazy. Courtney says since both of us are leaving, we have to get used to Mom ping-ponging between the two.

"What's happening?" I ask, because sometimes if I'm very direct with my mother, she'll stop being weird and just say what's bothering her.

"I'm just giving you this toaster for your dorm room," she says innocently.

"But what's *really* happening?"

"I don't understand what you mean, Eva."

I gently pull my mom onto the bed, so she's sitting beside me, the toaster between us. I glance around my room, which already feels like it has less of a sense of *me* about it. Soon it'll be my mother's *other* room, where she can go to watch TV shows no one else will watch with her, or read the long articles in her *Vanity Fair* she normally only has time to skim. "Call me a cab," my mother used to say whenever my sister and I would make simultaneous sleepover plans. I thought it was so sweet how Mom hated to be home without us, that when we left she wanted to leave too. But then Courtney explained that she didn't mean "call me a taxi," she meant "call me a Cab," like a *Cabernet*, her favorite type of wine.

"You're going to love it when we're gone," I tell her. "You and Dad are going to party all the time."

"Is that what you think?"

Her voice sounds hollow, like she's in her own world, which confirms the diagnosis: she's lonely. I open my arms to her, but she doesn't realize it's for a hug—she thinks I'm reaching for the toaster.

"Mom," I say, "I don't want this old-ass toaster."

"Why not?" she asks, her voice choked up and sad sounding.

"I'm not leaving yet. I'm not thinking about, like, appliances yet."

"So you're going to make me ship this to you when you change your mind?"

"Mom, don't give me that Mom Guilt, come on."

Then my mother tries to take back the toaster, but I grip the cord and won't let go.

"Wait, okay, leave it," I say. "I want the toaster. I want it, okay?"

"I'll give it to Courtney, it's fine."

"She won't even be able to use it in Amsterdam," I remind her. "The plugs are different there."

Then my mother tugs harder, yanking the cord from my hands, and that's when I realize maybe I misdiagnosed her: maybe she's crazy. But it's also early; I was woken too soon, so I'm grumpy and in no mood to comfort anyone. I don't feel like telling my mother, who knows I love her, *that* I love her, or telling her that I'll miss her when she obviously *knows* I'll miss her. *Call me a crab!* I don't care.

"You're crazy," I say, and grab my notebook off the nightstand and start scribbling notes. "I'm going to turn this into a short story called 'The Toaster.' It's about a mother's inability to let go, which manifests itself through the symbol of this toaster, which is just a cold, crusty, busted thing that represents the way she doesn't really know her daughter at all."

"Don't call me crazy, Eva."

"You don't even get that I don't want a toaster. I like cereal, hello! I need bowls and spoons!"

"You're grounded," my mother says, and then leaves the room without the toaster.

"I like being grounded! I'm *well* grounded!" I yell after her, already sorry and realizing I'm probably going to be late for camp this morning.

Courtney's in her room meditating when I barge in to ask what she thinks about the toaster fight. I tell her everything, every word I can remember.

"'The Toaster'?" Courtney asks, skeptical.

"At least it's good material for a story," I point out.

"Don't put us in your stories, Eva."

"It's what I know," I say. "It should be flattering!"

"You're saying it's an act of love to write about your family?"

"Basically."

"Then, *boundaries*. You can't just splay us out because you have"—my sister makes air quotes with her fingers—"a *gift*."

"Oh, I have a gift," I say. "It's a toaster, for you."

"I hate to say it, but you're in worse denial about moving to Boston than Mom."

"You don't hate to say it."

"I told you to have sympathy," Courtney says. "Remember what I said about empty-nest syndrome?"

I nod.

"You'll be living with Mom and Dad for, like, ten more minutes. So try to have a little patience, you know, some *understanding*." Courtney uncrosses her legs and starts positioning herself, to my total disbelief, into a handstand. "You've always been impatient, Eva. Maybe it's something from your childhood."

"I might still be *in* my childhood," I say.

"Tolerance," Courtney says, like an upside-down Buddha.

"I'm like the *Museum* of Tolerance," I tell her feet.

"I wouldn't phrase it that way," she says, and then kicks my chin a little, "counselor."

34.

ELEPHANTS

FORGET MORNING CEREMONIES. Forget free play. I miss them both.

In my absence the girls have been with Steven's assistant all morning, but when I finally show up, they mob me like they thought they'd never see me again, like I'd left forever. They hug me from all sides while I rotate, gushing sorrys, doing my best to reassure. "I'm not going anywhere," I find myself promising, and then realize: this is what Courtney means when she says I'm in denial.

I resist the temptation to ask where Foster is. I notice the tetherball court is empty, and so I lead the girls there to journal and reconnect.

"Anyone want to read something they've written?" I ask hopefully.

Nobody says anything or moves except Alexis, who covers her chubby face with her chubby little hands.

"You read," Jenna says.

I flip through my journal, which is pathetically mostly blank except for some scribbles from trying to get my pen to start.

"No one *has* to read," I say. "There's no pressure."

"I'd read my story about Mr. Baggy Jeans, but it's not finished yet," Lila says, and then Renee says, "It's really good because it makes you feel sad."

"Just read what you have," Rebecca says. "Don't be embarrassed."

"She's not," Renee says, and then Lila says, "Yeah, I'm not."

"Don't be shy either," Rebecca says. "Is anyone here shy?"

"Jessica and Alexis are shy," Zoe says.

"That isn't what they are," Billie says. "They're *introverted.*"

"They're *mute*," Jenna adds.

"Eva says there's no pressure," Maggie whispers. "Right, Eva?"

Then they all look at me.

"Be nice," I say.

It's the stupidest, most inane thing in the world to say, but so what. I *do* want them to be nice to each other, because I can only mentor them in so many ways; there's a limited amount of wisdom inside me, and most of it's about writing, not *being*. I don't know how a friend should be, so I'll probably fail if I try to teach them how to treat one another, but I feel like I could succeed if we can just focus on the journals.

"We're all friends," I tell the girls.

There's a single huff, a collective, jaded *yeah right.* Suddenly I feel so trapped in the role of the Adult, it's not what I was meant to do. I wasn't meant to lead them. It's never been my thing to take on leadership positions; I've never wanted to be captain of anything. I'm no Alyssa.

"Wait, where's Alyssa?" I ask.

The girls shrug.

"We have to find her," I say, and jump to my feet.

The girls rise slowly, awkwardly.

"Listen," I say, "who saw Alyssa last?"

"She was at the pool," Lila says, and then Renee finishes, "Swimming."

"Anyone see her after swim?"

Everyone shakes their head, so we walk to the pool. Alyssa's not there but Foster is, sitting next to the lifeguard tower, watching over his boys. I don't want to ask Foster if he's seen Alyssa, because I refuse to admit losing a camper *inside* of camp. I look back at my girls—who are rapt at the possibility they might get to swim again, a second chance to splash around—and notice Billie mouthing numbers, counting heads in the pool.

"Billie, what's up?"

"Eight boys," she says.

"Trevor," I start, but then lie, "is on vacation."

"Yeah but still," Billie says, "only eight. Corey's gone too."

"Everybody stay here," I tell them. "Whirled peas!" They don't hear me. Half of them are already taking off their shoes and socks, and the other half are huddled together, talking about which boy looks cutest with wet hair.

In the bathroom only one stall is occupied. I listen and hear the sound of lips smacking. I have to remind myself *not* to think about hypocrisy, but it's like trying not to think about elephants. Elephants! They're everywhere.

"I'm not going to come in there," I announce loudly, and the mouth sounds stop. "No one's in trouble," I say. "Hi, Corey."

"Hey," he says back.

I walk over to the door and lean in close, listening for zippers or the swoosh of shirts being hurriedly pulled on. It's silent. "Don't be weird," I say.

"It's *not* weird," Alyssa says.

"You don't have to be embarrassed."

"We're not."

"Okay, well, *I'm* a little embarrassed," I say.

"Everyone makes out," Alyssa says.

"I know."

"Camp is boring," she says, like it's a reasonable excuse.

"I know," I say.

"Besides, all the CITs come here to do this."

"They do?"

"*All* of them," Corey says.

I lean my back against the stall and glance up at the ceiling, where someone's written *SKUMMY SKIES* in a faded Sharpie scrawl. It looks twenty years old. Has everyone always been this cynical, this *disillusioned* with being young and sent off to summer camp to play stupid games in the stupid sun? The teenage exhaustion feels endless—not because it goes on and on forever but because it runs in a loop. Every kid starts where the last one left off.

"Fine," I say, "but if all the CITs jumped off a bridge, would you do that too?"

"Seriously?" Alyssa asks. "Jumping off a bridge?"

"Alyssa, people use clichés because they're universal. They make a point."

"Hell yeah, I'd jump," she says proudly. "I don't want

to be alone. That's lame."

"Also," Corey says, "if everyone's jumping, there's probably a good reason. We're not all just sheep. Maybe there's something really cool down there and when you jump, you find it."

I can't argue with that.

"Take your time," I say, and leave them alone so they can have some privacy.

35.

THOSE WHO CAN'T DO, GET TAUGHT

WHEN I WALK into the house, the last person I want to see is my father, but he's the first person I see because life is exactly like that.

"Evie," he says, his big palms shaking my shoulders, "be nice to those who made you."

"I'm nice," I say.

"We just want to help."

"Have you *seen* this toaster, Dad?"

"Honey, I haven't seen the *kitchen* in twenty-two years. And yet I'm always fed."

"I get it, I get it," I say.

"You don't have to apologize to your mom, but—"

"I *said* I was sorry," I tell him. "One of the many

things I said was 'sorry.'"

"Well." My father hangs his head. "*Needles* to say"—he pauses, gives my shoulders a pinch—"your words sting."

Needles to say, you're a prick. That's how he usually phrases it when he's talking to his racquetball buddies.

Then my phone beeps, and it's a text from Lindsay: Got a gift card 2 Target 2day!!! Before I can text back, my phone beeps again: DORM STORM!!!!

Cool, I text.

Beep, beep. So kewl.

I have a toaster, I text.

Beep, beep. Toe stir! *Beep, beep.* Grrrled Cheez 4 Life!

And even though I don't eat cheese, that still settles it: this'll be our first shared appliance. It's kind of exciting.

Later, my mother starts getting dinner together—grilled chicken breasts for everyone else and, like a saint, *St. Mom*, barbecue tofu just for me. The smell of soy and spices, wafting pleasantly up to the second floor, makes me feel hungry and sad. Penitence and piggishness swish around until my middle's gurgling, so loud Courtney hears it from the hall. She peeks her head in my room.

"There's that fault line rupturing."

"Why's everyone so clever in this family?" I ask. "Say something that isn't cute, say something heavy. Like, *weighty*."

"Forgive Mom her toaster-passes," Courtney says in a deep voice.

"I'm not *trying* to fight with her."

My sister stares at me, waiting for me to read her mind.

"I should be trying *not* to fight with her, I get it. But you fight with Dad and I fight with Mom. We can't get it out of our systems because it *is* our system, it's how we work."

Courtney frowns. She's sad to hear this, which is a sign I'm right. "It's not just that they won't be there anymore to enjoy, Eva. It's also that they won't be there to unload on."

"Fine with me."

"We're probably never going to live here again."

"I know that," I say, but knowing it doesn't mean I've thought about it. I look around my room. There's the desk I don't really sit at because I like to feel the heat of the laptop warming my thighs, and also because it's called a "laptop" and there's something to appreciate about the literalness of the name. It doesn't feel normal to miss a desk, since I'll have one at Emerson. Being a writer, I'll have one forever, I guess.

"Mom's like that desk," I start to say.

"I'm gonna stop you there," Courtney says, then grabs my hand and hurries me downstairs and into the kitchen.

"Teach us how to cook something," Courtney tells our mother, first pulling a skillet off its hook, then reaching into the dishwasher for a rubber spatula, flexing it back and forth.

"*Girls*," my mother says. "Don't make a mess before dinner."

"Really," Courtney says. "We need the skills. To usher us into the next phase of our lives."

"We want to learn, Mom."

"But something easy," Courtney clarifies.

"Rice-on-your-owni," I offer.

"Pasta prima donna," Courtney suggests.

"Now we're cookin' with sass," my father shouts from the other room.

"Okay, rice, pasta, we can do that, we can do that," my mother says, already browsing through cabinets and drawers. "This is going to be easy," she says, happy again, pleased to be needed, buzzing around the kitchen, talking and teaching, while we learn a few things.

36.

GOOD COUNSELOR, BAD COUNSELOR

MY GROUP STARTS the morning with Jan, the archery coach, who teaches the girls how to hold the bow and aim like Katniss, and not surprisingly they love it. They chant "Curl Powder!" every time they fire an arrow, whether or not it lands anywhere near the target. It feels like as good a time as any to sneak off and find Foster.

I've just crept away through some trees when someone taps my back: Alyssa.

"Bull's-eye," she says.

"Target's back there," I say, turning her around.

"I want to come with."

"You don't know where I'm going," I say. "Maybe I'm going to Steven's office to pick up some field trip slips."

"And maybe you're *not*," she says, seeing right through me.

"Alyssa, try not to know me so well, okay?"

"You're going to find Foster."

"What did I just say?"

"I want to see Corey," Alyssa says. Her eyeliner is especially flawless today. She's wearing lip gloss and a light bronze powder too.

"I'm starting to feel like your pimp," I say, then cover my mouth. "Oh God, I shouldn't have said that."

"So Foster's your boyfriend?"

"I thought you knew everything. What do you think?"

Alyssa considers it for a second. "I think he's not."

"Well, is Corey *your* boyfriend?"

"Hell yeah," she says, and fist-pumps the air.

"I never had a boyfriend when I was in junior high."

"And you don't have a boyfriend now."

"Actually, I *do*. His name's Elliot, he's in a band, and they're on tour this summer. They played Brooklyn last night."

Alyssa nods, a little impressed. It feels so satisfying that for a second I consider letting her tag along with me just to drive home what a cool counselor I am, how I can have Foster *and* Elliot—and maybe Corey too, if I tried. But then Seth walks by and waves, and it reminds me that I need to try and care more about impressing other counselors than impressing campers—even the supercool thirteen-year-old ones.

"Please go back," I say, clasping my hands together in a begging gesture. "The group really needs you there."

"That's, like, ironic," Alyssa says, "coming from you."

"What a mean thing to say."

"I just want to go with you."

"I'll let you do anything else you want," I tell her, immediately regretting it. The Sunny Skies Handbook would definitely classify making open-ended promises as bad, bad, bad.

"Can you take me to the party Friday?"

"What party?" I say, acting clueless.

"You know what party."

"I don't know, maybe . . . okay, fine," I lie.

"Yessssss!" she shrieks, jumping up and down.

"Now go, go, go." I give her a little push.

"Wait," Alyssa says. She reaches into her back pocket and pulls out a thick, folded stack of pages and hands it to me. "I told them to each put their names in the top corner like in school."

"How'd you get these?" I ask, astonished.

"I told the girls it was for the zine thingy."

"And they just . . . gave them to you?"

"Duh."

"Holy shit."

"She means, 'Holy cow,'" Foster says suddenly, from behind me.

"Oh fug," I say with a smile.

"Hi, Alyssa," Foster says.

"Bye, Foster," Alyssa says, and skips away.

Then Foster and I are alone together, strolling out along the sports fields. A stray soccer ball rolls our way, and Foster kicks it back. A counselor jogs by wearing an orange puffy vest, smelling like the bottoms of canoes, and nods at us. "Foster, Eva," he says.

"Let's go somewhere else," I say.

Somehow Foster looks distinctly better than he did yesterday, which was already better than he looked the day we kissed. Is this how it's going to be? Steadily rising cuteness, going up and up and up, like some graph problem from Mr. Laskin's trig class? I recall some deluded routine I used to rehearse, alone, facing my bathroom mirror: "I'm sorry, I just can't start dating someone right before I leave for college. I'd love to, really, but I can't."

"Where should we go?"

I shrug. I look at his wet, slicked hair, his damp basketball shorts, and get an idea: "Pool bathroom?"

Foster shoots me an admonishing look.

"I caught Corey and Alyssa making out in there," I say, and then, briefly forgetting who I'm talking to, laugh out loud.

"It's not funny," Foster tells me, his demeanor changing.

"Isn't it, though?"

"Do you want to get fired or something?"

"Not necessarily," I say.

"And we're cussing around eighth graders now?"

"It's *Alyssa*, she's down."

"Doesn't matter."

"She's like my co-counselor."

"She's your CIT," he says.

"Foster, you know how they say rules are made to be broken?"

"Don't do that, Eva. Don't be . . . flippant."

I try not to let that hurt, just keep things light, so I lean in close, raising his clipboard to shield us, and sweetly sing "Boom Chicka Boom," like it's a love song. Like it's *our song*.

"Did you hear what I just said?" Foster waits for me to stop singing and then, when I do, he shakes his head and walks off toward the cafeteria.

Usually I'm the one taking everything too seriously, because I like the idea of being thought of as a Serious Person. But this time it feels good to not to be the uptight one, walking away annoyed and let down because the other person doesn't get the gravity of being super intense all the time. So maybe, in the smallest way, this is a step forward, a sign of progress. I've got my eyes on the Big Picture, while Foster's still caught up worrying about the Little Picture. It's basically Life Camp versus Summer Camp. I guess we're on different wavelengths.

And that's the thing about wavelengths—they're not waves. You can't ride them alone; you have to ride them together.

37.

READING THINGS

I'M DYING SO bad to read what the girls wrote I'm barely able to make it through the day without peeking. When I get home, I dash upstairs and toss my cell phone across the room and lay the pages out in front of me on the bed.

There's a soft knock on the door—one of those respectful parental knocks.

My mother wants to know if I want a "going-away" dinner, like a bon voyage thing. But who would come? Not Shelby, she hasn't called in a while. Not Michelle and Steph, they're not so in love with me lately. Foster, probably.

Zack, maybe. Because yesterday, on a weird impulse, I

texted him hi and he texted back, im gonna call u.

Then, later that afternoon, he actually does. I'm too unprepared to answer, so I let it go to voice mail, then immediately check it. It's him inviting me to the movies, and more importantly, he sounds genuinely happy to be inviting me, about the prospect of seeing me. Throughout the whole message he maintains this genuinely happy-seeming attitude.

But near the end, after leaving his phone number—silly, because I obviously already have it—and asking when's a good time to call back, his voice changes. The vibe gets vaguely serious.

"Eva," he says, "you've been such a good friend to Shelby, and such a good friend to me, too. I know the two of you are close, but I hope that doesn't make it awkward for us to hang out."

Then there's a pause, and in a lower, smoother tone, he says, "I always liked you."

There's Reading into Things and then there's just Reading Things, straightforwardly interpreting signals that are right there in front of you. I don't have to study Zack's voice to understand the subtext of it—I just have to listen to the words he's literally saying out loud. It's all there. I'm not inventing anything.

The summary of his message is this: first Zack's genuinely happy, then he's vaguely serious, then he's something else: he's hitting on me. He even mentioned that if I need a ride, he can pick me up—maybe on his motorcycle, maybe not, he didn't specify. Either way, he's clearly moving on from Shelby—the best-looking, most together girl of all my high school friends, the one who's had sex a million times—to, quite possibly, *me*. Me: who isn't going to fall in love with him, who isn't going to try and date him because I'm not really dating before I leave for college, and even if I was, if I *wanted to*, it'd be with Foster. Or, I guess maybe Elliot.

Is it too crazy to imagine that Zack might be into me? And that, because I'm not some candidate for a long-term relationship, he might want to have sex with me?

I don't have to want it to happen to still be turned on by the idea.

There's hoping for the best, and then there's just hoping.

38.

SCRUTIN' EYES

I STAY UP all night scribbling notes in the margins of the girls' pages. I use two different pens, a green and a purple, because those feel like nonthreatening, nonjudgmental colors. When I like something, I circle it; when I love something, I underline it three times. And when I don't like something, or even hate it, I draw a question mark next to the sentence and write the word *WHY*.

I wake up in full-on workshopping mode. I organize follow-up questions, design writing exercises, and even sketch out a suggested list of related reading materials, as well as drafting a mock table of contents, where I number each piece in a potential order. For a second I wonder if I'm going a little overboard, but it's only for a second, and then it passes and I'm excited again.

"I'm inspirational!" I scream as I pass by the open bathroom door where Courtney's brushing her hair.

"Ahh," she sighs. "So the mental's become the mentor."

"Don't be jealous," I say, squeezing her face, kissing her on the cheek. "I still have so much to learn from you."

"*Bedankt*," Courtney says. "*Dank u*." She hands me a book, thick as the Lonely Planet, of English-to-Dutch translations.

"Dunk *you*!" I say, smacking her on the butt with the book.

But at camp that morning the girls are foggy with quinoa from the gluten-free muffins Jessica's mom baked. They move so leadenly I literally have to lead them by the hand to the Craft Shack for arts and crafts, where they numbly twist pipe cleaners into key chains, glassy-eyed, like they've been watching TV for weeks straight. They've got glaring farmer's tans and burnt red noses like little drunks and streaks of white on their shoulders where the sunscreen didn't get fully rubbed in. My girls didn't land on camp; camp landed on them. To stir them out of their funk, I tear up our printed-out schedule for the day and dramatically fling the confetti into the trash. No one notices.

Later in the afternoon we stumble through a very

sluggish session of Red Rover, followed by a game of handball that dissolves into formlessness about four minutes in. Alexis waddles off by herself, pulling at the jean shorts that keep sliding up her crotch.

"Curl Powder," I say, still trying to rally everybody.

"Can we go to the pool?" Zoe asks.

"It's not our swim time yet."

"Can't we just go anyway?" Jenna whines.

"Girls, come on," I say.

"Can we sing a song?" Rebecca asks. "And not like a camp song, a *radio* song?"

"Who listens to the *radio*?" Alyssa says.

"I mean a song from a video."

"What video?" Billie asks.

"Yeah," Maggie says, "we should sing a song."

"But I have your writing here," I interject, a bit exasperated, shaking a manila folder I took from my father's desk.

The group shuts up.

"I read everything you wrote and even took some notes to help guide your second drafts," I say, opening the folder, showing them pages.

"What does 'drafts' mean?" Jessica says.

"It means when we write them again," Billie tells her.

"Why do we have to write them again?" Jenna asks.

"Because she doesn't like them," Lila says, and then

Renee says, "Because they aren't any good."

"Of course they're *good*," I say. "It's just that every writer revises."

"What's 'revises'?'" Alexis says.

"Same thing as drafts, dummy," Billie says.

"So every writer writes their stories over and over?" Maggie asks.

"All of them," I say. "Zoe!" I point and snap in Zoe's direction. "Quick, what's your favorite book in the world?"

"*The Secret Garden*," Zoe says. "Tied with *The Golden Compass*."

"Well, those stories were edited and revised a hundred times before they became the books you love."

The girls look at each other, confused. They're baffled by the news.

"You can't get it right the first time," I tell them.

"Yes, you can," Alyssa says.

"No," I say. "Nobody does."

"Eva," Alyssa says calmly, jerking her head subtly in the direction of nine very crushed spirits, "you can *too* get it right the first time."

The girls look at me nervously. A distant group of boys chatter on the baseball diamond ("We want a pitcher, not a belly itcher! We want a catcher, not a belly scratcher!"). My girls are tense, anticipating, nine potential failures looming on the horizon.

We want a leader, not a book reader! We want a counselor, not a dream trouncelor!

"You're completely right, Alyssa," I say. "I was just talking about for *regular* novels. What you guys've done is totally different. You guys are like stream of consciousness, which is what the Beats did, very hip. It's kind of like the jazz of writing: improvised, raw, super unpredictable."

I smile to show them everything's okay. I close the folder with their inked-up pages, clip it to my clipboard, and hold it against my chest. They don't need to see the notes scrawled in the margins, the purple question marks and green delete lines, thick with finality.

WHY?

I can't believe I wrote that! The very phrase that was tossed at me like some hot potato, badly burning my self-esteem. And now here I am flinging it to my girls?

Why? I ponder the word and the instinct to ask it in every way possible; I ponder my itchy eyes, my *scrutin' eyes*, my consistent inability to see.

Why ask *why?*

They wouldn't have any more of an answer than I did.

39.

STYLE WAR

AFTER CLOSING CEREMONIES, I wander around the outfield of the empty baseball diamond, pretending to look for stray kick balls, taking a moment for myself. All the rubber balls are dirty and deflated and it's like, *I get what you're trying to say, World.*

Don't deflate, Eva.

Then I notice some campers by the pickup area, singing "Leaving on a Jet Plane" together and I'm like, *Good one.*

I cross the field slowly toward my car, hoping to miss all the buses and other counselors leaving, and when I reach the parking lot, everyone's gone pretty much except Foster, who's in the process of leaving. He rolls his window down as he pulls up next to me.

"Left a note on your car," he says.

"What's it say?"

"Omit needless words," Foster says with a squint and a *sorry* smile. "Shouldn't have called you flippant the other day." He reaches a tanned arm toward me and tugs softly on the sleeve of my camp shirt.

"It was very, very mean," I tell him, putting a hand on his. "What's the meanest thing I've ever said to you?"

Foster only takes a second to answer: "That I could use some *definition*."

"You've got nice muscles," I say, squeezing his bicep. "Super defined."

"You meant my writing," Foster says, pulling his hand inside the car. That's it—less than a minute in and we're done making up, done joking around.

"Foster," I say, "that was a hundred million years ago." I stoop down to meet his eyes. "Are you going to turn your car off?"

"No," he says.

"We just have different *styles*." I sigh, tired.

"So what's my style, then?" Foster asks.

"I don't know," I say. "Camp's over. I don't have any more answers today."

"Just because something isn't *your* style—"

"Yeah, you don't need to finish the sentence," I interrupt.

"Feel free to admit you've never liked my writing."

"Stop being so sensitive," I say, surprising myself, because don't I love sensitivity and rawness and realness and . . . Foster? "Stop picking a fight!"

"I'm not trying to pick a fight."

"Then what are you *trying* to do?"

"Sorry, forgot to choose my words perfectly for you, Eva."

And it's back to this.

Foster's engine begins to fume a bit in the heat, oily steam hissing from under his hood, getting in my eyes and making me tear up. I blink it away and look down at his lap, at his distressed jeans, and then I look down at my sandals, near my big toes where the soles have worn away, and it's like, *Enough of the symbolism already, World.*

Enough.

40.

PEDIATRICKS

"WHERE ARE *YOU* going?" my mother asks. I'm holding the keys and my backpack and standing by the front door.

"Um"—I look down at my Sunny Skies shirt and the pink-and-turquoise lanyard around my neck and wonder if it isn't apparent—"to camp?"

"What day is today?"

"Friday," I say, pretty sure it's Friday.

"And what did we schedule for Friday?"

"Mom," I say, "I think it's obvious I don't know, so just tell me."

"Your appointments," she says, drawing it out, giving me the opportunity to jump in. "Your *two* appointments . . . with . . . ?"

"I've never made an appointment in my life," I say.

"*I* made the calls, Eva."

"But I have work today."

"This is more important," she says. "You're leaving soon."

"I don't want to go to the dentist."

"And the doctor," she says.

This time I'm not the one to call in sick—my mother does it. If there's a lesson there, then I'm choosing not to see it, and if there's a story, well, I don't want to know about that either.

At the dentist's office Dr. Richardson gives me hell. He tells me to swear off sugar-free gum and avoid soda after seven p.m. He also says I shouldn't rip open bags of chips or candy with my teeth or chew on the insides of my cheeks when I'm nervous or grind my teeth while I sleep. And most of all, he doesn't want me to fly off to Boston and forget that *he's* my dentist, that he's got a say in my hygiene. It feels like Dr. Richardson exists just to make me feel bad—he's what Mr. Roush would call my *foil*, or my adversary—so I guess I should respect that.

I apologize for not flossing; I act sorry about not using enough Crest with tartar control; I promise I won't miss any more checkups.

"I'm afraid of it hurting," I say. He's heard that one before.

"You don't even want to *know* how many times I've missed my gynecologist appointment," I say next, trying to lighten the mood. He's never heard that one before.

I'm about to say, "Just kidding," when he abruptly fills my mouth with bubblegum-flavored fluoride and, not smiling, leaves the room.

A half hour later the checkup ends, and I go back to the waiting area, where Courtney's reading a *Vogue* alongside some other bored moms. My mouth's a little swollen, but I still manage a frown.

"Dr. Richardson said you can't eat or complain for an hour."

"I want to have all my teeth removed," I mumble, rubbing my gums. "I wish I had metal teeth, and I never had to go to the dentist again."

"You know how many cavities I've had? Four," Courtney says, opening her mouth to show me the silver fillings.

I've never noticed my sister's fillings before. When I look inside her mouth to count them—three on the bottom left, one on the right—I feel a sense of loss, as if something that should've always been mine had suddenly been stolen from me.

"Is it because you didn't floss?" I ask, sitting on her lap, leaning my head on her shoulder.

"No, it's because of all the Blow Pops Mom let me

eat when I was a kid. But now I'm an adult, Eva, and I don't go to pediatric dentists." Courtney scoots me off and starts heading down the hallway toward the elevators before I can even grab a complimentary toy from Dr. Richardson's treasure box.

At Dr. Connell's I get my knees tapped and my ears examined. He presses my tongue down and shines a mini flashlight down my throat. He places a stethoscope against my chest and listens.

"How ya feelin'?" the doctor asks.

"Great."

"Great?" Dr. Connell asks. "That's new."

"Yeah, well, everyone lies to their doctor."

"Not everyone," he says, moving the stethoscope higher up my neck.

"I'm a little tired," I tell him.

"How tired?"

"A little tired."

"Would you characterize the tiredness as lethargy or just drowsiness from not getting enough sleep?"

"The first one," I say.

"Do you ever feel dizzy?"

"Yes," I admit, without admitting that I haven't been wearing my glasses.

"Breathe deep for me," Dr. Connell says, placing his stethoscope on my lungs.

I breathe, but not that deep. He sighs and then stands. "You may be anemic, Eva."

It sounds character building—which I'm not against.

"I could take a multivitamin," I say.

"I've got something better," he tells me, taking out a prescription pad and scribbling something. He tears the page, folds it, holds it out for me. "Now that'll have you feeling great!"

"Great," I say, as he guides me by the shoulders back to the waiting room.

I hand Courtney the prescription. *Anemic,* I think, testing the word out in my head, seeing if I like the way it defines me.

"What is this?" my sister asks, staring at the page.

"Some prescription," I say. "For my *anemia.*"

"He's just written, 'Eat a cheeseburger.'" Courtney holds up the page so I can see.

"'Eat a cheeseburger'?" I read aloud. "That jerk!"

Just because someone's known you your whole life doesn't mean they can't be a jerk. Sometimes it means they're an even bigger one.

41.

THE FINALIST

I DON'T LEAVE my room for dinner, even though both my mother and father beg me. Instead I sulk on the bed, hungry and angry, when Michelle calls.

"You picked up fast," she says. "Were you reading old texts and acting weird about them?"

"For once, no," I say.

"I'm just calling to see if you checked your grades," Michelle says.

In this moment the word *grades*—a word I've felt enslaved by for at least the last six years—sounds totally foreign, like something I've never heard before. "My *grades*? No."

"When do you leave for Boston?"

I flip open my calendar, but there's nothing written on it. I never circle dates.

"No idea," I say.

"You're being kind of bitchy, Eva," she says.

"Sorry. I'm just . . . *hangry*, I guess."

"Like always," she says.

"Not like always," I say.

"So you haven't looked on the school's site?"

"I don't remember my password." Virgo? Vegan? Shakes? Something like that.

"So you haven't seen it."

"*Michelle*," I say.

"Then I'll be the first to tell you: you're a finalist for the Scholastic California Writing Award."

My mother knocks twice, calls my name, so I turn away from the door and lower my voice.

"What do you mean? What is that?"

"You're the only senior from our school on the list."

"I didn't apply for that," I say. "I don't know what that is."

"Whatever. You're on the list with four other people, and all of them go to, like, nightmare prep schools."

"Oh God."

"Roush must've submitted it. You're like his pet."

"He shouldn't have done that," I say. "I didn't ask him to do that."

"Are you going to be happy about this, Eva? Can you, like, *appreciate* good news?"

"*You* don't sound happy for me."

Michelle has nothing to say to that.

"Right now it just doesn't feel good to beat anyone at writing," I say. "There're different styles, you know, it's not all comparable. And what does it even mean to *win* at writing? And why would they even pick me?"

"Because you're better than everyone else," Michelle says. "You tell me that all the time."

"I guess I do," I say.

My mother knocks again. I can smell food; maybe she's brought up a plate.

"I have to go."

"Well, don't freak out. Maybe you won't win."

Finally my mother just enters and walks over to the bed. She puts a hand over my hand that's holding the phone.

"But you probably will," Michelle says, annoyed.

"Eat with us, Eva, please." My mother tightens her grip.

"Sounds good, Michelle," I say.

She squeezes tighter.

"Dinnertime," I say, and hang up.

"What did Michelle have to say?" my mother asks.

"That I'm a real winner."

"Oh, that's sweet," my mother says, and then hugs me, accidentally mashing her shoulder into my tender jaw.

"Ow!" I moan, a real winner—and a sore winner too.

42.

JOKES

I PUT ON my nicer lipstick for the party. I pick out a shirt that isn't my camp shirt and immediately feel prettier, rejuvenated. *This isn't going to be so bad,* I tell myself, stashing snacks and drinks in my tote bag. So far I've packed kale chips and flax crackers and a few little juice-box-size coconut waters. I've even got a plastic baggie of raw almonds and seaweed crumble left over from the last time Michelle and Steph and I went to the movies. I'm bringing enough to eat and drink for days—should the party last for days—but more importantly, it means I won't be the only one there not sipping or chewing something, awkward and excluded.

On the way to Nick's I drive down Thousand Oaks

Boulevard, where the trees are big and beautiful, and besides the brand-new mega-size Bed, Bath & Beyond, everything looks pretty identical to how it's been since I was thirteen. Roxy's Famous Deli closed, but there's a location in Westlake Village now where my family still goes for birthday dinners—though the Blockbuster nearby was torn down last year to make room for extra parking. It seems like something to potentially feel melancholy about or, like, protective of, because it reminds me of the opening to a short story about how the place where you're born and grow up can change so much when you leave that you don't even recognize it when you return.

"You can never go home again," Courtney once said to me bittersweetly.

"No, seriously," my father said, deadpan, "you can't come back."

Nick's house is in a suburb in the foothills, where the houses all have white two-car garages and Spanish tile roofs. It's a nice night out, and quiet, and I can't even tell there's a party going on until I'm at the front door, peeking through the frosted glass. Nobody answers when I knock, so I just go inside.

There're about twenty people spread out across the living room and den, most of them counselors. It's sort of dark inside, like mood lighting, but I notice Nick right away because he looks really different with his hair parted neatly to the side. He nods hello and then pauses, giving me a double take, as if he's not sure it's really me, which makes me worry most of us might not recognize each other just dressed as ourselves, not in camp clothes. But then I spy Foster across the room by the kitchen, and *he* looks like himself. Of course.

"I'll show you where to put that," Melly says, pointing to my tote bag.

"I'm just going to carry it, thanks," I say.

"Why?"

"It's just some food I brought, that's all."

"I never eat," Melly says.

"Never?"

"You didn't let me finish."

"Oh, sorry," I say. "Go ahead."

"I never eat," Melly starts, pausing, sucking in a breath for emphasis, "at *parties*."

"Me either," I say, swiftly dropping my bag in a dark corner.

Booth comes over as Melly wanders off down a hallway. Booth's wearing perfume, which I know because it's my mother's scent—Lancôme's Trésor—so I assume it must be his mother's too. I can't help leaning in closer for a longer, satisfying sniff. In a flash I'm transported, I can almost hear the clicking of high heels against a waxed linoleum floor; with my eyes closed I'm there, at school—my mom's come to pick me up. Another whiff though and it's just Booth. I'm not going anywhere. And no one's coming to take me home.

"Want to hear a joke?" Booth asks.

I'm not really paying attention. Booth notices.

"Looking for Foster?" he asks, winking.

"Not really. What's the joke?"

"What do you call a fish with no eyes?"

"I don't know." I shrug. "A fsh?"

Booth frowns. "I like that answer better, actually," he says. "You can go find Foster now."

"I'm not necessarily trying to find Foster."

Then Amanda and Kit and Jules see me and come over, and Booth slips away.

"Corey's here," Amanda says.

"Corey's hot," Kit says, giggling.

"Corey?" I ask. "The eighth grader?"

"Well, he's going into ninth," Amanda reminds me.

"I'd do him," Jules says.

"No, you wouldn't," I say.

"He can *surf*," Kit tells me.

"So?"

"So we can't all share Foster," Jules says, and they all laugh like it's an inside joke.

"He's mine tonight," Kit says.

"Who?" I ask, startled.

"Corey, stupid."

"Isn't this supposed to be 'Counselors Only'?"

"That's, like, only a friendly suggestion," Amanda says.

"You mean my friends could've come?"

The girls laugh again, probably assuming I don't have any friends.

I retreat to a bathroom off the kitchen and call Steph to see what she's doing.

"Before you say anything," I stop her, "I'm not going to just apologize and apologize. Instead I'm extending what the ancient Greeks called an olive branch."

After a little lull of silence, Steph says, "I'll be taking that."

"Oh, thank gods," I say, so relieved I sink down to the tile floor.

When I tell her I'm at a camp party, she seems happy for me. Although when I say *seems* I mean exactly that, because something distinctly *un*happy was stirred up by our fight earlier. Even with this surface okay-ness, an acidic feeling still bubbles around the edges of our chit-chat. This is the problem with getting everything out in the open, especially for girls, who *never* forget. My mom always says, "Put your issues in these tissues." But they're just tissues—soggy-ass tissues!—they can't hold the heavy stuff. So I'll just have to take the tissues, because I don't want snot on my face.

Steph says Michelle's on a date and that she's baby-sitting her little brother; they're making microwave brownies and homemade frosting. At first I don't believe her—about Michelle's date or the brownies and frosting—and then I can't believe myself: Doubting Eva, so distrustful. Then someone turns up the music in the living room so loud even Steph can hear it. "God, that's loud," she says. I tell her everything's about to get "camplified," which she appreciates, but not enough to ditch her brother and come save me.

Shelby doesn't pick up when I call her next, but Zack does. He says my name without even saying hello: "Eva." He almost sings it.

"Never mind," I say.

"Are we still on for tomorrow night?"

"Yeah," I say, not thinking, and hang up.

When I leave the bathroom, everyone's outside on the patio drinking. The warm breeze makes my eyes water, so I go back inside to find my tote and reluctantly dig out my glasses, stashed beneath Baggies and books. Once I have them on, it's heaven, I can see *everything*—even the words on the spines of my books.

"This is who I am," I say aloud, to no one. "The girl who brings books to a party."

"I'll show you where to put that," Melly says, suddenly

behind me. She's either on autopilot and doesn't remember talking to me earlier, or she just doesn't recognize me with my glasses on. That or she's just losing her mind from lack of food.

"It's okay," I tell her, clutching my bag, "I'll hold it."

She leads me down the hall anyway, into a bedroom with the lights out. At first it looks like there's a mound of coats on the bed, but then the mound moans, moves. It's two people, murmuring into each other's faces, one body underneath another body.

"I'm just dropping off my bag," I say, reaching for the edge of the bed but touching a foot instead. "Sorry, sorry."

"'S cool," a male voice says. Instantly I can tell it's Corey.

"Corey," I say into the dark. "It's Eva."

"Oh, hey, Eva," Corey says pleasantly, like we're at the supermarket and he's happened down my aisle.

"I see we're doing *this* again."

"What d'you mean?" he asks.

"Be careful," I say, for no reason, then leave.

Out in the hallway Booth's standing by himself, staring at a framed picture of Nick as a child playing in the sand.

"Don't go in there," I tell him.

"Wasn't going to," he says.

I try to slip past him, but his body's blocking my way to the patio. "Booth, move."

"Nice, nerd," Booth says in a dumb voice, finally noticing my glasses. "Foster's outside."

"I told you I'm not looking for Foster."

"Yeah, you are," Booth says, a sleazy smile spreading across his face. "You put your glasses on, so you're looking for someone."

"I *have* a boyfriend," I say. "Foster and I . . . we're not like that. He doesn't want to date someone, since he's leaving for college soon, and I'm already in a relationship with someone. He's in a band."

Booth looks like he doesn't believe me, so I start rambling details.

"His name's Elliot, but I call him 'Elli' or 'Smelly' or 'Smelliot.' He's only into music, he can't even watch a commercial without commenting on the music, and every time he reads a book, he has to make an iPod playlist to listen to while he reads, like a film score," I say, catching my breath. "And even though I'm leaving for Boston in August, and he's staying here, we're making it work."

Booth nods emphatically. He grabs my arm, wants to talk about love.

"I love Melly. I've never told her, though."

I accidentally laugh, then stop myself. "Melly?" I pat Booth's shoulder, slowly slip past him. "Well, there're other fsh in the sea, you know."

"He's with Amanda," Booth says, gesturing to Foster. "And the other girls."

He is. I see him. Right in the center of a circle of giddy, attentive girls. I join the conversation mid-giggle and catch Foster's eyes.

"Hey," he says, nodding at me instead of reaching out for a hug. "I remember those glasses."

I shrug and take them off, shove them in a pocket.

"What's up?" he asks stiffly, out of what feels like total obligation. He waits for an answer, and the girls, watching him wait, all wait too.

"Nada mucho."

"Foster says you're a writer," Amanda says.

"Yep."

"What's something you're writing now?" Melly asks.

"Oh, it's just child's play."

"Don't be modest," Amanda says.

"I'm not. It's a play for children. For a children's theater."

"See?" Foster says, smiling reluctantly, sadly even. "Told you she was smart."

The girls look at me, waiting for more smartness.

"I think I'm gonna go soon," I say.

"Okay, bye," Jules says, turning back around, closing me out of the circle.

"Foster," I say, over her shoulder, "want to go outside and talk for a second?"

"Why would he go with *you*?" Melly asks, and they all turn their stares from me to Foster, who looks uncomfortable.

"I'm staying, and you can stay another minute too," he says to me.

"I've heard it's cooler to leave a party before it starts to suck," I say.

"Maybe you suck," Jules mutters. The other girls pretend not to hear and avoid eye contact.

I've never cared about being universally liked—like, *across-the-board* liked—because I've always felt there was something unnatural about people like that. If literally everyone likes you, it's probably because you're generic and bland, which is the opposite of what I want to be. I know that having a way-too-specific personality inevitably bothers some people, and bothers them a ton, and that's fine with me. But I don't want to be disliked unless I'm *known*, I'm understood. I never had a chance with these girls, and to be real, they never had much of a chance with me. Still, even though I didn't really want to have to like them, I definitely wanted them to have to like me—to not be able to *help* but like me, to like me *in spite of* me. Of course, that's fantasy shit. They don't.

Then Foster shoots me a look—a conflicted,

disappointed, unsympathetic look that says: *You should stay and try and have a decent time and connect with other people, if not for yourself then for me, a little favor for me, Eva, who's sticking up for you and wants to respect you even though you're not helping, not at all.*

"Yeah, I have to go," I say, giving Foster my own look: *Forgive me.*

Follow me.

I head back inside the house, down to the bedroom, where the door's still closed, and I swing it open and flip on the lights. Corey's on the bed, and this time I can see the legs kicking beneath him—they're wearing Alyssa's shoes.

"Alyssa!" I shout.

"Oh, hey, Eva," Corey says again, just as casually as before.

"Alyssa, let's go. I'm taking you home."

"What?!" she yells, pulling off the covers and sitting up, furious. "You said I could come. You promised!"

"Yeah, but it wasn't a real promise—it was a camp promise. I can't keep all those."

"Well, we're not at camp. You can't tell me what to do."

I go sit on the edge of the bed and lean in closer. "No one's that into us," I say. "No one really wants us here."

"That's not true."

I stand, put my hands on my hips, try to project the

authority I've been seeking all summer. "You're *my* CIT. I'm leaving and so should you."

"I'm staying!"

"We're a team," I say, more forcefully. "Alyssa, c'mon."

I try and slide her off the bed, but she's stronger than she looks.

"You're just jealous!"

"You're not supposed to be here," I whisper. "I'm trying to look out for you. I have to redeem myself."

I grab her arm, pull her out the front door, and less than a minute later we're in my car. She sulks silently. I put the keys in the ignition so the radio plays. Corey waits on the curb across the street under a dim streetlamp, basically in the dark.

"Drive," Alyssa says impatiently.

"Please don't be so mad."

"Why are we still here?!" she screams, fuming, her black eyeliner smearing into streaks above her cheekbones. "What are you waiting for?!" A few tears hug the contours of her heart-shaped face.

"Foster," I say, not wanting to lie.

"You're fucking joking," she seethes.

I only wait another few minutes, but by then both of us are crying. He still hasn't come outside when I finally shift into drive and drive away.

43.

VANCOUVER

AT THREE A.M. my phone rings. I don't want to talk to any*one* about any*thing*; I just want to forget about the party, forget about the night, and forget about Foster and how he never came out to meet me. Because if he really liked me, he would have.

"We don't *pine* for boys," my mother always tells me. "We're not trees."

I answer it anyway.

It's Elliot. Tonight he's in Vancouver, tomorrow Seattle, the next night Portland, then Oakland, and then finally LA. Things have mellowed between his bandmates, but the vibe's not necessarily better. The bassist wants another singer—not *in addition* to Elliot, but *instead* of him—and he's hurt by it.

"Screw this band," he says at least four times, and the way he says *screw* makes me a little itchy.

Then Elliot asks what I'm wearing. What I'm really wearing is my underwear, but I tell him I'm wearing a party dress with tights and high heels. He wants to know if that's all I'm wearing and I laugh, tell him a top hat too. We talk for a while about his bandmates, 7-Eleven snacks, his big old cat back home. Then he tells me he misses me, and it's nice to hear someone say it, since it's not going to be Foster. Elliot's voice gets a little softer, kind of breathy. I don't hear a zipper unzipping, it's not that straightforward, but I can still tell what's happening.

I wonder if phone sex with Elliot is like what I assume real sex with Elliot would be like, where I don't make a sound because he's making enough for both of us. But unlike how a boy usually expects the girl to be loving it, never knowing if she's secretly just faking, it's the opposite with Elliot. He probably *assumes* I'm faking, that I'd pretend anything because I'm so into him.

But tonight I'm not pretending anything. I'm really doing it.

I assume it's going to be one of the strangest and most graceless things I've ever attempted, but impressively, Elliot doesn't let it be. Apparently he's a phone sex pro. Maybe the fact that he's so full of himself—which is a totally pointless expression, because what else would a person be full of?—helps somehow. Still, whatever he's projecting, I'm absorbing; he doesn't leave a single open moment to doubt myself or feel weird. I guess sometimes you do something you've never ever done, yet it's really not so pivotal. Sure, it's *notable*, so you take note—there it is, *noted*—and then the universe nudges you to just move it along.

When it's over, he puts down the phone to go get a tissue, clean up. I lie with the phone away from my ear, resting on my shoulder. When he returns, it's back to the high Canadian gas prices, a boring after-party with some local bands, a quick trip to a Vancouver art museum, money with the Queen of England on it.

Before we hang up, he asks about the earthquake that hit a week or so ago, wanting to know if I felt it. He says he felt it.

There's no point denying anything—we're all full of something—so I say I felt it too.

44.

IT'S ZACK

IT'S FOUR IN the afternoon on Saturday, and I've been reading the same ten sentences over and over—the final ten sentences of my best short story, the one Mr. Roush didn't like because it's fake. It's actually not that great, now that I'm really looking at it again. What it is, more specifically, is that it's not that *likeable*. I need to work on coming up with stories with more likeable characters; I should focus on that for my college writing classes. I wonder if maybe I should even try to *be* more likeable, but that'll be harder to figure out—in college or ever.

Then I get a text from Foster: Party got better. U shdve stayed. U mightve had fun.

I text back, 2 much competition 2 be yr date.

Oh.

Want to go on a real date.

When camps dun?

I'll be in boston!

And ill be tuff.

I stare at Foster's text—And ill be tuff—trying to decode what he meant to type, what was autocorrected. *And I'll be tough. And it'll be tough. And I don't feel like texting anymore.* And I don't feel like thinking about Foster for a while.

At eight, Zack picks me up in a Toyota Camry, saying the motorcycle's in the shop. It's fine, I don't want to ride it anyway, because those things are dangerous. He also tells me we're ditching the movie idea and instead going over to hang with some of his friends at somebody's house. "It'll be intimate," he says, in a smooth, buttery way, and for a moment I feel like how Shelby must've felt—like you're being taken care of. Zack also looks really good: his jeans are tight, his gray V-neck showing just the softest tuft of blond chest hair. When I look at him, I think, *There's a straightforwardly good-looking guy,* which makes me feel older, like I'm twenty, or twenty-three.

It's nice because I don't feel shy around him—he's Zack, Shelby's Zack, I've known him since forever—and I'm not shy around his friends either. I recognize a few of them from Shelby's birthday senior year: Leyna and Scott and Bobby, and over in the corner by the iPod player, Marta, the camp lifeguard. She waves at me and smiles. Zack's impressed.

"You know Marta?"

"I do, actually."

Zack's outside smoking most of the night, but it's okay, it feels good to not need him there by my side. Since I can tell this will be my last party of the summer—my last party before college—I decide I'll do this one differently. Not do it like Courtney ("liking people is *easy*") so much as do it like a Courtney/Eva hybrid, the best of both.

I make a point to say hello to everyone, that's the first thing: I'm Eva, hello, I'm Eva, hello. I cross the room to where someone's laid out carrot sticks and hummus and almonds and eat some of each, sampling anything that appears gluten-, dairy-, egg-, and meat-free. I let my T-shirt casually slouch off one shoulder like I'm also free, and loose, and down for anything—which, tonight, I kind of am.

A little later, when Zack comes inside to check on me, he seems pleased by how outgoing I am, how animated, engaged in Bobby's story about this video on YouTube that for once I don't have to lie about seeing because I actually *have* seen it, and have things to say about it too.

I've even positioned myself toward the center of the circle, and I'm laughing the hardest, touching Bobby's arm like he's really done it, really cracked me up. And, just like last night, I'm not faking any of it.

Suddenly it's late, and Zack starts saying his good-byes. Even though I don't need help—I'm sober, haven't had anything to drink but iced tea and lemonade all night—he helps me to the car. I assume he's driving me home, but he takes a route I don't recognize, eventually pulling into a driveway I've never seen.

"This is my parents' house," he says.

This is where he lives now, though he doesn't explain why. The place is nicer than the apartment he used to have in Thousand Oaks, but it also seems sadder. But maybe I'm just projecting that, I don't know for sure, I wasn't there for the end of him and Shelby.

Zack idles the car in the driveway and gently places his hand on mine, but I barely notice because I'm distracted.

Something's missing.

There's a lack of something, a vacancy, but just like with all my absences—with Foster, with Michelle and Steph, with Boston, with camp—I try to clear it out of my mind, like one of Courtney's meditations. Even as we tiptoe up the walkway, through the foyer, across the tile, down the length of the hall to the last bedroom, where I go into his parents' guest bathroom and stare into the mirror, I keep telling myself the same thing: *Don't think about it, don't think about it.*

There's nothing in the bedroom but a big-screen TV and a king-size bed. It's like a hotel room. Zack sits on the edge of the bed and starts whispering the sweetest things to me, which only makes everything somehow sadder:

"I thought we were going to get married."

"Shelby said she loved me, that she wanted to live together."

"You know how she is, Eva, how she can pull away sometimes and not mean it, how she really just wants you to pull her back and remind her you're not going anywhere."

I wait till he's finished before responding. "I don't know if I know her *that* well," I say.

Zack smiles. "You're cool," he says, patting the spot next to him for me to sit down. "And smart. And pretty." Then he pats a spot on his lap.

But that haunting sense of something missing doesn't go away; it seeps deeper into the walls and the carpet and the big-screen TV and the bed, until I know for sure there's no way I can have sex with Zack, partly because I don't *really* know how to have sex—at least, not good enough for someone like Zack, who's done it with dozens of girls, and probably even a few women. But I also can't make out with Zack because the truth is I like someone else more. And even if sometimes I veer pretty close to being an Unlikeable Character, I'm at least aware of the fact. Which means I have the chance to stop what I'm doing and change, before I become so unlikeable that the reader gives up on me, shuts the book, and sends it flying across the room, disgusted.

I'm not really sure what to do now, though. Zack doesn't seem ready to drive me home yet; he asks if I want to watch TV, and if he can take off my shoes and rub my feet. What do you say to that? So I surf around the channels while he massages my soles with his fingertips. It feels incredible, much better than kissing, and I drift away for a minute, not into sleep but some kind of foggy bliss.

I start picturing Foster. I conjure him in my imagination, but deliberately—because I *want* to imagine him. I don't want to keep being like Zack, searching for substitutions.

A few minutes later I rouse myself, slip my shoes back on, and stand to go.

Then finally it hits me what's missing, what's been lacking this whole time. It's so simple: Shelby. This entire scenario—the social hangout, Zack's parents' house, Zack lying in bed with his arms folded behind his head, waiting for me to lie down—they're all lacking the Right Girl, Shelby, or whatever girl out there is *supposed* to come after Shelby. A *Different Girl*.

But I'm not this Different Girl, I'm Eva, and he's not the guy I want, he's Zack.

Here's something else I know: I don't belong here. And if I don't belong here, then it's time to leave.

45.

PASSPORT

SUNDAY MY MOM'S sorting through a pile of old mail when she comes across an envelope addressed to Courtney and opens it without asking: it's my sister's passport. The problem is that six months ago Courtney told us at dinner that she'd picked up her new passport at the DMV and that everything was totally taken care of. My mother calls her downstairs to confront her, which Courtney deals with by *literally* backing up into a corner, claiming we misunderstood what she said. Then, when she tries to grab it, my mother holds the passport above her head, dangling it just out of reach like she's scolding a badly behaved child, and shakes her head, disappointed.

Eventually she lowers her hand, but not before launching into a speech on procrastination, which morphs into a speech on appreciation and gratitude and blessings.

My mother's never been to Europe, even once. She's been to Mexico (Cancún, on her honeymoon with my father) and Canada, but so long ago she never needed a passport. So her speech about appreciation, which began as a speech about procrastination, eventually transforms into a speech about reverie. Or not *about* reverie, but *of* reverie, my mother's reverie, her musings on the haves and have-nots of her life, the people who got it all and wasted it, and the opposite too.

Mom tells us what she would've done if she'd been given the chance to take a trip to Amsterdam, or even Boston, when she was young, her whole life ahead of her. The chance to live abroad, or across the country, even if only for a short time. The speech gradually transitions into other semi-related concepts and emotions, and slowly I realize it's not my mother's memories I'm listening to, but her lack of memories.

Lacking—it's everywhere!

At some point I stop listening, worried by the feeling that, underneath everything, maybe I'm just not appreciative enough, not grateful enough for the opportunity I'm being given. How can you make sure to get the most out of college—or at least get your parents' money's worth?

I run down my fall semester class schedule: Intro to Brit Lit, Writing the Personal Essay, Oral Narration, Geology. They feel like the names of my campers when I first read them: signifiers without meaning. Emerson College is just this abstract thing I've committed to be a part of, and so far it's committed nothing to me except these four classes, which hardly sound life changing or door opening or mind expanding. What do I know about making the best of a situation when it seems obvious that I'll just keep avoiding what I'm prone to avoid, which is basically everything outside of what I already know, which is still barely anything at all?

Courtney's stopped listening too, distracted by her passport photo, her face faintly flushed with panic.

I glance at the photo but can't tell what's wrong; Courtney just looks like Courtney, standing against a white wall—it's no disaster. "Hey," I say, reaching for her hand, "you're really doing it."

"*We're* doing it," my mother chimes in, huddling us all together, proud, the soft-lit glow of reverie still beaming in her eyes.

"Aren't we annoying?" I joke to Courtney. "You definitely won't miss *this*," I say, laughing, poking her playfully.

But Courtney's too wise to believe it's that simple. She knows it's not the absence of memories that keeps a person from being happy; it's the absence of certain people from the memories you're making. Traveling forward means leaving behind. Stamp the passport, write it all down.

46.

DEADJA VU AND THE CURSE OF THE COYOTE

WE'RE ON OUR way to the sporting goods storage closet to get bases and a ball for kickball. I wave at Foster as we pass by the amphitheater, where he and his boys are painting the benches for Parents' Day. He holds up his arm in a vague salute, but it's not quite a wave. It's one of those extra-hot, sweaty days, and my girls are feeling it, bleached and parched and straggling behind me. Alyssa's brooding and won't make eye contact—not when she hands me today's schedule and not even when she coldly informs me she's going to the bathroom and will be gone awhile.

"The *bathroom*?" I ask, dipping my head, trying to catch her eyes.

"Yes."

"*Alone?*"

"Fine, I'll take a buddy."

"I'll go," Rebecca says.

"I want to go," Maggie says.

"No one's going," I tell them.

"You can't, like, outlaw me from using the bathroom," Alyssa says.

Of course I can't. So instead I stall, poring over the schedule. The truth is I actually *feel* apologetic but I'm *being* antagonistic, and coming off as petty, which is embarrassing even in front of a bunch of nine-year-olds. I was praying Alyssa would be over it by now, but since she isn't, I can't be either, and that's frustrating. When you can't be the Bigger Person, you end up the Same-Size Person: pretty small. I kill almost a full minute just tapping my pen against the clipboard, pretending to examine our itinerary, hoping that by the time I look up, the girls will be bored and oblivious to me and Alyssa's looming showdown.

"Fine, I'm going," Alyssa says, sick of waiting. The rest of the group watches.

"No way."

"Um, *yeah.*"

"Here's the keys to my car," I say meanly, shoving my keys into her hand. "Why don't you just take Corey there?"

"I have to *piss,*" Alyssa says, throwing my keys in the

dirt. "And *shit*," she shouts, grinding the keys into the ground with the toe of her sandal.

The girls gasp. I don't. I've heard thirteen-year-olds say a lot worse, so I can take it. And that's what I'm going to do: Take It.

"Oh, I had no idea," I say, mock-concerned. "Please go ahead then."

But Alyssa just stands there, fuming. The girls huddle closer, hypnotized by the drama.

"Fine," I say to her, "hold it in."

Alyssa huffs, but the moment passes. Suddenly I'm sick to death of Sunny Skies, sick of summer in general. It feels like we'll never get to the ball closet and back to the amphitheater, back to Foster. I miss him. I want to lift whatever weight might be between us. I don't care about motivating my group anymore—I don't want to waste another minute here.

What's worse, I wonder: summers that race by breathlessly, or the endless kind? Mine feels all monotony, yet no routine.

"Come on," I say, walking ahead, not even checking to see if the girls are following. But they are. I hear their sluggish, flip-flopped feet shuffling to keep up.

When we get to the playing field, I pause. We don't need to play kickball—this summer's already kicking us around. We have an hour to kill, but Foster's boys are covered in paint and won't be done for a while. There's no place else to go really, except up to the lookout at the top of the hill, with all the brambles and the dead shrubs and the holes in the ground where furry groundhogs pop out and little ankles get caught and twisted.

"Up?" I ask, but the girls don't realize it's a question—they just obey. So up we go.

Soon we're outside camp; we're above it. Up here it feels like I'm no longer the counselor and they're no longer my campers. The transformation does us both good. We hold hands while we hike, carefully picking a path through the desert bushes and spiky plants. We bypass the hostile, alien cacti and the huge boulders that look poised to tumble down the hill and crush everyone below. We're being active for a change. But we're also *escaping*.

"Somebody say something," Alyssa says.

"Something," I say, and the group laughs.

"No, say something *besides* that."

"Something besides that." Everyone laughs again.

Higher up, the hill ramps at a sharper incline. I wonder for a moment if what we're doing is safe.

"Maybe we should turn back," I suggest, and the girls immediately agree, making me wonder if this was a forced march. We've only just begun slow-stepping our way back down when we see him: a gray-brown coyote, scraggly and skinny, facing us, panting in the heat.

I throw my arms out in the same motion my mother does when she slams the brakes at a sudden red light, her arm whipping across my chest to keep me from flying through the windshield. An involuntary protective impulse.

"Don't move," I whisper. "Don't move and don't run."

"And don't look it in the eye," Alyssa adds.

"Why?" Zoe asks. "What happens if you look it in the eye?"

"You get cursed."

"Alyssa, shut up."

"It's for reals," she whispers, serious. "It's like a Southwestern thing."

The coyote just stares at us, its tongue lolling out like a dog when it's hot. Alexis whimpers, faintly. I coo to her, "Shh, shh."

"Hey," I shout at it. "Go away!"

"That's not going to work," Billie says. "You have to really scream."

"Please don't scream," Jessica pleads.

"You gotta jump up and down and throw stuff," Billie says. "Coyotes hate people."

"If we were a puppy, it'd eat us," Lila says, her voice shaking, and then Renee says, "Or if we were a cat like Mr. Baggy Jeans, we'd be dead."

"Don't say *dead*," Maggie says.

Then the coyote cocks its head slightly, staring at us sideways, and I get an eerie, creeping, familiar sensation: *deadja vu.* I've been feeling and refeeling it for weeks.

"Let's all scream at the same time," Billie says. "Let's jump around like we're crazy."

It's our best—though admittedly *only*—idea, and it's Billie's, not mine. I knew I wasn't cut out to lead these girls. I don't know any more than they do how to stave off evil coyotes and cruel summers.

"Yeah, let's act crazy," Jenna agrees.

"Someone count down," I say.

Maybe seventeen is just one of those years during that annoying phase of life called Immaturity when you haven't experienced much more than a nine-year-old but you're supposed to act like you have.

"Three," Rebecca says.

I'm smart, but I have no firm philosophies. Not like I did when I was ten, when I had it all figured out, and not like I will when I'm twenty-five, when I've lived through everything.

"Two."

When someone calls you a Know-It-All, it's only meant in a negative way. It sounds like it should be a compliment, knowing so much that you *know it all*, but in fact it's a terrible thing.

"One and three-quarters."

Man Versus Nature. Man Versus Self. I can still picture the words scrawled on Mr. Roush's whiteboard, concepts to help us make sense of the writing we're reading, and to make sense of ourselves, too.

"One and a half."

Eva Versus Coyote.

"God, Becks, c'mon already," Zoe says.

Eva Versus Eva.

"One!" Rebecca screams.

Turns out coyotes *do* hate people—especially screaming girls throwing sticks and pinecones and acting like lunatics.

It also turns out you don't have to look them in the eye to get cursed.

47.

I AM IN TROUBLE

LATER THAT NIGHT Shelby texts me to meet for coffee drinks. We always order the exact same thing—her a chai iced tea, me a blended soy mocha—but predictability sounds comforting right now. At this point it feels like I should try and do all the stuff I usually do at least a few more times before I'm gone and can't do it anymore. But then Shelby changes her mind, tells me about a vegan place in the city called Café Gratitude, and she's not exaggerating or implying something, it's actually called that.

I make it to Larchmont right on time, at 7:58. Shelby's standing by the hostess, her phone to her ear.

"I'm calling you," she says.

"Why? I'm here."

"They wouldn't give me a table until the rest of my party arrived." She rolls her eyes at the inhumanity of it.

The hostess leads us to a two-top by the door and leaves a pair of menus. Cool air breezes in every time a waiter enters or exits with dishes for the diners on the patio, and soon I'm shivering. Shelby passes me her cardigan without even asking if I'm cold, a move so smooth and intuitive I assume she picked it up from Zack.

"You're cold in August—in *LA*," Shelby says, laughing at me. "Good luck making it to Thanksgiving in Boston. You're going to hate it."

"Thanks a lot."

"I just mean it's going to be *cold*."

"Yeah, I don't know. You might be right. Maybe I'll hate it," I say. "It's possible."

Shelby's been to Boston, and New York, of course, and she's even been to Maui multiple times. Zack took her to Palm Springs twice, and one weekend he rented them a suite at the Luxor in Vegas. They used to weekend down at his grandmother's beach house in Redondo too, and once in a while they'd invite me to come along, but I always declined. I don't remember why; I think at the time it just seemed like something I wasn't interested in doing. I guess if they were still together now I'd be interested, but now's too late.

"Everything looks good," she says, scanning the

menu. Every dish is named like an affirmation: *I Am Open, I Am Adventurous, I Am Transformed.* "Writing anything?" Shelby asks, flipping the page to teas and desserts.

"No," I say.

"That's what you always say when you're in the middle of something really good. You are humble," she says, reading a dish: Indian curried lentils with spicy mint chutney.

"You think my writing's good?"

Shelby looks up from her menu, smirks, and puts a hand on my hand. "I know what this is. This is about Foster, right? Now that you're at camp together, he's messing with your head. You're starting to think you're not as good as him."

"Pretty off base," I say. "About as off base as Alexis Powell during pretty much every sport."

"Who's Alexis Powell?"

"One of my campers. She's fat."

Shelby gives me a look.

"What?" I say. "She's a fat little kid."

"One archenemy at a time, okay?"

"Who's my archenemy?" I ask, loud enough for the woman behind Shelby to swivel around and glance at me.

"Foster."

"Hardly. And don't say *archenemy*—it makes it sound

like I'm in a comic book or Greek myth or something."

Shelby shrugs. "How are Michelle and Steph then?"

"Fine, you can say archenemy."

Finally the waitress approaches to take our order. I watch Shelby as she explains what she wants extra of and what she wants on the side, and try to soak in her whole aura so I have a mental image to refer to when I'm away. She actually looks really great, maybe better than she's ever looked: tan, her bangs growing out in a chic way, her eyebrows elegant and manicured. I've always thought of Shelby as my best-looking high school friend. That's not the *sole* reason she got Zack, but it's part of it.

"What do you want, Eva?" she asks.

"Is it too late for I Am Satisfied or I Am Free?" I ask the waitress.

"Sorry, we don't serve those for dinner."

"I Am Happy is fine then."

"You are happy," the waitress confirms, writing it down.

"Oh, and an I Am Loved too, please," Shelby says, pointing to the tea selection, "Iced."

"You are loved, iced," the waitress says, then walks away.

"What should we talk about?" Shelby wonders aloud, which reminds me of a reason I like her so much: she speaks her subtext. She'll say, "Well, this is awkward," or

"I shouldn't have said that," and then pop an olive in her mouth or flip her hair, like *oh well.*

"We can talk about you," I say.

Shelby's fine with that. She tells me she's dating someone new but doesn't offer details on who or how or why. This is one of the things I *don't* like about Shelby: she prolongs her gossip.

"You know him," Shelby says.

Shelby's been having sex longer than any of my other friends, and when I used to ask her about it in tenth grade she'd tell me everything. Then one time I asked her about when she lost her virginity, and she shoved me against some lockers, said it was none of my business, and didn't speak to me for a full semester. Ever since then I've been a little hesitant to ask her about sexual stuff. So I sip my drink and listen quietly, trying to focus my thoughts on this new guy instead of her old one.

"His name's Anthony," Shelby says, blushing. "You know him—*Anthony.*"

But I don't know an Anthony. I tell her this, but she insists. She keeps saying his name: "Anthony, it's Anthony . . . you *know*, Anthony!"

I can't picture an Anthony at all, but partly because I'm picturing Zack.

The third time we all hung out, Zack tried to persuade me to ride on his motorcycle. "Eva, you'd look great on the back of my bike," he said—but not in the way it sounds. He had his arm around Shelby when he said it, and when he turned to her to be, like, *Right?* she nodded and laughed wildly. Then they kissed. Right in front of me. They kissed and kissed.

"Does Zack know you've got a new boyfriend?"

"Why do you care if Zack knows or not?"

"He'd probably be sad, that's all," I say.

"You only care if *I'm* sad, okay?" she says, basically commanding me. "Because—and it goes without saying, or at least it should—you're *my* friend."

"I'm not saying not to date anyone, I'm just saying Zack would probably be hurt if he found out."

"And how exactly would he find out?" Shelby asks, eyeing me suspiciously.

"Come on, Shel."

"You saw Zack," she says, with such witchy certainty it's pointless to deny it.

"Yeah, I *saw* him," I admit.

"What'd you do?"

"I didn't tell him anything. I didn't even know you had a new boyfriend."

"No," Shelby says slowly, closing her eyes for effect. "Not 'what did you say?' What did you *do*?"

"Nothing," I say, but it comes out hollow. Not just a lie, but a quarter-assed, lazy lie.

Then the waitress interrupts to inform me I can't be Happy because they're out of cashew feta, but how about I Am Present with a complimentary extra side of buckwheat crackers? I'll settle for that.

"Go back to Anthony," I say, hoping she'll move on.

For a moment she does: "Anyway," she says, "Anthony's a brother."

A brother of who? Michelle has one sister, Shelby two, and Steph has a half brother, but everyone else—every single other person I know—is an only child.

"Whose brother?" I ask.

No, she shakes her head, then leans in closer. "Like a *brother*," she says, enunciating the word in a slangy way, her manicured eyebrows arching higher.

"*Oh*," I say. "You mean like a black guy? *That* Anthony—why didn't you just describe him? Use another adjective."

"God," she says, downing the rest of her iced tea, sliding the empty glass to the center of the table. "It's called reading between the lines, Eva."

"If you're going to bother with a cliché," I say, "try 'the truth is in the details.'"

"The truth is it's going to be crazy cold in Boston," Shelby tells me, abruptly pulling out her phone to text someone—maybe Zack, to cross-examine my lie, maybe Anthony. Shelby's never more than a send button away from cooler plans. "And you'll probably hate it. But you really *do* need to travel."

She pauses, raising her glass at the waitress, shaking it for a refill, before finishing: "And, you know"—*clink, clink*—"grow up."

48.

CRYING THROUGH CONFETTI

"WHAT SHOULD WE talk about?" I ask the girls. We're sitting around a circular wood table, squeezing puffy paint onto a giant poster board.

"Coyotes," Jenna says.

"Not coyotes."

"Mountain lions," Maggie says. "Or, um, bobcats."

"How about our par rents?" Alyssa says, pointing to the sign, which I now notice reads *PARRENTS DAY*; another error, another omen of the curse.

"Lila wrote a poem," Renee says, and then Lila says, "And Renee wants to read it out loud."

"You wrote a poem?" I say, clapping glitter all over my lap.

"It's called 'Bad Day,'" Lila says, and then Renee says, "No, it's called '*The* Bad Day.'"

"Don't read it," Alyssa says.

I shoot her a look. "Alyssa!"

"What? It sounds upsetting."

"Wait—*is* it upsetting?" I ask Lila, a little worried myself.

Lila shrugs.

"Read it," Zoe says. "Read it, read it, read it," and then all the girls are chanting.

Renee stands and pulls a folded piece of blue construction paper out of her pocket. A poem on blue construction paper? It's sad already. Renee clears her throat, shakes the bangs from her eyes, takes a small sip from her water bottle. The girls watch and wait, and I watch and wait too, afraid to give any constructive construction paper criticism.

I'll just lie. No matter what, I'll lie.

"Okay," Renee says. "Ready?"

This is true suspense, actually—the kind I've never been able to write myself.

"'The Bad Day,'" she begins, "by Lila Kissling."

Lila claps.

Renee goes on: " 'Camp is a place where the kids all race. Where the sky is sunny and the counselors are funny and it's green like money on the dodgeball field.' "

Alyssa starts giggling a little, so I step on her toe.

" 'But on a bad day the sky is gray and there's nothing to say and there's nowhere to play and it feels like May when we were still in school.'

" 'We walk but don't talk and think about the clock and wish we had chalk to draw on the sidewalk or be like birds in a flock, flying far, far away.' "

"Jesus," Alyssa whispers, and I whisper back, "Oh my God."

" 'What do you do when you feel so blue but can't go to the zoo? How do you smile when it takes a while like running the mile or crossing the Nile like in the Bible?' "

The Bible?!

I can't deal. I start to spin out, remembering Courtney and the poetry she used to scrawl in secret in her black leather notebook.

"What're your poems about?" I asked once.

She bent down so we were eye level and said, without any feeling, "Whores."

Whores! I was eight. The word alone gave me nightmares.

If only Lila's poem was about whores. Whores would be much less devastating than this Biblical torture.

Renee continues, " 'You'd rather be alone or on the phone or giving your dog a bone or licking an ice cream cone or—' "

"Renee," I interrupt, at my limit. "You have to stop."

"Why?" Renee asks, and Lila says, "It's only halfway done."

"*Because* . . . I want the ending to be a surprise for everyone when they read it in our zine. This was like the movie preview: you give us a little bit as a teaser and leave us wanting more."

"Pbbth, *more*," Alyssa says, with an overdose of sarcasm.

I ignore her and turn to the rest of the group for affirmation. "Right, you guys?"

Their eyes are empty, drained by rhyme.

"Curl Powder," I say, but no one says it back.

This is what it feels like to try and *not* succeed, to try and to fail. To utterly bomb. I scramble for ideas on how to turn this around.

"Free play!" I shout, but still no one moves. "Free play!" I shout louder, and finally the girls lurch to life and hustle outside. I can't do anything but bury my head in my arms, which are covered in dried glue and paper scraps.

Alyssa puts her hand on my shoulder. "Crying through confetti," she says, "like Gatsby in *The Great Gatsby*."

It's kind of a profound thing to say. I tell her so.

"That book is dumb," Alyssa says. "The twentieth century was so *emo*." Then she walks away, phone in hand, texting.

I take out my phone and call Foster's number.

"Hey," he says.

"Hi."

"Where are you?"

"Craft Shack. Where are you?"

"We're not supposed to be on our phones," Foster says.

"I know."

"Eva."

And I know he doesn't mean to, but the way he says my name sounds somehow sensual, like he's reclining, lying down.

"Can you ditch the boys for a minute? Leave them with Corey."

"Okay, but only one minute."

"Meet me in the break room."

Then I run, faster than I've run in my life, a real Camp Champ, a real Camp Tramp, ready to repair and reroute the Eva/Foster Arc. When I get to the break room, Foster's already there, in the dim light, clicking and unclicking a pen. He doesn't say anything but instantly I feel it—true sexual tension—the kind we've never had, not as rivals, not as frivals, not as archenemies, not as co-counselors or friends. This is the daydream stuff; the heart of so many young adult novels, where first love blossoms outside the bunkhouse, after a sweaty three-legged race. Everything's

hot and dizzy and everyone's loose and lusty, and touching him is like two liquids joining to form one warm
black puddle. . . .

"Will you take your shirt off?" I say.

Foster shakes his head no, and then he lets out a
depressed sigh, which comes out all heavy, and weirdly is
almost as good, almost as poetic, as taking off his shirt.
I reach behind me for the doorknob and feel for a lock. It
has a lock! I lock it.

"Fos-ter," I say, pronouncing both syllables, then com-
mand him one word at a time: "Take. Off. Your. Shirt."

I take mine off too, for encouragement, fully aware
that my sports bra is stained with perspiration and a
crude, half-finished pink-and-turquoise lanyard is hanging from my neck, drawing attention to the starchy white
of my untanned stomach. What's next? I wonder, sliding
my shorts off to reveal a mismatched bikini bottom, still
crunchy with sand from Courtney's beach bag. I slip my
fingers under the elastic.

"Don't," Foster says. He hesitantly steps closer,
reaches a hand toward me.

I grasp it, guide it to my sports bra. But instead Foster
pulls his hand away, then begins picking bits of confetti
off my skin.

"Stop doing that," I say.

He wipes disinterestedly at some glitter on my cheek.

"Lick it off," I say, then laugh because it sounds corny

and desperate, and not kinky at all.

"Should I even ask where your group is?" Foster says. He's unamused, still brushing at my neck and cheeks, peeling off sparkly shreds of paper.

"They're off on their own."

"You are a bad counselor."

"Definitely bad," I say, laying my head on Foster's shoulder.

"What are we doing here?" he says.

"Well, we're never going on a real date," I say, feeling more emo than Fitzgerald, more emo than the twentieth century. "Did you ever have a crush on me in high school?" I ask.

"No."

"Just say yes."

"Because it's better for your story?" he asks.

I nod.

"Then fine," he says. "Write down: since freshman year."

"Do you want this one?" I ask. This is the stuff good short stories are made of. The stuff Shakespeare and the other Classics skip over because it's too stupid, too sad, too tragic.

"You can have it," Foster says. "You'll write it how you want to remember it anyway."

49.

A BREAK

AN HOUR LATER I've got my shirt back on, and I've gathered the girls by the drinking fountain.

"We're going to finish strong today," I tell them. The girls look tired. Alyssa looks extra tired. *Eat a cheeseburger!* I think, not because I want to, but because it's the only professional advice I've been given by someone whose job it is to know how to improve people.

"Shake it off!" I say, throwing my arms in the air, shaking them like crazy.

"You're so weird," Alyssa says.

"*You're* weird," I say, then grab her arms and shake them. Soon the whole group has joined in, shaking, jumping, flailing like little crazies, giggling.

An instant later Jessica starts crying, swearing she got stung by a bee. But now I'm invigorated, I'm *on* this problem. "Alyssa," I call out, "take the girls up to the stalls for horseback riding, I'll come there once we're done with the nurse." I stoop down and let Jessica climb up on me, promising she can piggyback all the way to the first aid station.

But Alexis Powell wants to come too.

"No horses," she says. "Uh-uh."

Jessica whimpers in my ear, wrapping her arms around my neck, moaning how much it stings.

"Alexis," I say, as stern but sympathetic as possible, "it's just a horse, okay? You're going to be fine."

She shakes her head.

I swear to her I'll be there in ten minutes, less even, but as I shoo her off to catch up with the others, an expression I don't fully recognize—of what, pure dread?—flashes across her face.

"Go on," I tell her, gently but with a counselor's insistence. Finally she goes.

By the time we're at the nurse's station, Jessica's stopped crying, but she starts up again when the nurse pulls out some tweezers to remove the stinger.

"It won't hurt, sweetie," the nurse says, rubbing iodine on the wound, which is small but swollen and red.

For a second Jessica literally faints—not from the pain

but from the anticipation.

"It's too hot today," I tell the nurse, trying to sound like I notice these things. "Maybe she should stay inside and cool off, avoid heat stroke?"

The nurse agrees, but Jessica shakes her head no, gripping the sleeve of my shirt until her knuckles are white. It feels good to be needed, but we've been gone twenty minutes; I've got to get back to the group.

"Stay and rest," I tell her. Amazingly, she obeys.

I jog across the lawn, past the water fountain, the basketball court, a younger girls' group finger painting. It's only when I reach the foot of the hill that I hear screaming. I sprint to the top of the ridge, and then I see the scene: two counselors, plus Macy and Rico, the horse trainers, all trying to heft Alexis onto a spotted brown Clydesdale. She's screaming, pulling up her camp shirt to cover her face, her little fat stomach exposed for all to see. There's laughing, plenty of it, and some horrified faces, some concerned faces, some bored, blank faces.

It's yet another moment of realizing that I need to be more like Foster, more clued in. I should *know* who's allergic to what and who takes karate and who has a celebrity mom and who needs an insulin shot before lunch and who has a twin brother in another group and who, absolutely, with the *fear of God inside of her*, does *not* want to ride the horses.

I rush over to the Clydesdale and rip Alexis out of the saddle, stretching her shirt back down. She sobs into my chest, inconsolable. I position her fat little body behind me, sheltering her.

"What were you thinking?!" I yell at Macy and Rico, at Alyssa and the rest of my girls. "What were you thinking?!"

Then I heft Alexis into a sloppy piggyback position and hike her down the hill. It takes some serious effort; by the bottom, I'm definitely out of breath. I march her to the shady spot she likes—the one she wanders off to during free play, close to the sandbox under the big elm—and give Alexis two juice boxes: hers and the one for Jessica.

I tell her she doesn't have to do anything she doesn't want to do.

"I swear," I say. "If you don't want to do it, I won't make you."

"I want to go home."

"I know it's a cliché," I tell her, "but they do say it's good to get back on the horse."

"I want to go home."

It's all she can say. She keeps saying it. But I can't give her that.

"Let's just sit here," I say. "Let's stop thinking about home. Let's stop thinking about going anywhere for a while."

50.

VHS

AFTER CAMP I want my mom, I want my dad, I want my sister, but they're all gone. Courtney's on a random date, and my parents are at the Hollywood Bowl. It's the first time in my life I've longed for a dog, just some lapping, licking, living thing to show me love. A friend to miss and be missed by; it sounds nice.

At eight, Elliot calls from Melrose, seeming pretty drunk. The band got into LA early, and he's either ecstatic or miserable about it, it's hard to tell.

The fact that Elliot's back in town, that he's *here* in the same city as me, should feel so giddy and exciting, but honestly I have no idea how to feel.

Today was too much drama, so I tell him I can't come

to the record store and watch what might be his band's last show. For some reason he's not upset.

"Does the whole band need somewhere to stay?" I ask, afraid of the answer.

"Just me," he says, which is potentially an even worse answer. Me and Elliot, utterly, totally alone.

He says he can score a ride to my place but not for four hours, which means I have the whole evening free. I dig through our movies and pull out an old VHS of *Good Will Hunting* that my dad recorded off HBO. I take it into his office, where the VHS player is, and curl up on his leather couch with a blanket. The machine is boxy and clunky, a lame leftover from the Emo Century, nothing really to miss.

But the degraded picture quality and warbly sound transport me to this blurry, muffled, dream version of Boston, and it makes me wish the city was actually like this: color-bleached, hazy, homemade. Even though I want my memories and experiences there to be fresh and vivid, I know they'll just be taped over other stuff, whatever was there before. And each time you do, the quality gets worse.

I finish the movie, but the house is still empty. Performances at the Bowl rarely run this late, so I focus and really try to remember where my parents said they'd be tonight. Something about Santa Barbara, maybe? For an anniversary? Exercising my memory wears me out for some reason (*Eat a cheeseburger!*), so I fall asleep on the couch, still in my camp clothes.

I wake up later to the doorbell ringing, the TV a solid blue screen. I rub my eyes, unsure how long I was out. Elliot's at the door, bag slung over one shoulder, guitar case in hand. He does this move where he leans against the door frame, but not in a sexy Foster way, more in just a stupid drunk way, and I can tell by the way his eyes swim that he's seeing two or three of me, instead of just the one pissy me.

He stumbles inside, dropping his stuff at the foot of the stairs, and follows me up to my bedroom. Even though he's out of it, I'm happy to see him—we're friends after all, we *are* friends—I just don't know what to do with him. What not to do with him too.

I mention that my parents are gone. I try not to make it sound like an invitation, but how could it not?

"They're in Santa Barbara," I say. "Or possibly Ojai. For the night."

"Oh hi," Elliot whispers into my ear, "for the night."

Once we get to my room, he walks straight to my bed and flops down on it.

I say his name a few times, but that's it, he's out. For the night.

To myself I say, "Oh, Elliot," and I mean it in a

frustrated way, like "*Oh God*," but it comes out sounding tender, forgiving. Finally I flop down too, next to the bed on the carpet.

I guess I did want him to come back. I guess I needed to see him, to see what I felt when I saw him.

Hours later, in the early morning, I wake to a weight on my back. It's Elliot, snuggled against me, nuzzling into my hair, rooting around sleepily for a kiss. My face feels like it's sewn into the carpet, or made of carpet, so I don't even try to lift my head to return the gesture—not even when he traces one finger lightly along the elastic of my bra strap.

Everything in front of me is a wash of blurry, color-bleached textures, real but not really, my room but seen through a degraded, muffled haze.

And when I say, "Oh, Elliot," this time, I can't tell which *Oh, Elliot* it is.

51.

CHRISTY AND THE CASE OF THE MISSING CLIPBOARD

WHEN I WAKE up, Elliot's gone, but there's a scribbled note on my dresser. All it says is: *Texted you.*

Something about his lazy scrawl on the back of an envelope makes it clear to me in a uniquely official-feeling way: Elliot's wasting my time, and I'm wasting his.

This is what Mr. Roush would call an Anticlimax. Curiosity, anticipation, *promise*, all building toward a Significant Moment—Elliot's Return!—but then it happens too quickly, fizzling out without even feeling like much. Mr. Roush has always pushed me to work harder on my plots and engage a deeper, more descriptive language, but it's not easy.

I do want to be relatable, to be *related with*, and to

craft a story that's memorable, that reflects something thoughtful and crucial—the difference between some random romance and an epic one, between a Naive Eva and a potentially Wiser one.

It's just that last night with Elliot lacked the right adjectives. It can't really be described as anything particularly resonant, or specific, and the main word that comes to mind is *ambiguous*, which is basically the *opposite* of specific, and rarely means anything good when it's written in red ink at the top of one of your pages. Even now that he's come and gone, Elliot's still What I Don't Know. I guess he's sort of a Rough Draft person, no matter how many times I try to revise him.

I didn't change out of my camp clothes last night, so I just leave for work, doubtful my parents will even notice I came home.

After my girls swim and sunbathe, we move on to pottery, where the previous group's already fired up the kiln. I help the girls roll clay snakes and shape little clumsy cavewoman bowls, listening to them chatter about who's cute on TV and who isn't, and the repetition soothes me. Even Alexis seems relaxed, therapized by the soothing rhythm of her thumbs pressing into stiff, cold mud. She's happy as a fat little clam.

"Let's finish up soon," I say to the group, "so we can get our projects in the oven."

Everyone cheers.

"Where's the clipboard?" I ask Alyssa. Today there'll be no wasting time, and no one's time will be wasted.

"I dunno," she says, shrugging.

"Anyone?" I ask. "Clipboard?"

"Oops," Alexis says.

"Where'd you leave it?"

"Changing room."

I ask the girls if they can be good and watch themselves while I'm gone, and they nod and mumble, "Yes, Eva," without looking up from their gray blobs. I make my way back to the pool, where now the twelve-year-olds have taken over, splashing around in the deep end and diving off the diving board.

Inside the changing room it's dank and drippy like a cavern, and smells of old towels, the concrete floor slick with water. I do a quick walk-through, looking for the clipboard, and that's when I see Katie—or is it Christy?—one of the older girls. She's over in the corner near the showers, facing the wall, crying it looks like, staring down at her hands.

"Katie," I call out. She doesn't move.

I try "Christy," and she turns.

Even in the dim light I can make out the blood on her hands. But the color of the blood isn't the normal bright red I've seen running from my campers' noses or down their scraped knees; this blood is brown, and clotted, and tacky on Christy's palms.

"You got your period," I say. My voice echoes off the concrete.

I walk closer and notice the crotch of her bathing suit is brown and damp. She's also left a few faint, bloody fingerprints on the skinny wooden bench next to her.

"It's okay," I say. "Let's wash your hands." I lead her over to the sink and turn on warm water. She's shaken, but not actually crying. I help wash her hands and dry them.

Next I tell her to take off her bathing suit so I can wash it. She doesn't react.

"Christy?" I say, and then she reaches back into her bathing suit, and when she pulls her hand out, it's streaked with brown blood again. I'm too stunned to say anything, especially because what she does next is touch her fingers to her tongue.

52.

ANOTHER IDEA FOR A PLAY

THE REST OF the day I map out an idea for a new play:

There's a husband and wife. She's pregnant in the first act, with a giant round belly. She shuffles around the stage in pain, grasping at her back, and the only thing that takes her mind off the pain is tending to a garden she's started in the backyard. So even though her husband's concerned for her health, he lets her spend day after day—each day leading closer to the due date—on her knees in the vegetable garden, planting and cultivating and sweating in the sun. He lets her root out weeds until her hands are blistered and raw, because it makes her happy and because it gives her a different kind of pain to focus on.

At the beginning of act two she loses the baby; or she doesn't lose it, it's a stillbirth. Then the husband and wife begin to drift apart, slowly losing interest in one another. The husband spends most of his time at work, the wife in her garden. Each day he comes home she's prepared dinner and feeds him vegetables that look like nothing he's ever seen before. They almost aren't recognizable, these vegetables. A squash, but not. A zucchini, but not really. That sort of thing.

She begins acting strangely—as all my characters tend to do when they're hiding a secret. And her secret is that she's planted the placenta, the nutritious afterbirth, the blood and all its bloody mess, in the soil of the garden. It's what's fertilizing the vegetables.

"What have you done?" he says. "What have you given me?"

Then one of the vegetables falls off the table and rolls down into the audience. Then the curtain lowers and the stage goes black.

It's a compromise, I think. Something for Mr. Roush, and something for me.

53.

DIFFERENT TYPES OF CAMPS

IT'S THURSDAY, ONE in the afternoon, and I can't understand it.

"Are you *sure* it isn't Friday?" I ask Alyssa. She's holding her face in the high, wet arc of the drinking fountain, letting it splash all over her like a shower. "It's Friday, I know it."

"*Thursday*," Alyssa tells me.

"Thirstday, Frieday," I say, and stick my head in the water too.

We're walking toward archery—nine sunburnt girls and a dripping CIT and me—when Rachel, the camp activities coordinator, comes up and tells me Steven wants to see me in his office. She tells me that she'll be taking over my group and supervising our bow-and-arrow safety lesson, and that I should go now.

"Now, Eva," Rachel says.

Her voice is sunny but stern, like she's trying to convey something serious without seeming too serious. I assume I'm in trouble. Maybe the girls do too, because they cling to my legs, begging me not to leave. I have to physically pry them off, which for some reason makes Rachel look away.

I walk across to Steven's office at the center of camp. I don't feel nervous, I know what to say in these situations:

I did my best.

I'm trying to do my best.

We all like to think we're basically doing our best.

Steven greets me at the door and ushers me in with a hand on the middle of my back. We sit. He asks if I know why I'm here, and I say I do.

"It's about Christy," I say, sitting up straight in my chair.

Steven's confused. He flips through some papers. His face says, *What Christy? Who's Christy?* I worry for a second that I've switched the names again, that Christy is actually Katie, and that's when a man and a woman, holding hands and Sunny Skies packets, come into the room.

"Eva," Steven says, "this is Mr. and Mrs. Powell. Mr.

and Mrs. Powell, this is your daughter's counselor, Eva."

Apparently they're Alexis's parents, but that seems impossible because they're both extremely fit. Not skinny but muscular, toned. And they're tan; maybe too tan.

I say hello and they say, right off the bat, "Alexis loves you."

"She *really* loves you," Mr. Powell says.

"She does," Mrs. Powell agrees.

"Well, I love Alexis," I tell them. Once I hear myself say it out loud, I know it's not a lie.

They want to know if I've noticed their daughter's weight problem.

She's a little fat, but I don't say that. Instead I say, "Yes, I've noticed it."

The Powells look at each other, give a collective sigh. Then the mantra begins, like a family slogan, and it speeds up into a chanting march:

She's got to get on that horse. She's got to get on that horse. She's got to get on that horse. She's got to get on that horse.

I smile while they talk and consider whether it'd be too straightforward to point out that not only does Alexis Powell *not* want to get on that horse, but that she basically shits blood whenever she gets near that horse, that she breaks into tears just *thinking* about a horse.

"And she needs to play *all* of the games," Mr. Powell says.

"Especially the ones with running or climbing," Mrs. Powell says.

They go on like that for a while, listing everything Alexis should be doing, and all the various reasons why she should be forced to do them.

Then Steven interjects. He tells me that this is what camp is for, this is what camp's all about: to shape Alexis Powell, literally and figuratively, until she's a skinny little thing and not a fat little thing.

"But this isn't fat camp," I say.

"You should always be promoting health," he says.

"But this is summer camp. This isn't some, some, *concentration camp.*"

"What did you just say?"

But I don't have to say it again. I'm told to leave the campgrounds immediately, because I'm fired—and with only three weeks of summer left.

54.

DROPPING IT

WHEN I GET home, Courtney's sitting silently at her desk—something she never does—her body stiff, her eyes locked on the computer screen. I notice too that her room's not the tornado it's been the past few weeks, full of clothes and bags in a state of mid-packing; right now it's almost tidy and smells of sandalwood and shower products. Courtney's wearing a damp towel twisted around her head like a terry-cloth turban. She hears me enter and tilts her head in my direction, causing the towel to loosen, slip down the back of her neck, and fall to the floor. But Courtney just leaves it there; that's how I know something genuinely bad has happened. Maybe something even worse than what's happened to me.

"What is it?" I say.

"Someone in the Amsterdam program died. I guess yesterday."

"What do you mean they died?"

"It was an accident," Courtney tells me. "This girl had an allergic reaction. Something she ate."

"Are you *serious*?"

"Yeah," Courtney says.

"Well, that's not the program's fault, right? I mean, it's not like she was in a dangerous situation. That's not, like, Amsterdam's fault or anything," I say.

Courtney puts her head in her hands and breathes in an overly focused way. When she looks up, her face is a mess, on the verge of losing it. I walk over to her and bend down and grab the towel. When I hand it to her, she doesn't take it; I keep my arm extended anyway, the towel an inch from her head, basically hanging next to her hair. Still she won't take it.

"You're going to go anyway, though, right?"

"I don't think so," Courtney says.

"You have to," I say. "This shouldn't have even happened."

"Aren't you supposed to be at camp?"

"Like, this wasn't some normal thing," I say.

"What time is it?" she asks, glancing around for a clock. Then she puts it together: "You got fired, didn't you?"

"But no one *else* has died! It was a food allergy. Accidents happen."

My arm's still out, but it's beginning to shake.

"Hey," Courtney says, "I'm sorry you got fired."

How can I be sad for myself when I'm so, so sad for my sister?

"You *have* to go," I say, my voice breaking. "We *both* have to go."

"Not anymore."

"Yes."

"Eva, just drop the stupid towel."

"Fine," I tell her. "I'm dropping it."

55.

BLACK-AND-WHITE

AT THE TABLE my parents don't know which daughter to be more devastated for, so we all sit and eat quietly, no puns, no jokes, no laughs. But after dinner my sister has plans and leaves, so my parents zero in on me.

"I didn't do anything wrong," I say.

"But did you do anything *right*?" my father asks.

"No," I say. "Nothing."

"That's not true, Eva," my mother says. "You stood up for that little girl. You didn't let her down. You did your best."

"My best?" I say. "My best?" I repeat. "Nowhere close."

"You did your *burst* then," my father says. "Your bust."

"I could've gotten a warning at least," I say. "They didn't have to, like, throw me right out."

"They had to make an example out of you," my mother says.

"Usually you *like* being the example," my father says.

"Why don't you just go back down there and explain yourself? You're a very smart girl," my mother says.

"Mom, I'm just smart. I'm not *very* smart."

"Well, you're smart enough to know this job doesn't really matter anyway," my father tells me. "You're leaving soon. This was only a temporary position; you didn't want to be a professional camp counselor. In a way it's better. Absolutely okay."

"All jobs matter," I say. "Everything matters."

"Not *everything* matters," he says.

"That's vague."

"That's the vague of the vorld," my father tells me.

Then my mother pivots straight into Preservation Mode, asking about my various possessions and how many of them I want to take east with me, and maybe having things from home will help me adjust more smoothly? There's a lot to sort through. She digs out an unused suitcase from the hallway closet and assaults me with suggestions of items I could fill it with: used textbooks, jeans that don't fit, scratched CDs of bands I don't listen to anymore, group photos with friends I barely know, high school yearbooks, holiday socks, tampons. None of it's coming with me to Boston, but I do appreciate the urge to clean house, get rid of extra baggage, and not be misrepresented by old stuff you don't want around anymore.

My mother anxiously discusses packing strategies until some instinct or thought process prompts her into feeling like she has to drive to the store this second. I don't bother asking for what.

A half hour later she's back, loaded down with shopping bags. Courtney pulls up a few minutes after.

"Home again, home again, jiggity-jig," Mom says, pulling out packs of diet soda and Weight Watchers frozen dinners and paper towels.

Around nine there's a Hitchcock movie on, one I've already seen, where Jimmy Stewart loses his mind because there's a murder. No one else in my family's seen it, so they all watch it silently, shushing me every time I try to say something. When it's over, Courtney vents how stupid and staged it was.

"Too Hollywood," she says.

But I wish it was more Hollywood. I wish everything was a lot more black-and-white.

56.

CHECK HER

TODO I DON'T know what to do with myself.
I check if Lindsay's online, but she's not. I call Foster,
but he doesn't pick up. I heard Steph's in Waikiki, but I
almost don't believe it. It's ninety-five outside, so the air
conditioner's on in every room.

I can't help wondering who my girls are with right
now and what they're doing—and if it's more fun than
what they did with me.

I need company, so I text Shelby even though I know
it's not my best idea. She always replies faster when I ask
her nicely if she'll trim my bangs. A half hour later she's
at the door, with haircutting scissors, hair clips, a smock,
but no smile.

"So, how'd you get *fired*?" Shelby asks, hungry for gossip. "And don't give me some Eva Answer."

"How's this for an Eva Answer: I wanted to make a little girl happy, and everyone else wanted to make her sad."

"Perfect. No one gets fired from being a camp counselor," Shelby says. "Unless they did something seriously messed up."

"I *may* have referred to my boss as a Nazi."

"Or that," she says.

"Foster hasn't called or texted since it happened, though. I think I really let him down. Or maybe he's not that mad, I don't know. But if he never calls again, I'll just assume he hates me now."

"So you're back where you started."

"Shelby, you're supposed to be cheering me up," I tell her.

"No, I'm not."

After she finishes blow-drying my hair, we go outside and play checkers on the patio. I'm black and she's red. I don't say much except "King me, king me, king me," because I'm on a roll and winning every game. It's really effective at helping me not think about Alyssa or Jessica or Zoe. If I keep winning at checkers, eventually I'll be fired up enough to drive my ass to Sunny Skies and demand my job back. That's one strategy at least.

Then, out of nowhere, Shelby says, "I know you made out with Zack."

"I didn't, though."

"You kissed."

"No, Shel, I'm telling you."

"Fine, say exactly what happened—*exactly*."

What *did* happen? Not much. But, yes, something. Definitely something.

"Never mind," she says, homing in on me. "I'd rather you answer this: Why even do it? Why even call Zack, or pick up when he calls you? Why go out with him wherever you went, and do with him whatever you did? Like, what's even the point? What is there to *gain* from seeing Zack? I'm just curious what the hell the point is."

"There's no point," I tell her, looking down at my lap. "There's nothing to gain, literally. Only something to lose."

"What did you *think* you were doing?" she asks, and I'm pained by how genuinely she wants to know.

"I guess—and I know this sounds kind of psycho, *I know*—I just wanted to see if I *could*. I wanted to see if the option was even there. I think I wanted his attention, but then got it and realized I didn't actually want it." I try and beam this truth out as clearly as I can, so she can sense the purity of it. "I do like Zack, but I like him for *you*. And you for him."

Shelby doesn't look at me in disbelief; she looks at me in utter *belief*. The Eva Answer she was expecting was the Eva Answer she got. "You're selfish," she says.

"And you're Shel-fish."

She looks sick of me. "You're always . . . quipping."

"I'm well e-quipped," I say, playing the smarmy bitch Shelby's cast me as.

"You had sex with Zack—admit it."

I almost wish I *could* admit it, because then I could confess it, have it out, be forgiven, and move on. But now we're stuck: I'll keep denying it and she'll keep not believing me. How do I explain to her that for one night I almost experienced what it was like being Shelby? And now I'm seeing what it's like to be Zack—broken up with, gotten over.

"You're making me sad," I say.

"*I'm* the sad one, not you. It's my relationship, not yours."

"I know, I swear. Trust me, I felt it."

There's a pause, and she leans in. "Know what your problem is?"

There's never any satisfactory answer to that question, so I ignore it, refocusing on the checkerboard. It's my turn. I pick up my piece and double-jump.

"Your problem is you were there to do a job," she says, cycling back, "to do something different from what you normally do, to act a way you don't normally act—and you *just couldn't do it*."

I look at her numbly but apologetically, and shrug.

Shelby hops a checker, shakes her head, and laughs an incredulous laugh. "It's the same with your glasses," she says. "You just don't want to *see*." She makes an expression like she's amused.

"I see what I want."

"You have to think about the entire story, Eva, not just what you feel like writing," Shelby says. "You say that you think of yourself as one of your characters—well, then your arc's moving backward."

"My arc's fine."

"Is it?" she spits, snatching a piece from my hand and holding it out of reach. "What's your personal journey, or whatever? How are you going to resolve it all?"

"I won't know until it ends," I say, and then flip the checkerboard, spilling pieces everywhere, because that's something her character thinks my character would do.

57.

MUDDY WISDOM

AFTER SHELBY LEAVES I go inside, rattled, and find Courtney in my room, in the dark, in her underwear, staring at my laptop screen.

"I just wanted to look something up," she says. She's clearly been crying. And eating. There are crumbs all over her bra.

I look at what she's looking at. It's a Gchat conversation with Lindsay.

"I needed advice," she says.

"What'd Lindsay say you should do?"

Courtney points to the screen, but there's a lot to read. I scroll up and down, trying to find something that reads like advice, or makes sense:

me: right now it just feels good to be home.

Lindsay: i get that, totes.

me: maybe there's more of this country for me to see, do you know what i mean?

Lindsay: listen. when I wuz in Japan last yr I totally couldnt handle my feelings of like displacement, u know? Evn in Tokyo, where there's like millions of ppl, it wuz still so . . .

Lindsay: lonely

Lindsay: n then when I came back, eating burgers, fries, drinking coke with ice—the best! 2 miss smthng as dumb as ice! I mean, wow, u know?

Lindsay: Tkyo Dizney just felt, like off or smthng. like how there's Mickey but he's not OUR Mickey. I dunno, it wuz weird. like I shldn't have felt this way, Mickey shld belong to evry1, but I kept thinkin Mickey belongs to us! he's such a symbol.

Lindsay: n whut he symbolizes is . . . home. u know, america.

Lindsay: I mean, don't u feel like being abroad makes u question yr whole idea of identity on like a personal n national level???

Lindsay: n don't u sorta feel like now u'll know more bout whut it means 2 b american or whtevr than u ever did? or maybe, tragically, even less?????

Lindsay: i mean, srsly, doesn't it feel like the world's just so small???

"It's not a particularly insightful thing to say," I tell Courtney.

"I don't know," she says. "Isn't it?"

It isn't! And that makes me want to say something a thousand times more insightful, because if someone's going to blow Courtney's mind with clichés and stupid Disneyland truisms, like It's a Small, Small World, then I want it to be me. If my sister's currently a mess and therefore more of a receptacle for thrift-store wisdom, then it should be my lazy knowledge lifting her up, not Lindsay's. Not Lindsay's Wisdumb.

"You know how they say, 'This too shall pass'?" I ask.

"Yeah, of course."

"Well, what they're really saying is 'Everything passes.' But I think the saying should really go, 'This all shall pass, even this moment, and *this* moment, and yes, even *this* moment, right now, that we're living through *right now*, even if it's a wonderful moment, doesn't matter, it's just got to pass. There it goes, and there *that* goes, and there this moment goes too.'"

Courtney stares at me.

"Gone," I whisper, and blow invisible dust from my hand.

"I love you," my sister says, kind of sadly, and she pats me on the head.

"Are you going to Amsterdam?" I ask.

"Are *you* going to *San Diego*?"

"For what?"

"Lindsay's play," she says.

I forgot about Lindsay's play.

"I can't," I say.

"Why not?"

"Because I don't want to see her acting like someone else before I've even seen her acting like herself."

Courtney nods, typing something on the laptop.

"How about meeting her at a bookstore?" She types a few more words. "Tomorrow."

"I'm busy," I say. "I have to work on getting my job back pretty much all afternoon."

"I thought everything passes."

"Okay, well, everything *does* pass. I just want it to pass my way."

"If only they had a saying for that," she says, mock-wistfully. Then she gives me a little kiss on the cheek and pinches my arm.

"Fine. So do I have to drive to a bookstore in San Diego tomorrow?"

Courtney skims the screen. "No, she was planning to come to LA, actually. She wants to see the La Brea Tar Pits."

"Doesn't she know it's just some stinky pond off Wilshire?"

"Actually, she doesn't," Courtney says, snapping the laptop closed. "And you're not going to tell her."

58.

UPON MEETING LINDSAY

AT ONE, I'M at the Barnes & Noble at the Grove, waiting to meet Lindsay, trying to remember the last time I was in a bookstore, which makes me realize I haven't read one book since I graduated. Emerson sent me a summer reading list at some point, but I never got around to looking at it. Why not?

I scan some book jackets, flip through a few chapters, killing time.

It feels unusual to be out in the real world in the middle of the day, among adults, rather than at camp surrounded by kids. But instead of bonding with family or old friends, instead of Frenching Foster for what would be the third, and most likely, final time, I'm idly combing through magazines, waiting for someone I've never met, who I'm about to spend every day of my life with. Is this the end or the beginning? I can't tell.

Today I've got my glasses on. I found them in the top drawer of my desk, the single unpacked item left rattling around, appearing very much like a symbol in some Fitzgerald novel about flappers and car crashes. In the end, it's about what a character does as much as what she doesn't do—what she sees and, maybe more importantly, what she's seen as. Dorothy Parker may have been right, but who cares, she was so sad, and I want to be a Great Woman Writer but not one who's as sad as she is clever.

Anyway, with my glasses on I look like the Old Me and, because it's been so long since I've worn them, like a New Me too.

I wander back to the corner of the store, near the sale stuff, hiding, I guess. It's not so much hiding from Lindsay—that's just delaying the inevitable—it's more just generally hiding. I people-watch, playing the game where I imagine different people from high school that I would or wouldn't want to unexpectedly bump into. I'm picturing Kerry Ward, standing next to a Mara sister, scowling at me, and that's why I don't notice Lindsay, even as I stare directly at her, at her waving, at her whole body approaching me down the aisle.

Now I'm wishing I'd seen her in that play.

Although all first meetings are sort of like a play. Lindsay will definitely be doing some acting, so I should probably work on the writing. I'll establish a few contextual details first, before I get into the dialogue.

Lindsay's walk can be described as confident, self-possessed. Every few steps she seems to grow slightly taller, and more confident, as if every book she passes gets instantly absorbed into her, the words spiraling off their pages and into her spine. Maybe Lindsay *does* have wisdom. Maybe, like Courtney, she's actually read a lot of these books, has digested the knowledge and drawn interesting conclusions about them. The closer she gets, the more ridiculous I feel at having been found hiding in a bookstore, imagining showdowns with enemies and archenemies from high school, faking that I've even read a book this summer.

Lindsay looks tan—a better word would be "honeyed"—but the more general impression she gives off is that she looks *healthy*. I realize that's kind of a clinical term, like you're describing a purebred puppy or blood cells under a microscope, but I don't mean it like just physically, I mean it of the mind and the spirit too. Lindsay's giving off really good vibes, as my sister would say. A very positive energy.

"Eva?" she says, and, even when she's right in front of me, she waves and waves. "Eva! Eva!"

Then she's hugging me and I'm hugging her, and then she pulls back, smiling the fullest smile, with her lips *and* her eyes. It's not the fake smile I throw out dozens of times a day when I'm annoyed or bored or don't care, wide and meaningless, the one I use for strangers, neighbors, friends I don't really know, counselors whose names I've never learned. Lindsay gives me the real thing.

"I didn't know you wore glasses!" she says, really looking me over.

"I didn't either," I say. I notice a La Brea Tar Pits key chain dangling from her keys. "How was it?"

"The Tar Pits are awesome," she says. "Just awesome."

"I haven't been since I was a kid."

"You should've told me! I could've met you there instead," Lindsay says.

"It's not really my thing."

"No way, you've got to go again! I mean, you *have* to go before we leave for school."

"I don't need to go to the shitty Tar Pits," I say.

"Oh, okay."

"I'm sorry. I didn't mean that."

"I get it," she says. "You've been a hundred times. You're tired of the Tar Pits. Makes sense."

"No, you're right. I really should revisit some of the places I used to go, all the old spots."

"Soon there'll only be new ones," Lindsay says, already positive again.

"Totally," I say.

Lindsay turns to her left, noticing a particular book, and strokes its spine absently, like she's petting a kitten.

"Know something crazy? Like a month ago I made this decision to stop reading new books. And not just *new books*, but also books that are *new to me*. I kind of felt like, if there's something I haven't read by now, I should probably just keep it that way until college, because once I'm there I'll find out about all the right books I should read," she says, glancing at me, to see if I agree. "But the problem was the only books left are, like, Harry Potter and the stuff I read in high school. I mean, at first it was fun, digging into a bunch of my kid books I'd forgotten about, but then it's like, come on! So after a while I just stopped reading. Period. It's kind of sad."

"Lindsay," I say, stunned, "we're so alike."

We talk about some other topics—San Diego, the Sea World there, driving on the freeway and how weird it'll be to not drive in Boston—while Lindsay idly touches an atlas someone left on the shelf next to us. Soon I'll know more about her than I do about anyone else. I'll watch her talk on the phone to her parents, type emails at two in the morning, do her homework or ignore it. Whatever she's interested in that I don't care about—geography, history, current events—will rub off on me, because she'll be so close. I don't know if she's a Star Student, but I can already tell she probably gets passable grades and knows some interesting stuff, like details about how certain celebrities died and which tampon brand is best. She'll be my first college friend. Maybe she already is.

"Hey, this one looks pretty good," she says of some generic-looking book on our aisle. "I think I'm going to buy it." She winks at me.

She changed her mind. I'm impressed.

We go up toward the cashiers but don't get in line. We both realize that a purchase means the completion of the bookstore experience, and the conclusion to our meeting, so both of us just stand there, not really knowing what else to do.

"Well," Lindsay says.

I've learned from listening to a lifetime of my mother's phone conversations that the word "well" is the beginning of every ending.

"Anyway," she continues.

I've also learned that an "anyway" followed by a sigh means that a talk is over, that it's time to leave. So I don't bother Lindsay with what the rest of her LA plans are, if she's seeing other sights or if she's just getting back in her car with her generic book and tourist key chain and driving home to San Diego. I don't try to extend the hangout, even though I'd like to, since I have nowhere to go and nothing to do until my flight to Boston leaves.

I don't tell Lindsay to call me or Gchat me because what's the point, we're about to be together basically forever, but I do hug her because right now she's as new as she'll ever be, and in a week or so, when we get to the dorms, she'll already seem familiar. I hold her for a minute, burying my face in her soft hair. But when I feel her start to pull away, I also feel a tug on my earring and realize that we're attached—my hoop to her hair.

I rub my head against her, trying to loosen my earring from whatever strands it's knotted in, but she doesn't understand that I'm caught, that a part of me is attached to her and if she pulls away she'll rip my earlobe and I'll scream.

"Sorry," I say.

Lindsay thinks I'm having a moment, that I'm overwhelmed by our meeting, by college looming so close, the separation anxiety. So she strokes my back, staying still, letting other customers slip past to make their purchases.

I keep trying to untangle the hoop, get it free, but I can't see my hands, can't tell what I'm doing, if I'm getting closer or just making it worse. I wonder if Lindsay will have something wise to say about it, some easy advice like she shared with Courtney.

And then she does.

"Let go, Eva. I need you to let go."

59.

YOU WITHOUT ME

ON MONDAY I set my alarm for six thirty, because seven is when the copy shop opens. I'm the first one in the door, and when the bell chimes, it's like the bell chiming in my head, *Happy Day, Happy Day.*

I make ten copies of each of my pages and then take the fat stack of pages up to the counter.

"Can you bind these into ten books?" I ask. "And can you use the spiral binding, and can you make it with this Curl Powder page on the cover and this dedication page on the back?"

When the zines are finished, I carefully write each girl's name on the top of her copy in my fanciest cursive, with my coolest colored pens, and then personalize each one with a note and a *Love, Eva*. Then I gather every-thing up and drive to Sunny Skies with no real plan. As I'm cruising up the entrance, four big yellow buses rumble past me going the opposite way. I U-turn and follow them as they cross up and over the mountain, heading for Zuma Beach.

Once we're there I park at the edge of the lot and stay in my car, watching kids pour out of the buses and sprint across the sand toward the ocean. I see Booth; I see Melly; I notice Christy/Katie laying a towel down. Then I spy Rachel holding hands with Alexis, leading the rest of my girls to a little dune, where they all drop their beach bags and snacks. Alyssa's in a purple bikini, holding a bottle of sunscreen. Closer to the water I make out Corey and his group, and Foster.

Maybe I technically don't deserve it, but I feel like I belong out there on that beach. There's an Eva-Shaped Hole in this scene, and it's all wrong. I've never felt so apart from something I wanted so badly to be a part of.

This lack, this Eva Absence, starts to depress me in a way I can't deal with, so I turn up the radio, some song about being a teenager. It takes a few verses before I hear Alyssa calling my name.

"Eva!" she yells, jogging toward me, barefoot. "Hey, Eva!"

She knocks on my window, and I roll it down.

"Alyssa, you should go back to the group," I say.

"What are you doing here? Why are you in your car?"

"I got fired."

"Duh," she says. "No duh."

"So, I don't think Steven would want me out there, around you guys."

Alyssa hops from one foot to the other, her feet burning on the hot asphalt, and I'm about to ask her if she wants to get in the car, but then worry that'd seem really sketchy, and I didn't come here get in any more trouble, I came here to do the right thing. I slip off my sandals and hand them to her.

"Thanks," she says, putting them on. "What'd you do anyway?"

"To get fired?"

"Yeah."

"I wasn't a very good counselor to you guys, that's all."

"That's horseshit," Alyssa says.

"Hey," I say. "C'mon."

"You're my favorite counselor I've ever had."

"How many counselors have you had?"

"One million," Alyssa says, and sticks out her tongue.

"How's Corey?"

"You mean how's Foster?"

"Alyssa," I say, holding her wrist, "if you were four

years older, you'd be my best friend and I'd worship you."

"I know," she says.

"So how is Foster?"

"A little sad, I think. Corey told me he tried convincing Steven to let you come back for a day so you could say good-bye."

"Guess that didn't work."

She shrugs.

"I miss you guys," I say, looking out across the beach where Rachel's helping the girls bury Alexis in the sand. "I don't like seeing you guys without me."

"Rachel's nice, though."

"I'm sure."

"But she's kind of boring, and she makes us do all the stuff on the schedule and even forced Alexis to jump off the high dive without her goggles or nose plug."

"Was she okay?"

"Obvi, Eva."

Obvi. Obviously I screwed up majorly. I feel sicker, and sorrier.

We listen to the waves crash a little. Alyssa squints in the sun. She seems kind of anxious now, like she doesn't know whether she should stay here with me longer or go back to the group. She glances in Corey's direction and then inside the car at me. I must look upset, because she pats her hand on my shoulder, like she's reassuring me.

"You're stoked for Boston, right?" she asks.

"*Obvi*," I say. "What about you? Stoked for high school?"

"Pbbth," she says, rolls her eyes.

I reach over to the passenger seat and grab the thick brown envelope with the zines inside.

"Listen, Alyssa, take these and give them to the girls for me. At first I was trying to edit and improve them but later changed my mind and whited out all my notes. So this is just everything, as is. Every page you gave me is in here."

"Even Lila's crappy poem?"

"All the crappy poems," I say. "Every one."

"That's cool," Alyssa says.

"You should go back."

"Okay."

"Don't tell *Corey* that you saw me."

"I won't," she says, smiling, and slips my sandals off and takes off running across the parking lot.

But I can't stand it, letting them all go like that, so I jump out of my car and run after her, catching her as she gets to the edge of the sand.

"Tell the girls to sneak off over by the showers. Go, I'll wait there," I say.

Alyssa nods and leaves, and I jog toward the beach showers. It's blazing out today but I have on a hoodie because, once again, I'm hiding from people. I loiter on the shady side of the shower building, my head down, my hood up, waiting for nine girls who I know for a fact move very, very slowly.

For some reason I think of Tiffany Lee and her valedictorian speech. If she's right, and the University *is* the Universe, then my Universe is only just about to begin. What an amazing feeling. Because my life so far, even with the bad parts, has been pretty great, which means everything I'm about to do should be even more amazing.

I think of all the side characters I've known, and still know, that make my story layered, complex.

I imagine my readers, and how they'll judge me, and I think ultimately it's okay to be judged, because all that truly means is that you're being thought about, looked at, considered.

I think about what I know, what I've learned, and it's not a lot. But it *will* be, eventually.

Then I think about the lesson of charades, about teaching yourself to communicate without speaking, without writing, for the times when you don't have the right words, or when what you're trying to express is too huge, too deep. When you're faced with the Whole Thing.

That's when my girls jog up, a squealing, open-armed

mob. I crouch down and let them crush me, a frenzy of Curl Powder and Whirled Peas, and then I hug them one by one, squeezing until my arms feel sore, and it's time to let go, for good.

60.

IMAGINE ALL THE PEOPLE

ON THE DRIVE home I break the law and scroll through the contacts on my phone. I call Steph first just to touch base, to tell her flat out that I love her.

"I love you."

"What's wrong?" she asks.

Then I call Michelle. "I love you, Michelle," I say when she answers.

"Totally," she says, not exactly paying attention. I'm happy with that; I'll take it.

After that I'm on a roll—I can't stop checking in. I text both Lindsay and Shelby noncommittal single-word messages: hi, hey. I text my mom, Comin home soon. Then, on a long stretch of empty highway, I call Courtney, recite every word out of Alyssa's mouth, and a third of the words out of mine, but she says to save it.

"Save it for what?" I ask.

"*Savor* it," she says, and I can hear her smile.

I hang up just as I'm pulling off the freeway. I'm wearing my glasses for dusk driving, even though this particular route's basically ingrained in my sense memory. I could probably do this route blindfolded, because patterns you've traced a thousand times stay burned in your memory forever. As long as I can count, I can see. One, two, three, four speed bumps, and then a left. One, two, three weeks, and then I leave.

I pass Agoura Road, Foster's street, which makes me miss Foster's voice: the lowness of it, humming through my phone, tickling along my neck. The best way to break the ice is with a hammer, my dad always tells me—not a hemmer or a hawer. What he means is you shouldn't hold back.

So I don't: I call Foster. As it rings I envision the conversation I'm hoping we're going to have, one of those really sprawling endless ones that lasts so long it actually gets kind of boring, spaced with calm silences; the kind that ends with you each describing random items from your dresser, sunlight starting to bleach away the night, while he keeps reminding you there's only an hour or two left to actually get some sleep and make it to work before the first camp song.

I imagine all this while the phone rings: how to

instigate such a connection after so much teenage tension, how to design my night so it seamlessly interlocks with his. But when Foster finally answers, he sounds rushed.

"Eva," he says. "What's up?"

"I just wanted to call. To talk, you know."

"Cool, yeah."

"Thought I'd let you know I got fired from our job. It was a pretty fair slash unfair firing."

"I was going to call," Foster says. "I didn't know what to say."

"You basically predicted it."

"Eva. I never wanted you to get fired."

"But you thought maybe I deserved it."

"No," he says. "You're wrong."

"Look, I just wanted to say I'm sorry," I tell him, "for being so lame at that party. I could've tried harder. Or honestly, at all."

"The party wasn't your thing, I get it. I didn't mean to, like, force it on you."

"I don't have a thing," I mumble.

Foster laughs, so sincerely it kills me, literally makes me die. Then I hear some clicking, followed by a spry computer bell, the bright ping of Microsoft saving a document.

"We can talk tomorrow if you're busy," I say.

"I'm just working on a new story," he tells me. "I can take a quick break."

"No, don't. You're in the zone, keep writing."

"You sure?" Foster says.

"Tomorrow," I say. "I'm sure."

"You know I'll be at camp till four."

" 'The horror! The horror!' " I say.

"So you *do* remember *Heart of Darkness*."

"Impressed?"

"Eva," he says, before slumping into a soft, extended silence, during which my mind skips ahead to the end of some fictional future life in which the two of us are much older, and falling in love. "Always."

After he hangs up, I have a long talk with Foster anyway, sustaining the dialogue in my head like characters on the page, a scene from our story. I work on it all the way until sunrise, when I hear my father's alarm go off, followed by the whirring of my mother firing up the coffee machine downstairs.

That's what lifts us up, us writers: we have our imagination, if nothing else.

61.

POSTCARD FROM THE ISLANDS

LATER THAT AFTERNOON it hits me how much I need to see Michelle and Steph, because time isn't holding on, it's running out, and who knows what we'll all be like by Thanksgiving, or if we're not all home for that, Christmas? At first I'm brainstorming ideas on how to solidify this, like, *fragile harmony* we have going, even if only for a few hours, but then I stop because the truth is it's *not* so fragile—they love me, I love them, and they're not going to stop loving me just because I acted like an ass this summer and then moved three thousand miles away.

I propose meeting at the mall food court, but Steph says she and Michelle have been at the mall all day.

"We obviously would've invited you," she says, "but we thought you were at camp."

"That's over."

"What happened?"

"Doesn't matter."

"I just got back from Hawaii yesterday, actually," Steph says. "That's why I haven't called."

"It's okay."

"Did you get my postcard?"

"No."

"I sent one," she says. "You have to believe me."

"I do," I say. "I can't wait until it comes in the mail."

"Let's meet at Islands then. You can get a veggie burger."

"I think those veggie burgers have cheese in them—" I start to say, but then say, "Never mind, I'll be there."

When I get to Islands, Michelle and Steph are in a booth with a tray of fries, already laughing. I love them. I've seen every movie they've seen; I've heard every joke they know. We don't have plans to marry brothers or live on the same street when we're older or anything corny like that, but we do have firm plans for New Year's Eve that I'm really looking forward to. I pause in front of their booth, not sure which side to sit on, because neither of them scoot in.

"What's the grace period for being a jerk?" I ask.

"You mean grace*less* period," Michelle says. "One summer, I think."

"We were all jerks," Steph says. "Some of us just tanner jerks."

"Will you sit on the same side of the booth?" I ask them. "So I can see both of your faces?"

They move to the same side, and I slide in across from them. They're sharing fries and smiling easily, and every impulse I have is to totally degrade myself so they'll permanently forgive me. But I should know by now that you don't have to do that for real friends, and I should also know that ultimately there's no imbalance because we're all equally awful and awesome, just at different times.

"If there was one thing in the universe I could do to make you guys happy, what would it be?" I ask.

"Write to us," Steph says.

"Write *about* us," Michelle says.

"I thought you hated that," I say.

"How could I *really*, though?" Michelle asks.

"It should be flattering," I say.

"We know," Steph says.

"I wish we'd known each other when we were five," I say. "I wish I had a million more stories I could tell about you guys."

Michelle and Steph smile and dip fries in ketchup.

"I wish I knew every story in your lives. Or at least all

the stories of your *summer*."

Michelle nods and Steph sips some water.

"At least we have, like, ten days—right?" I ask. "That's some time. We can hang out every day and do everything we want."

"My college starts next week, actually," Steph says.

"And I leave on Friday," Michelle tells me.

"No," I say, crushed, but they both just nod.

Then the waiter comes, and I order a bun with lettuce and tomato and guacamole and that's it. Michelle and Steph cock their heads, shoot me knowing looks, those vintage *Oh, Eva* looks, and I shrug.

"I'm saving all my changes for Emerson," I say. "Once I'm there I'll start eating cheeseburgers and writing about my childhood and getting into everything I used to hate, even beer."

"Don't do that, Eva," Michelle says.

"Yeah," Steph says. "Don't ever change."

I wish I'd brought my yearbook.

62.

THE WEIRDEST DATE IN THE WORLD

OVER THE NEXT few days I get a couple texts from Elliot—some sweet, some shameful—and even a couple from Zack—*very* sweet, *very* shameful. I don't text back. What's the point? I'm allowed to say that now—*What's the point?*—since their chapters are over.

I'm still playing a game with Foster, though, and that game is Who Texts First. I knew going into it I'd lose; I *want* to lose, right . . . this . . . second.

I miss you.

I miss you too, Foster texts. Want to c u.

2nite???

Can't tonite.

Oh ok.

Unless yr free l8tr?

I look at the clock. 9:18. How much latr? I text.

Midnite.

Just the word alone, misspelled, makes me feel sexy.

Where? I text.

U pick.

What's open?

Hmm, Foster texts, and then there's a few minutes where neither of us text. I open my laptop and type in the search bar: *open 24 hrs Agoura Hills CA*. The first result is CVS.

CVS? I text.

U want to go to a drugstore?? Ha.

Yes, I text. Want to go n e where w/ u.

At midnight Foster and I are the only ones in CVS. There doesn't even seem to be one stock boy or security guard on the clock, which makes it feel intimate, despite all the fluorescent lights. My heart actually beats faster, like I'm on a date—a first date even—but we're just standing by the magazine rack, flipping through a *GQ*, eyeing expensive suits and exotic vacation destinations. Tropical Muzak wafts down from tiny speakers in the ceiling.

Foster looks at me. "So what do you need?"

"In life, or . . . ?"

"In CVS, Eva."

"Oh, right," I say. "Something, I'm sure."

"Let's shop then," Foster says, taking my hand and swinging it.

He seems a little nervous too—though not as much as me—because his palm is sort of sweaty and he's reading aloud the names of pain relief pills we pass by: "Advil, Excedrin, Aleve, ibuprofen."

"Foster," I interrupt, "I like you so much."

Foster smiles, caught off guard. "You should win," he says. "That writing award, I mean."

"I don't think so," I say. "You should win!"

"Now I *know* how much you like me."

"It's just that I have so many *other* awards to win," I say, tugging a little on his shirt.

"You've already got the Junior Nazi Whistle-Blower Award," he says.

I hide my face behind my hands. "Steven thought I was going to be great, remember? Great, great, great."

"You *are* great," Foster says, "but you're also Eva."

"Shit," I say, and we laugh. "Oh! I know what I need!"

"What?"

"A toothbrush."

Foster leads the way over to the mouth-care aisle, and at first it's just rows of picks and flosses and whiteners and gels and washes. We start combing through the options, and soon I'm thinking more about my teeth than I ever have, and how I guess I've always hated my teeth, or at least never felt any positive emotions toward them, but now I'm being forced to assess minute preferences for hundreds of teeth-related products. My whole life I've just used whatever toothbrush and toothpaste has been given to me by my mother or dentist and never thought twice about it. But starting this fall I'll have to buy my own toothbrushes, my own shampoo and deodorant, my own *everything*.

"Well, what kind of toothbrush do you like?" Foster asks.

"What kinds are there? Mine was always just like regular, with a regular handle."

"There're a lot of choices," Foster says. "Like what about the coarseness of the bristles? There's hard and soft and medium and also sensitive, which is different from regular soft, and also extra-medium."

There are rows atop tiers atop columns atop pyramids of toothbrush options. I reach for a straight-handle brush with a purplish sparkly color that reminds me of my old one, but it's hanging within a galaxy of other handle styles: flex-y necked, travel-size, cartoon tie-ins, sports teams, ones with a plastic pick on the end. I realize I'm concentrating so hard I'm chewing on my knuckles.

Foster starts pulling down one of every type to show me. He even grabs an electric toothbrush, which I'm embarrassed to admit I've never seen before.

"What?" he says, shocked. "How's that possible?"

"I don't know!"

"They're kind of expensive, but look, they rotate and vibrate and you can just replace the head when it gets old. You don't have to buy the base again."

"How do you know when you need to replace the head?"

"It probably says on the instructions."

"Ugh, I can't decide," I say.

"The store's open twenty-four hours."

"This is the weirdest date in the world."

"Why's it so weird?"

"Because we're at CVS, and now you can see how, I don't know, like, *inept* I am."

"It's the best date," Foster says. "Hey, relax, Eva."

"Yeah, okay." I try to seem light, but I feel heavy.

"Come on, don't cry."

"I'm not," I say, but I touch my cheek and it's wet, so maybe I am.

I close my eyes for a second and breathe. I picture a zero. Then I picture a one, a two, a three, and a four. I stop at five and visualize myself inside the number, sitting at the bottom of the dip, my legs dangling off. I don't need Courtney's zero protecting me, creating a barrier between my body and the world, because I have my own number—the five—and the loop of the five is open, it never closes.

I can enter it, and just as easily, I can leave it. There's a beginning and an end. Even though nothing holds me in, nothing holds me back either.

I can choose any of these toothbrushes!

The idea suddenly overwhelms me with happiness, making me cry more, but these are happy tears, because I can see myself inside the five and Foster inside with me.

"I want to kiss you," I say.

"Here?"

"Yes!"

"Let's go outside," he says. "We can go in my car."

"No," I say, "Here, now." I grab his collar, pull him close.

But he pulls back.

"You might never see me again," I say.

"Eva," he says, and touches my face, my neck. "I'll see you in Boston. At Tufts."

I have a true, crazy Eureka Moment. *That's* what he meant in his stupid cryptic text weeks ago, *And ill be tuff*: Tufts University, just outside Boston, only a few subway stops away.

"Tufts," I say. "Tufts!" I scream. I jump up and down, then stop myself. "But wait, stories don't end like this. It's too neat, too perfect."

"So what?"

Impulsively I grab a polka-dotted toothbrush, hold it tight against my chest.

"Is that the one you want?" Foster asks.

"I *want* you to clean my teeth with your tongue," I say.

"Very . . . *forward*," he says, laughing, and then I'm Frenching Foster, over and over.

Forward's the only way.

63.

THE ROUSH SOLUTION

MY MOTHER PROPOSES we all go to Whole Foods on one of my final nights at home so she can spend hundreds of dollars on a lavish family meal.

"It's our last dinner all together, as a family," she says.

"Technically Eva's got a few more days, Mom," Courtney says.

"Yeah, Mom, you can dial it back," I tell her.

"What do you girls always say?" my father asks. "'Save the drama for your mama'?"

So we drive to the store and fill an entire shopping cart with glamorous groceries.

"Anything you see that you want, throw it in!" my mother keeps saying. "You're gonna miss all this pampering!"

I grab a nine-dollar pack of gluten-free muffins and throw them in the cart.

"Maybe I'll be gluten-free now too," I say.

"Oy, Boston," she says, "you can have her!"

Later, over by the olive oil, I notice Mr. Roush. He looks sheepish and polite, like a teacher glad to be done with summer school, so I don't want to bother him. I try to maneuver around him and hurry down the aisle, but he sees me and calls my name. "Eva!" he says again, and then I stop. "Were you not going to say hello?"

"I'm just acting weird," I tell him, and he smiles.

"There's that Kramer candidness, that honesty. I'll miss having it this year."

I shrug, give him a look.

"Oh," he says, "you're not happy with me for submitting your story for that award."

"No, I'm happy," I say. "I'm grateful."

"Grateful?" Mr. Roush asks, impressed.

"And guess what else?" I say. "I don't know *anything*."

Mr. Roush laughs. "What does that mean?"

"On the last day of school you said I should ask myself, 'What do I know?' Remember?"

"Mostly," he says.

"Well, I thought about it, I asked myself, and I realized it's nothing. Pretty much nothing."

Mr. Roush sets his basket down, places a bottle of

olive oil he's holding back on the shelf. He looks at me with saddened, sorry eyes.

"That wasn't at all what I meant, Eva."

"No, I know that," I say, though I'm not sure if I do.

"Have you been writing this summer?" he asks.

I shake my head. "Not a single word."

"Congratulations!" he says, enthused.

"What? But I wanted to redo my story, fix it, you know?"

"But you went out and lived. You *experienced. That's* how you add to what you know."

"I got *fired*," I tell him.

"That's good!"

"It sucked," I say. "It was painful."

"That's *even better*!"

"The whole summer was kind of painful, actually," I say, laughing.

"That's a sign, Eva," he says. "A sign you're a real writer."

That's the sign I've been waiting for. And now, maybe, it's time to write—about me, and about all of this.

64.

NOT ALWAYS

COURTNEY'S OFFICIALLY NOT going to Amsterdam. She's not getting her own apartment either. She's not going anywhere.

"Don't feel bad for me," she says, but I do.

We're lying on her bed, facing one another, in the dark. It's night. Courtney was supposed to go to a party, but she changed her mind.

"I was never going to go," she says, but the way she says it I can't tell if she means Amsterdam or the party.

"Yes, you were," I say. "You *go*—that's your thing."

"I don't have a thing."

"You're a *fountain* of things. You're totally defined."

"I don't want to be defined. Being defined is very Eva."

"Okay, but you represent something, and that something is Going."

"That's you now," she says.

Virgo. Vegan. Writer. I guess I can add a word to my list.

"I pictured the zero," I tell her.

"What zero?"

"Your zero, Courtney, the ring around you."

"The hollow ring." She shakes her head, remembering. "You know, you don't need everyone's advice as much as you think you do."

"I need *your* advice, though. Always."

"Well, this time I don't have any," she says.

"I'll just recycle then."

Courtney rolls onto her back. "So what are you going to write about next?"

"Whores," I say.

"Ah, okay then, maybe I *do* have some advice," Courtney says.

"Can I give *you* advice, Courtney?" I stand, turn on her bedroom light. I want to tell her that she should go to that party, go see her friends right now. I want to say that it's just Amsterdam; it's just one city; there are a million cities you can go to. And when you go, there you'll be.

It's Courtney's advice—I just want to give it back to her.

65.

THOROUGH

THE NIGHT BEFORE I leave, my mother helps me finish packing the very last of my clothes. She's always been a champion packer. She can fold shirts until they're so compact they look like trim linen napkins. She can ball socks into a perfect sphere, round as a tennis ball. She can also stack sweaters, roll scarves so they don't wrinkle, and bundle jeans into flat little denim bricks to maximize luggage space.

My mother forgets nothing. She packs toiletries in separate plastic Baggies, so if anything spills, no clothes get ruined. She has different packing strategies for different types of luggage. For square-shaped traditional suitcases, she lines the bottom with shoes and layers clothing on top; for duffel bags, she positions the shoes around the sides like a wall to protect the rest of the contents.

And my mother knows everything there is to know about weather. She checks the forecast for her destination city daily for weeks leading up to a flight. She's been following the highs and lows for Boston since June.

She hasn't forgotten school supplies either. My mother's filled a whole corner of my room with zippered pouches full of pens and colored pencils and Scotch tape and extra binders and even a mini stapler with mini staples already loaded inside.

She's so committed and thorough that I start to forget it's me who's leaving and not her. I lie back on my bed, hypnotized by her assembly line, watching the master at work, and I listen to her talk—occasionally about Boston but mostly about folding methods—and eventually my eyes close.

And then my mind floats, and I imagine my mother folding me up into a compact, little form, instead of my clothes. My mother folding me up so small that I stay stuck in that position, and by the time they finally unfold me the plane's already taken off, it's landed in Boston, everyone's learned all their lessons, made all their memories, and now they're on their way back home.

ACKNOWLEDGMENTS

FOREVER THANK YOU to Tara Weikum and Ann Behar, my counselors, guiding and cheering me on.

Please don't ever, ever change, Jen. Stay the exact same, Katie.

Walk through all the open doors with me, Jillian.

Matt, the undisputed camp champ, who literally helps me dye.

Kim, let's make everything together, okay?

Elizabeth, endless gratitude, my favorite second chance.

Rachel, I think I just end up with you.

Mom, it's true, you're the best at folding and the best at holding, too.

Ben, all the toast, we can have all of it.

And Britt, my DB, what can I say, what can I write, that isn't perfect until you've fixed it?